Stuck In Paris

A love Story

Nikki Khanna

A Chick Lit in the City of love

Creator: Nandika Khanna

Title: Stuck In Paris
Subtitle: "A Love Story"

Printed in India
First printed in 2020
ISBN: 978-93-5416-292-3

Publishing Rights with Sava International Pvt. Ltd.
545 Pace City 2, Sector 37, Gurugram, Haryana 122001 India

Disclaimer

Dedications & Acknowledgements

I would like to dedicate this book first to myself and my mind that ran these stories along with dusk till dawn.

To my dad, who pushed me to my limits until I became a published author.

To my readers, who showed love and support for my work.

This book is for all the hopeless romantics out there, who can't help but create such vivid moments in their head that they only dream to have.

This is for you.

I would like to acknowledge how grateful I am to the people who stuck with me through this book. To everyone who supported it from the start, showed their appreciation, read, commented and have a soft spot for liking this book.

I want to thank all my readers that appreciated this book and my parents for supporting me through writing from the beginning to the end. I would like to thank my dad for pushing me to my limits until this book was published, and my mom for constantly appreciating and acknowledging my work.

Most importantly, I want to thank all those that came here from Wattpad. You have seen me from beginning till now; with and without my mistakes and errors and for that I am thankful.

Last but not least, I would like to apologize to the ones that I have not named but have stuck with me through the whole ride.

Thank you to all.

Author's note

If you've come here from Wattpad, then first I want to take a moment to thank you for coming this far with me! I started writing as a fun little hobby and before I knew it I was hitting thousands and thousands of reads!

So thank you for coming on this journey with me and sticking it all the way through.

-- **Nikki Khanna**

CHAPTER ONE

RILEY

"I hear there's a rumor going around that our French class gets to go to Paris!" Allison squealed beside me.

Did I forget to introduce myself? Probably. I'm Riley Blakely. I'm seventeen years old, I go to Greenview High and am currently suffering from the worst period cramps in my life. That's me. In a nutshell.

"That's great, Ali. I am so thrilled, gleaming with joy!" I spoke sarcastically.

"Look, I get that you're on your period but can you not dampen the mood so much? We're going to Paris! We get to see the Eiffel Tower and Disneyland Paris!" she squealed for the billionth time.

"*Might*. We might get to see all that. It's just a rumor." I'm not usually this pessimistic, I promise.

"I don't like this version of you. Bring the happy one back please?" she whined.

"Wait till next week." I huffed as we stopped at my locker

where I grabbed my books for the first two periods. "Math and Bio, great," I uttered sarcastically. I use sarcasm a lot if you haven't noticed.

"Do we have French today? What period is it?" She tried to look into my timetable.

"Eighth period, patience honey, patience." I shut my locker before we headed to math. She wasn't in my math class so I headed to mine and said goodbye. I sat in my seat in the second row from the back before groaning and resting my head on my arms.

"Wakey! Wakey!" I heard someone mumble before I looked up, resisting an eye roll. Of course, it was him, Asher mother fucking West. I'm gonna give you guys a quick over view on this guy.

Dick, egoistic, full of himself, sometimes funny, devilishly charming although I'd never admitted that to anybody except for myself and a huge pain in the ass. "Morning, asshole," I mumbled to myself as he took the seat behind me as usual.

We don't talk, At all.

Just snide remarks to each other. It's a hate-hate relationship. I hate his player ways, cockiness and existence and he- well I wouldn't know, we don't talk.

"Pencil please?" He pulled my hood off my head. I rolled my eyes far back into my head before running a hand through my hair.

"Shove it up your ass." I smiled at him while handing him a pencil. Our teacher Mrs. Mathews walked in before he could say something witty.

"Morning class! How many of you have done the homework?" She was a very straightforward teacher but a bitch sometimes. I was on her good side for the most part. "Ms. Blakely?" she asked me, a little surprised that my hand didn't go up.

"Ooh, someone's becoming a rebel," Asher snickered.

"I was attending his funeral," I mumbled before answering, "I was sick," I lied.

"I'll let it slide. Mr. West?" she turned to him as I turned in my seat, amused for his excuse this time.

"My notebook was finished so I couldn't exactly do it." Liar. "Learn to lie," he whispered in my ear from behind.

"And you did not have one sheet of paper at home?" she glared at him. He was stupid.

"I didn't think of that, Mrs. Matthews." He is in such deep shit, again. She smiled sarcastically.

"You can use your time in detention to think of that," she announced before beginning to teach. I turned to look at him with a grin. At least something cheered me up. "Shut up, Ry Ry." He kicked my chair from behind while I chuckled before beginning the work.

I remarked, "Whatever you say, Ashy Bashy." That only triggered him more. Oh, how I love this.

The bell rang after class ended and the class began to file out, Mrs. Matthews being the first one out.

"My pencil?" I held my hand out, blocking his way. That was a good pencil and I shouldn't have given it to him.

"I thought you told me to go shove it up my ass?" he feigned confusion. I rolled my eyes before turning around and walking out only for him to come up to me and place it behind my ear before jogging away, catching up to Ashley Simpson.

The girl for the week I assume.

"Cute style of carrying stationary." Ali pointed out the pencil while walking with me to bio.

"Hmm, I have Asher to thank for that," I mumbled. She laughed before nudging my shoulder with hers.

"I still think you two would make a great couple. It worked in third grade," she shrugged.

"Yeah and then he pushed me off the swing." I pointed out as we walked into class.

"Honey, you stabbed him with a pencil." She gave me a pointed look. I have an explanation for that.

"He stole my baby! I was taking care of that damn doll then he took it! Into the sandpit!" I explained.

"And I'm sure he has a great reason for that." This bitch always sides with that manwhore.

"Say that one more fucking time. I dare you," I challenged her while she put her hands up in surrender. "That's what I thought," I mumbled as Mr. Davis walked in.

Bio went by quickly since we weren't doing much just

taking notes from the textbook and then we were off. I got to my locker and grabbed my books for my next three periods since they were all on this floor.

I walked there while Ali left for history, only to see Asher and Ashley Simpson snogging. I groaned, "Can you guys take this somewhere else please?" Nope. No response. Fine then. "Oh Ashy Bashy!" I said extremely loud in a sing-song voice. He pulled away and glared at me. "Get the fuck out of my way. You're at my locker," I demanded while he looked at me challengingly.

"Oh, I can yell your name again and ten times louder." I shrugged nonchalantly.

"You will one day, Riles. Wait for your turn." He winked before grabbing Ashley's hand and disappearing in some corner. I rolled my eyes before grabbing my books for English, business, and geography before heading to class. I got to class, took my seat and began going through the extract placed on my desk.

To Kill A Mockingbird. Classic.

I read it twice before annotating it as the class settled in. "Annotate and I'll give out instructions then," Mr. Wayne announced.

"I'm done." I went up to his desk. He sighed before typing something out on his laptop.

"Slow down Ms. Blakely. The class has a tough time keeping up with you. I've sent a print-out for the comprehension sheet and the essay question, as well as the summary, write up for you. Go get it please." I nodded before heading out of the room and to the printing office.

I walked into the dusty, old and abandoned room of the school where the printer lied. I walked in and saw Asher sitting on the ground, leaning against it, puffing out clouds of smoke Of course.

"Don't you have something better to do Asher?" I asked as I stood and waited for the print out only for the printer to be out of ink. I sighed before walking over to the drawer and grabbing an ink cartridge, inserting it into the printer.

"I didn't feel like doing English," he shrugged nonchalantly.

"Oh that's right, you're in my class. I wouldn't know since you're never there," I scoffed.

"You notice my presence and absence? I'm flattered," he scoffed while smoking his cigarette.

"That'll kill you one day, you know." I looked at his cigarette with disgust. I despise smoking.

"That wouldn't be so bad, would it? I get to be away from you in hell." He stood up and killed the cigarette with his foot.

"Don't worry, you'd see me there one day, I'll pay you a visit." I smiled as I got my print out. I placed the extract in the photocopier. I got the copy and handed it to him. "Catch up on the work." He took the sheet and looked at me with surprise.

He narrowed his down on me. "Why are you helping me?" I could sense the suspicion in his voice.

I'm not that mean even when I'm on my period. "We can't have Grandview's delinquent failing, can we?" I arched an eyebrow before walking out.

A part of me cares for my third-grade boyfriend. But then I look at him and see the asshole he's become. What the hell happened to him?

Before I could leave, he grabbed my wrist and pulled me back. "Get me a copy without your annotations," he demanded.

"I won't always be here to help so take it when I offer." I pulled my wrist out and left.

— CHAPTER TWO —

RILEY

I had ten minutes till lunch followed by a free period and then French. The ten minutes went by and the bell rang. I grabbed my books and headed to my locker before going out to sit in the field where Ali and I usually do.

I turned around after closing my locker to see Asher an inch away from me. He pushed me, slamming my back into the lockers, making me wince. "Ow!" I hissed.

"Next time, help instead of giving me the answers or just don't." He aggressively placed the annotated sheet in my hand before glaring at me.

"Okay, I'll do it. *Next time.*" I said as I shoved the sheet against his chest. "But this time, keep it." I shoved him back and headed for the cafeteria.

"Why are you helping me?" he shouted as I was halfway down the hallway. I knew what he was doing, trying to get rid of me by making me the center of attention which I hate being.

"God knows, all I know is that you were my third-grade boyfriend and deep down inside..." I stopped as I walked over to him until I was an inch away. "He's still there." I had no clue what I was saying. "Not the one that pushed me off the swing, the one who bought me candy and a teddy bear with roses glued on because it didn't come with them," I said softly before walking away. *It's not that deep, Riley. Relax.*

"He's gone, Riley Blakely!" he shouted from across the hallway. I laughed before yelling back.

"I'm not too sure he is!" before turning the corner and going to the stairs, heading to the ground floor to get to the cafeteria.

Lunch went by way too quickly with Ali still thrilled about the Paris trip which has not yet been confirmed and Asher glaring at me from his table while Mason kept smiling and I'm very sure it wasn't meant to be for us but I don't know, Ali possibly?

We headed to the room where we had our free period in and I managed to grab a book to read from my locker. Let It Snow. A very good book is you ask me. I got to class and saw Ali sitting with Mason?

"Excuse me?" I asked as I approached their table to see him charming her. If I said Asher was a player then Mason is next level. "Move, that's my seat." I furrowed my eyebrows at him.

"There's a special reservation for you." Mason smiled while gesturing to the seat behind him with his eyes and just my luck, it was next to Asher. Great day, isn't it?

"What do you want?" I groaned while setting my books down and taking a seat, moping already.

"I didn't ask for this seat, it's not my fault my friend can't keep his dick in his pants." He is such a prick.

"Who's friend is he? Yours. So who will I blame? You." I smiled at him sarcastically before plugging earphones in and blasting music only for him to pull one out.

"Okay, at least help me out and keep me from third-wheeling?" he asked with slightly pleading eyes.

"Why would I do that?" I shrugged before taking my earphone back, blasting music as he groaned. The teacher was walking in as Asher was walking out.

"Right..." Mr. Brown sighed while strolling in, setting his books and laptop down on his desk. "Now who will get Mr. West for me?" His eyes trailed across the classroom, eyeing us all. I ducked my head down, hiding behind my book while praying he wouldn't choose me.

"Ms. Blakely, that's a lovely book. I'm afraid you're going to have to put it down and get Mr. West for me." He smiled at me.

Annoying little brat.

I rolled my eyes and let out a groan before putting my book down and heading out the door, not missing the suggestive looks Ali and Mason gave me, which only made me clench my jaw harder.

I stopped and looked left and right to see if I could still see him, and when I couldn't, I came to the conclusion that he had gone to the printing room. Again.

I walked to the printing room, going a floor down in the process and opened the door to see him once again sitting against the printer, on the floor, drinking what I can assure you, is not water.

I sighed before walking over and dropping my arms to my sides, uncrossing them. "You're being summoned," I huffed as I sat down on the ground beside him, resting my head on the printer, tired and exhausted from the day.

"I don't want to be summoned, tell them you couldn't find me." He shrugged casually.

"How rude! You think I'd lie to my respected teachers?" I spoke with sarcasm seeping through my tone.

"I actually think you would. You did it in third grade," he smirked before taking a drink.

I shook my head before talking, "To get you your football that you lost." I pointed out the facts. He has a habit of not telling the full truth anyway.

"You lied, either way, do it for me again," he shrugged.

"You're not my friend anymore." I shrugged, staring ahead and the pile of books and jackets students had lost. This room kind of became the lost and found too.

"Ouch!" he laughed.

"Get your ass up, Ash. We have to get to class even though it's a free period." I sighed before standing up and dusting my legs.

"Tell him I went home. I don't feel like coming so I won't ok?" he glared up at me.

"I've been told specifically to not come back without you." I gave him a pointed look.

"Then don't go back, take a walk around the building just leave me alone," he groaned before taking another drink.

"I can't do that Ashy Bashy. Get your ass up!" I kicked his leg slightly. He just stared at me blankly. He thinks he's so tough but he's not. Trust me, I've seen the best and worst of both worlds.

"Come on... we don't want to be late for French, which we will be if Mr. Brown comes looking for us after his lesson. Let's go!" I kicked his legs a few more times before he sighed and finally stood up. And tossed the empty plastic bottle in the trash.

"It was water, Ry Ry. I could have consumed alcohol on school premises but what kind of a disrespectful student would that make me? A rebel? Never in a million years. Right Riles?" he smirked at me as we approached the class.

"I brought your favorite student back," I said to Mr. Brown as we walked in and over to our seats.

He was a chill teacher too and extremely funny, liked by everyone and liked everyone back.

"Thank you, Ms. Blakely. Where were you, sir?" he turned to Asher.

"I felt nauseous and went to the bathroom. Riley found me on my way back," he lied while giving me a look as Mr. Brown shook his head.

"Take your seat please." Sometimes I feel bad for the nice teachers. Students go to such a high extent to annoy them. I'm not saying Asher walked out of the class to annoy him, but he managed to do it anyway. He said down beside me with a sigh.

I kicked his leg under the table, "Liar." He kicked my leg back.

"I lied for you. Don't want Ms. Blakely to get in trouble now would we?" he spoke tauntingly.

Asshole.

"In trouble for what? I didn't do anything except bring you back and do as I was told," I said defensively.

"You sat with me and skipped a total of..." he checked his phone. "Twenty minutes." I wish I could slap that smug look off his face.

"In trying to convince you to come back!" I whisper yelled. He simply shrugged and stared ahead with a smirk.

"You missed twenty minutes either way."

He is so aggravating.

This guy genuinely gets on my nerves to the point where I am screaming in annoyance. "Why would anyone believe that? Everyone knows I hate you," I mumbled before trying to go back to reading, only for his voice to disturb me. Again.

He scoffed, "Everyone also knows how charming I am. Aren't I Ry Ry?" he whispered.

He's enjoying this way too much. "Let me read in peace, Ash shut up." I nudged his leg before he nudged mine back.

Ignorance is bliss, Riley. Ignorance is bliss.

"You can't ignore me forever," he whispered in my ear before nudging my leg one last time.

"Watch me," I whispered back. Soon enough, class ended with Ali shrieking.

"We're going to Paris!" she screamed.

God, please help this lost soul of who I call my best friend.

CHAPTER THREE

ASHER

Mr. Walker was taking even longer than usual to come to class and I am one hundred percent sure it's a strategy of his to get the students excited and then ultimately tell us that we're not going anywhere.

It's just not realistic for our school to take us to Paris. "Since when?" I heard Riley asking Allison something while Allison shushed her, smacking her arm aggressively. "Ow!" She rubbed her arm, seated in the seat in front of me while Mason went on about something besides me.

"Are you even listening to me or are you admiring a certain brunette?" Mason nudged my elbow with his.

"What the fuck has been up with you and pressing me about her?" I asked him, curious to know why lately he hasn't shut up about how I'm in love with Riley. I hate her. And she hates me.

It's a hate-hate relationship.

"Were you listening?" He gave me a pointed look.

"No, but that has nothing to do with her. Why are you acting as someone told you-" I shut up as it dawned on me. *"You've been hanging out with a certain brunette and she's filled your head up with the bullshit that she believes,"* I scoffed while shaking my head and laughing at how pathetic this was.

"I can hear you." Allison turned to face me. "I didn't say anything," she shrugged before turning back to face the front as Mr. Walker entered. I gave Mason a look, speaking with my eyes and the faint blush and embarrassment on his face, gave his answer away clearly.

"Okay, okay! Settle down everybody!" Mr. Walker exclaimed and the class immediately died down unlike usual since everyone wanted to know if we were going to Paris. I rolled my eyes at how pathetic the people were acting and listened in. "I've heard a few rumors that we'll be heading to Paris..." Mr. Walker began, "I would like to know who started that rumor. Any clue Mr. West?"

What is with people thinking that I am some huge trouble maker? Well, I am, but that's beyond the point.

"No clue at all, sir. But I'll ask the long-awaited question, are we going?" I stood up dramatically while Riley turned around in her chair and looked at me weirdly, before rolling her eyes and facing the front of the class again.

He waited for a long, *long* moment of silence just for the sake of being dramatic. "Yes, we are indeed!" he spoke cheerfully as the class erupted in cheers. "Listen up now! There are some rules and instructions!" He clapped and everywhere actually listened.

"We'll be leaving this Friday. The flight details will be emailed to you all as well as your parents. Make sure to bring your passports and all the things necessary. I'll be sending you all a list of things you require for the trip, make sure to check that, I will attach it in the email. We'll be in Paris for *three weeks*. It's a long time and we have a lot planned since your trip last year to Toulouse was canceled."

People began getting excited while Allison squealed not so quietly and Riley smiled. "For the first half of the trip, we will be doing solely school activities and the second half is for you all to explore the city." People broke out into soft chattering.

"One rule." Everyone fell dead silent. "No rooming with the opposite gender."

As those words escaped his mouth, a domino effect of groans shot through the class.

Well damn.

Tyler Davidson glanced around the class, giving certain people a look and I already knew what was going to happen in Paris, and it is not what Mr. Walker said, which automatically means I'm in.

"I'm sending out the emails right now, I want everybody to go through them and ask if they have any doubts or questions about the trip. I expect the forms to be signed by parents and given back to me tomorrow since I have the first period with this class. And after that, you all have the remaining time of the period as free. You're welcome," he smiled at the class as everyone began getting more and more excited.

Today is Wednesday. Two more days and we'll be off to Paris for three freaking weeks.

"Hear that Ry Ry? You can't room with me." I tugged at her hair. She'll kill me one day.

"Make sure to remind yourself that when we get there." She rolled her eyes before pulling out her phone and reading through the email. She stood up after going through the email and walked up to Mr. Walker.

She asked him a question, showing her phone in the process as her eyebrows creased slightly.

Why am I paying so much attention to her?

"Oh, thank you for reminding me. We'll be staying in two hotels. Since the class is too big, we'll be split up into two hotels, two teachers in each hotel. Le Regent Montmartre and Hotel 121 Paris. The four teachers going will be Mr. Brown, Mrs. Stevenson, Mrs. Williams and of course me."

Everybody groaned as they heard Mrs. Williams' name. No one likes that bitch. She's a pain.

Mrs. Stevenson is a history teacher, Mr. Brown is an English teacher but not mine, he's just there for my free periods, and the devil's bitch teaches us homeroom while Mr. Walker is here for French.

"Now, relax. Mrs. Williams has not yet been confirmed so we might have Mr. Davis fill in," he informed and everybody let out a sigh of somewhat relief. If Mr. Davis decides to come then we'll have the best trip of our lives since all the teachers would be good, chill, and funny ones.

"Now, if anyone has questions feel free to ask while I send hotel and flight details and then get back to whatever it is that you kids do, just don't get too noisy," he warned as Riley came back and sat down.

"What the hell am I going to need a flashlight for in the city? It's the city of lights?" Riley mumbled while sitting down and going through the list.

"And the city of love, who knows, maybe you'll find your lover and soulmate there. I'll cross my fingers and hope you do." Allison teased her. I rolled my eyes before going through all emails and the list before taking a screenshot and going onto social media on my phone.

"I'm not even gonna say anything," Riley sighed before plugging her earphones in. It's that time of the month for her. It has to be. She's being nice to me, sort of, and helping me, has major mood swings and complained about her stomach hurting throughout the day and also has close to no but somehow a lot of patience today.

It feels weird talking to her again so consistently after not talking for a long time. I almost missed our friendship/relationship as third graders and up till freshman year but then we grew distant. I found new friends which I now don't speak to at all, and she grew to hate me, I still don't know for what.

Maybe I'll get a chance to ask about this trip. Do I want to know? I don't think so.

New plan: Avoid Riley Blakely as much as possible and make her stay away. Steps: Be a dick.

That shouldn't be too hard, it's in my veins. Allison turned in her seat and began speaking to Mason, occasionally rolling her eyes at me or glaring at me, and soon enough Riley joined their conversation.

"Are you going to do the English work? If you're not then-" I cut her off.

"You can't take it back now. When I was giving it back, you didn't take it. It's mine." I shrugged, trying my hardest to get on her nerves. What? It's what I do best.

"Okay," she just shrugged. That didn't get to her one bit? That work was rightfully hers and she didn't give one shit if I called it mine? "It's just the annotations anyway." She shrugged before turning her back to face me and going on her phone for a little bit. She turned it off and set it on the table, and soon enough, it rang.

Loud

She jumped before excusing herself and stepping out of the room after seeking permission.

An amused smile made its way to my face.

She hasn't changed at all.

I rolled my eyes when I saw the look Mason was giving me. "It's not going to happen, you both need to lose hope for that." I said to Allison and Mason who were giving each other the 'I told you so' look.

"Whatever you say." They said in sync.

CHAPTER FOUR

RILEY

The bell rang and French was done and so was the school day. I went to my locker and put any books away that I didn't need to take home and began walking to the gate. "Heyyy!" Ali skipped beside me, linking her arm with mine.

"What's wrong? Don't have your loverboy with you?" I teased as we walked together.

"How rude of you to think I'd put a guy before you!" she argued while turning slightly. I followed her gaze to see Mason and Asher walking out the building behind us. My eyes met with Asher's and we both just glared before he rolled his eyes and broke away. "Paris is going to be fun! Don't you think?" Allison raised her eyebrows at me before narrowing her eyes down.

"Disney is. And so is the Eiffel Tower. Nothing else. I'm just going because it's a chance to see the Eiffel tower glimmer and light up the night." I kind of have an obsession with the Eiffel Tower. It's the most beautiful piece of architecture to be created in my opinion and the way it glimmers for ten minutes in the hours is stunning to me. I even have a little Eiffel Tower with a switch to make it glimmer like that.

My dad got that for me when he went to Paris for work. It's my prized possession.

"You know according to the schedule, we don't see the Eiffel Tower until the last few days with the rest of the class. How are you going to go at night?"

See, that's a good question that I did not think about but should have.

I shrugged before answering, "I don't know. But I'm getting out of that hotel at two am and watching that show," I replied as we walked out the gates. I began my walk home as she headed over to her car where her mom came to pick her up.

I waved bye to her and her mom and began my daily walk home. About three minutes into my walk, I felt someone walking behind me. I turned around slightly, just enough to see who it was.

Asher West.

My *lovely* neighbor and peer.

How fucking cliche and ironic that we're neighbors am I right?

It was nice when we were friends but now, not so much. "Hey loser," he said as he caught up with my pace.

This is weird.

He never talks to me while we're walking home. "What do

you want, loser?" I asked as I kept walking, squinting slightly at the brightness of the sun.

"Why do you think I want something from you?" he asked in confusion.

"Wasn't your little plan to be a dick and shoo me away?" I asked nonchalantly while walking. He stopped walking and stood in my way. "You're standing in my way, loser." I squinted at the sun that was heavily blinding. He took a step closer to the point where he was towering over me and blocking the sun.

"Now you're not going blind. Did you know? How?" he asked in confusion.

"You forgot that I've known you for a long time. We used to be friends and as much as the word makes us cringe now, we knew each other inside out. Plus, you're easy to read." I shrugged before maneuvering my way around him and turning the corner to my street.

"Am not," he argued.

"Are too," I countered. "Look, let's just stay away from each other, okay? It worked for the past year and it should continue working. I don't want war going on between us when we're in Paris. I'm actually trying to enjoy this trip." I turned when I reached my house and looked at him.

"You just want the trip to be good so you can see the Eiffel tower. I don't get your deal with it," he scoffed.

"There's a lot that I don't get about you, don't get me started on that list. So just leave me alone, alright? Glare at me and snicker comments all you want. Just don't talk to me." I sighed, leaning on my little gate we had.

"You're the one who started by helping me!" he exclaimed.

I groaned, "Okay! I'm sorry I won't ever help you again. Happy?" I threw my arms up in frustration.

"No," he shook his head, "Now this game works my way." I am going to kill myself.

"Why is everything always a game with you? Why can't you just let it go?" I huffed in annoyance.

"Because if I let it go, then you win. And I can't let you win, you know that," he shrugged casually.

"So what are you going to do? Annoy me for eternity?" I rolled my eyes. He smirked in amusement before answering.

"If that's what it takes." He began walking away but I grabbed his sleeve.

"If that's what it takes to what?" I asked as I heard my front door opening behind me.

Oh no.

He needs to leave before my mom invites him in. She likes him a lot since the third grade for the teddy. "To make you crack and like me first," he winked before getting away just in time.

"Oh honey, why didn't you invite him inside? Your dad would've liked the company," my mom laughed as she came and stood next to me.

"I still hate him mom, still hate him," I sighed before turning around and going up to my room. I walked up to my room and tossed my bag carelessly onto the ground before face-planting on my bed, groaning into my pillow.

"Already annoyed?" I heard his voice peering through my window. I need to learn to close that damn thing.

"Asher, please can we just put your game on pause until Paris? Start then just let me be!" I screamed as I marched up to my window.

"Why did you help me?"

Oh my fucking god this little piece of shit is still going on about that.

"Is that what this whole thing is about? I'm sorry!" I whined before groaning.

"Sorry doesn't cut it, Riles," he shrugged while chuckling as his hand slid into his pockets.

"I'll cut you. Let it go, Ash. I made a mistake, okay? I was being nice and human!" I reasoned.

"We don't play nice with each other. You dug yourself deep into this one," he snickered. I turned to my desk and looked around for the heaviest yet most useless thing. I didn't exactly find anything, like at all.

"Explain your game to me. I wanna know all the rules." If he wants to play a game where I have a shot at winning, then I'll play too and I'll win. He arched an eyebrow at me.

"Intrigued are we?" he teased while I rolled my eyes. "First one to stop hating the other loses."

Are you serious? That is the most bullshit, boring, and useless game that I've ever heard of. "You want more? Fine. First one to like the other person loses, confessions only."

"I sense a challenge and just because I like to see you lose, I'll accept it." I arched an eyebrow at him. "Time limit is up until we come back from Paris. Time starts tomorrow so now shoo!" I closed my window along with the blinds.

"Time starts now, Riles!" I heard him shout. I groaned before pulling out the form for the Paris trip and taking it downstairs to my dad.

"Hey hun," he greeted me as I walked into his study.

"Hey. I'm gonna need you to sign this, please?" I placed the form in front of him. He went through it before grabbing a pen without hesitation and signing it.

"No hesitation at all, dad?" I asked in a little surprise. I didn't think he'd be so chill with me going for so long.

"You've wanted to see that tower glow and sparkle since you were three, no hesitation," he smiled at me.

I gave him a quick kiss on his cheek before heading back to my room to begin packing. I wanted to start packing today and finish by tomorrow so I was ready to go the day after.

I'm going to get to see the Eiffel Tower. This is unbelievable to me.

Just one thing that sucks about this trip, Asher is going and from what I know, he's going to take this game very seriously, in fact, maybe too seriously and something is going to go very wrong. I also don't know about the roommate thing because I think the students have something else in mind, I can only hope we abide by the rules just this once.

I don't understand why people have such a hard time following rules. What is so cool about being a rebel? I don't get it.

"Honey, someone's at the door for you," my mom came in and informed me with a look in her eyes.

I went downstairs to see my dad at the door, talking to Asher?

—— CHAPTER FIVE ——

RILEY

"Come on in," my dad patted his shoulder while stepping aside and letting him in. I stood at the end of the stairs with an exhausted look on my face while his eyes locked with mine. He smirked as he gave me an amused look.

"So, will you be going on that trip to Paris?" my dad asked as he got them both a glass of water.

"I will indeed, thank you," he replied as he took the glass of water.

"Well then, you better take care of my daughter, you've known her the longest," he smiled.

"Dad, I can take care of myself," I groaned while staying rooted to my spot. I raised my eyebrows expectantly as Asher walked up to me.

"I took your notes down." He handed the annotations sheet in front of me.

"I don't need another copy, just keep it." I shrugged as he sighed.

"You're going to get in trouble for giving me the answers," he gave me a pointed look.

"So pretend like you never got a copy and re-write my notes on the new copy you get." Does he not use his brain?

"How rude! You think I'd lie to my respected teachers?" he smirked at me.

"I'm pretty sure you have many times, not just in third grade. Did you come here for this?" I looked down at the copy.

He shook his head, "It was just a chance to annoy you," he shrugged.

Asshole.

"Great. Bye now." I placed my hands on his chest and began pushing him towards the door.

"So eager!" he teased while laughing as his back hit my front door. "See you later," he winked before opening the door and leaving.

"Oh my god, I hate him!" I yelled before sprinting up the stairs and into my room. I grabbed my pajamas and went into my bathroom, taking a shower before stepping out into my room in a pair of shorts and a full-sleeved t-shirt with my towel in a hat on my head.

I stood in front of my mirror before getting rid of the towel and brushing my hair through. I grabbed my bag and got all the homework, sitting on my bed to finish it earlier so

I had the rest of the day to myself.

English, great. I wrote the summary and wrote the first essay draft before putting it away and deciding to begin packing. I grabbed my suitcase from under my bed and placed it open on my bed.

I opened my closet, sighing as I checked for clothes to take. I grabbed my phone and checked the weather, it was clear for the most part.

I'll take a little bit of the basics. I started by packing my bottoms. Shorts, leggings, and some jeans and joggers. Then my t-shirts. Tank tops, graphic tees, and off-shoulders. Socks were followed by one pair of shoes and some sandals. That was one side.

On the other side came all my undergarments, pajamas and space for toiletries. I was pretty much done with my packing except for the toiletries which I would pack tomorrow after school.

I sighed, zipped it up and placed it in a corner of my room before going downstairs to get something to eat. I went downstairs and grabbed a packet of chips before sitting on the couch, watching tv.

"Are you excited about Paris? You've wanted to go since forever, honey!" my mom spoke in a cheery voice as she sat down beside me.

"Not with my class but I'm excited nonetheless." I gave her a small smile. By 'my class' I mean Asher. I've kind of spent the whole day trying to figure out what he has in mind but I haven't been able to come up with a logical answer and he's a very logical person.

I think.

I'm starting to get frustrated with the fact that I don't know what he's about to throw my way and that I can't do anything but get stuck with him for three weeks.

Think about Paris. The tower, Riley.

"Do we have ice cream?" I asked my mom. She shook her head in response while standing up. "I'm gonna go get some from the store." I stood up and grabbed the keys before taking my wallet and throwing my slippers on.

I stepped onto my porch and saw Asher leaving his house simultaneously.

Oh god, no.

I turned around and tried to open the door but it was locked and using my keys would make it too obvious.

Do I care?

No.

As I'm about to unlock the door, his voice interrupts me as I cringe. "Hey, Ry Ry!" he exclaimed while running over to my gate. I rolled my eyes before turning around, plastering a smile to my face and walking over to him.

"Yes, Ashy Bashy?" I asked while opening the gate and beginning to walk to the store.

"Where are you heading off to?" he questioned while

walking by my side. I resisted a groan,

"Does it matter? Why do you want to know?" I began picking up my pace, desperately wanting to get away from him.

"It doesn't matter but I bet I can take a guess," he smirked, "You're going to get ice cream."

Has he been stalking me?

"I don't want to know how you know that." I rolled my eyes and continued walking. "You do realize this is only making you more annoying and not-likable, right?" I asked as I crossed the street and got onto the one with the store.

"Oh really? Is it?" he asked sarcastically.

"Asher," I stopped abruptly and turned to him, making him crash into me. "Stop," I demanded. He just smirked at me. "Looking at you is making my blood boil. Please stop," I huffed before turning on my heels and heading into the store.

I walked straight to the ice cream aisle and looked around the fridge for the flavor I wanted. Where the hell is it?

"Ouch!" he laughed while following me. I looked around the whole place to see it on the topmost shelf.

Are you fucking kidding me? I groaned while trying to look around for my second favorite ice cream flavor only to see they were out. God, why are you playing with me?

"Do you want chocolate?" he asked while looking at the flavors.

"No," I lied while looking for another flavor to buy. This is what I get for being picky.

"I'll get it for you," he shrugged.

I looked at him in disbelief. My eyebrows raised, "Really?" Before I could process anything he picked me up. I tensed up but grabbed a tub anyway before he put me down. "You could've grabbed it for me." I maneuvered around him and headed to the counter.

"I just chose to grab you. See you around." He nudged my shoulder with his before heading out while I stared at his retreating figure.

"Seven dollars." I snapped out of it and gave the cashier ten dollars before telling him to keep the change and taking my ice cream and leaving. I got home and saw Ashley Simpson standing at the West's doorstep.

I resisted a groan of disgust and rolled my eyes before opening my door. "I'm back!" I announced while placing the ice cream in the freezer. I headed up to my room and turned to my bed after closing my door, only to feel someone clamp their hand over my mouth, muffling my screams.

"Please don't scream, Riles!" he whispered in my ear pleadingly.

My eyes widened as I tapped his arm. He let me go as I spun around to face him.

"What the fuck is wrong with you?" I whisper yelled.

"Ashley's there at my house please help me hide?" he asked while closing my window and closing the blinds with it.

"You can't just break into my room, Ash!" I smacked his arm repeatedly. "You're not supposed to be here, you need to leave right now!" I demanded while sighing and sitting on the foot of my bed.

"Please! How was I supposed to know she won't understand the word 'no'? Riles, please just for an hour, please?" I have to admit, it was fun to see him beg.

"Are you begging?" I smirked at him. I watched as his jaw clenched while he closed his eyes tightly.

"Yes, I am." That was so hard for him to admit.

I contemplated for a minute.

"Just an hour," I spoke warningly. He nodded, agreeing almost instantly. I shrugged before grabbing a book and sitting on my bed.

"What do I do here? I don't have my phone," he mumbled to himself.

"I know it sounds absurd, but you grab a book, and read," I smirked while throwing a book at him.

— CHAPTER SIX —

ASHER

This is boring. Just blatantly boring. We were both sitting on the floor now, her leaning against her bed while I leaned against her closet. My eyes are peeking from above the book while hers are curiously scanning the pages of hers.

"Can we please do something?" I asked while nudging her leg. Her eyes shot up to meet mine from her book. She glared at me before going back to reading. "Ry Ry," I nudged her leg again. Her eyes didn't leave her book, she just nudged my leg back.

"I'm willing to talk. Let's talk about how our best friends are so in love." I nudged her leg, again. Her eyes met mine, more intrigued now, as she put her book down and gave me her undivided attention.

"Spill the beans, Ashy," she sighed while hugging her knees, waiting for me to begin.

"Only if you spill them in return."

She nodded before holding out her pinky which I entangled mine with. "He's been trying to impress her and get close to her for a while. It started as just another girl but I think he's starting to genuinely like her. He doesn't tell me much about his love- or well, lust life. But he's different with her. He's more... careful." I explained everything in a nutshell.

"She usually tells me everything but she's very secretive about him. I think she's trying not to like him because of the image he carries and the number of girls everyone's seen him with. She's different with him too but she's trying to be cautious. I don't know if it's working. I don't trust your best friend with the heart of mine." She has a valid point there.

"I don't think he'd risk fucking shit up with her, I think he likes her," I shrugged, genuinely not knowing what's been going through Mason's head.

"Well, I hope he does," she sighed before stretching in her seat.

"You know that the students aren't going to follow rules in Paris," I began.

"There's only one rule?" she asked in confusion. She's so innocent sometimes. Most of the time.

"Exactly. No one's going to follow it. Everyone's already thinking of ideas." I informed her.

"Ideas to what? Find a roommate?" she asked with curiosity while I nodded. She sighed in exhaustion. "Are the teenagers of our generation really so desperate and sexually frustrated?" she groaned into her hands.

"They're just horny, Riles. You're gonna have to deal with it," I laughed and shrugged.

"No, I won't. I'm rooming with Allison," she pointed out. Way too innocent for her good.

"And what if she chooses to room with Mason?" I arched an eyebrow at her.

"Then I'll just have to room with whoever, it doesn't matter. It's just for the nights," she shrugged.

"Not if they choose the most popular method so far," I paused, waiting to see if she'd get it.

"No!" she groaned, "They are not considering picking chits, please no!" she screamed into her pillow while I chuckled.

"I hope I get you, your reaction would be so priceless," I laughed.

Her screaming stopped and she immediately turned to me with a death glare.

"I will kill you." She acted so serious that I genuinely got scared for a second.

I sighed before continuing,

"You're not as sly as you think you are. I know you put up a tough front and try being mean like you hate everyone and everything around you, but I know that's not true. And whether you admit it or not, you are *thrilled* to be going on this trip because you want to see that tower. Stop lying." I shrugged.

"You don't even know me anymore. What makes you say

that?" she raised her brows at me curiously.

"You forgot that I've known you for a long time," I smirked, using the words she used earlier.

"Did you though? Or did I just know you?" she arched an eyebrow at me, making me second guess my words.

How much do I know? To be honest, compared to how much she knows about me, I don't really know much.

"Give me a chance to get to know you then," I suggested.

"Why?" she scoffed, "So we can go down the same path again?" she stood up while I mirrored her actions. "So that we get close only for you to turn into a dick and leave me?" she had pent up tension and this was the boiling point.

"We weren't together?" I voiced my confusion.

"That's not what I mean! We were friends! I trusted you and then you became a dick!" she exclaimed.

"I didn't do anything, Riles!" I paused, "I just came to school and you hated me!" I explained my side of the story.

"Did you ever wonder why?" she paused, "I know what you said, Asher!" she used my full name, no Ashy Bashy or Ash. This was way worse than I thought.

We hated each other but the nicknames were always there. Not anymore I guess.

"You talked so much shit on me the day you found new friends! They're not here anymore but now our friendship is down the drain because of what you did! You hurt me!" she reasoned.

That's what this has been about all along. "It's been a year, Riles, come on," I countered.

She scoffed, "I didn't know there was a time limit on healing from the hurt you feel?"

I hurt her badly.

"I'm dumb, okay! It was my mistake for doing that, I am sorry!" I wanted this feud to be over, I was tired of our hatred. I wanted my friend back.

"No, you're not." I don't blame her for not understanding but I want another chance. "Why do you suddenly want to be friends with me?" she asked, thinking out loud.

"I'm tired of acting like we hate each other!" I let out an exasperated sigh.

"We do hate each other! I'm not acting, Ash!" she argued. That hurt just a little.

"You don't miss the relationship- friendship, we had?" I corrected myself.

It was just a friendship.

"It was a toxic one. We kept hurting each other. It's better this way." Her voice was dying down. That's how I knew she didn't mean that.

"You don't mean that. Not one bit." I argued.

"I don't want to be friends with you, don't you get that? I never did!" she lied. I didn't want it to come to this.

"You're right, you wanted to be more!" I blurted out as confusion clouded her eyes. "You liked me, Riley. Admit it!"

As those words escaped my mouth, her right hand made firm contact with my cheek.

"You are so full of yourself! Open your fucking eyes! Not everybody likes you, Asher! Not everybody is willing to die just for you to notice them! You were my friend! And when you left me for other people and talked shit about me, I lost all feelings of friendship that I had for you! And that's all they were! Feelings of friendship!" she clenched and unclenched her fists.

"You were my friend, but you betrayed me. I don't want that again." Her voice cracked so slightly that I thought I had imagined it. Maybe I had? I bit my lip, not knowing what to say to her.

"I didn't mean to hurt you," I tried explaining my sad excuse.

She chuckled humorlessly.

"No," she shook her head, "You just meant to talk shit and me to never find out."

She's going back to being cold. She barely started warming up to me today and it was already all gone.

"Just trust me. Please?" I tried to take a step closer to her but she stepped back, increasing the distance between us.

"I can't. Even if I wanted to, I couldn't," she shrugged, her voice soft.

"I won't ever hurt you again, I promise." I tried. I don't even know why I want her in my life so badly. She was a person I could always talk to. And now I lost her.

She shook her head before speaking, "I'm not willing to risk that for the friendship we had because I don't think we can even get close to the one we had earlier. It's gone, Ash. We're not getting it back," she shook her head slightly. "We'll only ever be acquaintances now," she paused, "You should go."

She walked over to her window and opened it. I looked at her, trying to find a sign that contradicted her words. "Riley," I whispered, taking a step closer but she only distanced herself more from me.

"Go," she whispered. I got out of her room and swung into mine.

That last thing I saw was her locking her window, and closing her curtains.

— CHAPTER SEVEN —

RILEY

I cried that night. A lot. I got that friendship back and lost it again in one day. Well, kind of got it back. I know I'm the one who told him to leave but I did not want him to want to become friends with me just because of the guilt or just ask me so blatantly.

I wanted to be friends again but I couldn't forget everything that happened so easily. It put me through hell then and letting him in would just do that again. After everything that happened last year, Allison joined our school and I found a new best friend. Just as good as if not better than him.

I don't want her hanging out with Mason because it automatically means that I have to hang out with Asher. But she's my best friend and it's the least I can do for her. I was leaning against my locker, waiting for Allison to get to school when Tyler approached me.

"Hey Riley," he greeted me white leaning on the locker beside mine.

"Hi?" I said but it came out more like a question. We never

talk so this is confusing.

"So listen, Hotel Le Regent Montmartre is thirty-two minutes from the Eiffel Tower and Hotel 121 Paris is twenty-six minutes away, we used google maps, which one do you want to stay in?" he asked me while going through his phone to double-check the distance and then putting it away in his pocket.

"Students get to choose?" I asked as Allison entered and walked up to me.

"Students that make their choices first do, others just get whatever is available," he explained, "And I'm going around asking the people in our class that I like so we can get the same hotel."

That was the reason. He wanted to throw parties even on the trip as if one every weekend at his house wasn't enough.

"Majority has been choosing Hotel 121 Paris so you want..." he trailed off.

"Um- Hotel 121 Paris. It's not for the parties, it's closer to the tower, that's why," I clarified.

He cheered before nodding and typing my name and preferred hotel in his notes before walking over to Asher who was standing a few lockers away from me with Mason.

"Can I see what people chose?" Asher asked while Tyler handed him the phone. "I'll take the hotel 121."

I turned to see him looking at me. I clenched my jaw before sighing and walking with Allison who much to my dismay, was walking over to Mason. She glared at him before walking right past him.

I guess not. "What happened right there? Everything okay between you two?" I asked worriedly.

She huffed.

"He didn't call me and say goodnight last night so now I'm acting mad." She blushed crimson as we sat down in homeroom.

I rolled my eyes.

"You're perfect for each other," I chuckled while thinking about how childish both of them are.

Asher and Mason came in and sat down in front of us.

"Ali, I'm sorry I was with my mom helping prepare dinner we hosted." I feel bad for how hard the guy's trying and she's not even actually mad. "Please?" he took out a basket of chocolates.

"Oh my god." Asher, Allison and I spoke in unison. Well, food is the way to a girl's heart I guess.

Not to mine though, I'm more of an old-school roses kind of girl.

She laughed before taking the basket and analyzing the chocolates. She's a very picky eater. She giggled before placing a kiss on his cheek.

"Get a room," Ash and I mumbled simultaneously before glancing at each other.

Mrs. Williams came in and homeroom began with the best news. "For all those people in Mr. Walker's French class, I will not be coming on the trip. I have a wedding to attend," she announced.

The class erupted in silent cheers. "Mr. Wayne will be the fourth teacher." That just made the news a whole lot better. Homeroom went by quickly after that and I headed for business only to find Mr. Brown as my substitute.

I was the first one in class and he greeted me with his warm smile. "Mrs. Grimwald has quit her job, she probably got sick of it," he shrugged while writing the date and title on the board. "Welcome to my class, Ms. Blakely." He smiled as I took my seat.

"I love you, Mr. Brown, you are my favorite teacher!" I laughed while throwing a scrap piece of paper I found in my notebook in the trash. Before I could get back to my seat, the door opened in my face, making me stumble.

I glared at the person who walked in and of course, it was Asher West. "Sorry, are you okay?" he asked with concern.

I simply rolled my eyes, "Whatever," before going and sitting down in my seat. He sat down behind me before greeting Mr. Brown. The class eventually filed in, gleaming with joy after learning that Mr. Brown was our new teacher.

School is kind of getting better.

We were halfway through class and we were actually

having fun and getting notes down. This is why everyone likes Mr. Brown, he teaches but makes it fun.

Unfortunately, Asher behind me wouldn't stop whispering. "Do you have glue by any chance?" he asked someone. "It's okay, do you?" he asked another person while I turned in my seat to glare at him. "Do you?" he asked me nervously.

"Mr. West, can I help you?" Mr. Brown turned to him patiently. "What do you need?" he asked.

"Glue," Asher spoke with embarrassment painted all over his face. I stifled a laugh while Mr. Brown smiled and tossed him a glue stick.

"Thank you, sir, you're the best." Asher caught it with ease.

"I know, let's get back to class, shall we?" Everyone chuckled before beginning to take notes while Mr. Brown told a story about how he went to the store and ended up accidentally buying a whole aisle.

Don't ask, I'm not paying much attention, I'm trying to get the notes down. "I didn't know the worker misunderstood my words and thought I wanted to buy the whole aisle!" he exclaimed while the class began laughing hysterically. "Alright, alright. Let's get back to sales revenue."

He laughed himself before changing the slide, moving to the next. The class was over and he was asking people a few questions to make sure everyone understood. "Mr. West, can you tell me the formula for sales revenue since you were so dedicatedly looking for a glue stick while I taught my class."

He looked at Asher with a grin. I smiled to myself, ducking

my head while Asher stuttered. "Ms. Blakely?" Mr. Brown passed the question onto me.

"Price into quantity," I answered correctly. Mr. Brown nodded before sighing,

"Please give Mr. West your notes, the boy could use them," he huffed before packing his stuff up as the class laughed. "Class is dismissed." He left before the bell rang and since the class was dismissed, so did we.

"Ry Ry," Asher jogged up to me. "Notes please?" he smiled and held his hand out.

I sighed and placed my notebook in his hand.

"I need them back by tonight," I huffed before speed walking away. The rest of the day went by pretty fast and soon enough I was out of art and into lunch. "I forgot my lunch in my locker, I'll meet you in the field," I informed Allison before heading for my locker.

I dialed the combination but it refused to open. What the hell? I tried again but it still didn't work.

"Come on, third time's the charm," I whispered to myself before yanking it open.

It opened.

And I found a gift box inside.

This felt a little like a stalker horror movie, not gonna lie. I looked around to see nobody there. There was no note, nothing with it that hinted who left it there. It was definitely someone who knew my combination.

I unwrapped the box and opened it to find a teddy bear inside.

What. The. Fuck?

I pulled the teddy bear out and looked inside the box for a note but found nothing.

When I finally looked at the teddy bear, I found three roses glued onto its arm, holding it.

I sighed and rolled my eyes before letting myself smile and laugh. I looked around while holding the bear to see Asher peering out from the end of the hallway, hiding behind the wall.

I laughed before smiling to myself.

This boy.

—— CHAPTER EIGHT ——

RILEY

I walked out into the field to see Allison sitting and talking to Mason. I went down and sat with them. "Hey you two," Allison smiled. Two? I turned to my right to see Asher walking up beside me.

We sat down and soon enough, Allison and Mason got back to their conversation, leaving Asher and me out. "Did you get my gift?" he asked discreetly while drinking from his water bottle and putting it back in his bag.

"I don't know, did I?" I glanced at him with an expressionless look.

"Riley," he whined like a child.

I bit my lip and tried not to smile or laugh and turned my head in the other direction, avoiding his gaze.

Since my actions are obviously contradicting my words, let's just lay it all out on the table.

I hate him. I'll always hate him for hurting me the way he did, however, the boy will always hold a soft spot in my heart, and I will always care for him. Maybe it's because he was my third-grade boyfriend and first kiss, maybe it's because he's the bestest friend I've ever had, maybe it's the memories or maybe it's something else. But I'll always care about him, even if he hurts me.

I bit the inside of my cheek while nodding and turning to face him. "Yeah, I got your gift." I laughed slightly while taking my lunch out and beginning to eat my cold spaghetti. Not that cold, surprisingly.

"Should I be looking for it in a trash can?" he asked, sounding slightly disappointed.

"No," I laughed, "You can look for it in a backpack," I shrugged.

"You kept it?" he asked, his eyes gleaming. I haven't seen this side of him since freshman year and here and there last year before we stopped talking.

"Of course I did." I squinted at the sun while looking at him.

"I'm sorry." His voice was barely a whisper while the wind blew his hair, whipping through it.

"I can't forgive you," I whispered in response, giving him a small sad smile.

"I understand that. You can't forgive me," he nodded, "Can I get another chance though?" he asked, squinting at the light too while Allison and Mason were too engulfed in their conversation.

"When you earn it, then maybe you can someday." I looked

straight at him.

He smiled,

"Acquaintances?" he reached his hand out for me to shake. I looked at his hand before chuckling.

"Acquaintances." I nodded before placing my hand in his, shaking it. "Still hate you." I looked out into the field.

"Feeling's mutual, Riles." He too looked around before we both went back to just that. No talking.

Soon after, the bell rang and lunch was over. Two more periods before the day ends and then I can finally get home, finish packing and I'll be all set for Paris.

I still can't believe I'll get to see the tower.

"You better keep that bear, Riles. It took me forty-five minutes to glue them on and make it look presentable. I wanna see that every time I look into your room like I see the one from third grade," he spoke as we began walking to English together.

Why are we walking to class together?

"Why don't you buy the ones with roses?" I asked as we approached our classroom.

"It's a tradition between us. I have to glue them on," he shrugged nonchalantly.

"Right," I nodded, "And why would you be looking into my room?" I narrowed my eyes down at him as he continued walking ahead of the class.

"Why not?" he yelled before turning around, heading to the printing room.

I scoffed to myself before heading into class to see Mr. Wayne sitting there on his computer. "Ms. Blakely, please do me a huge favor and get print outs for the class?" he requested. I nodded before putting my bag down and heading to the room. I walked in there to see Asher sitting and smoking.

"He always sends you," he laughed while blowing out puffs of smoke.

"You're very weird. I don't understand what's so addictive about that cigarette." I looked at it with disgust before the sheets began to print out.

"I'm not addicted, Ry Ry. It's an escape." That's a new one.

"From your tragic reality?" I scoffed while leaning against the printer and looking down at him.

"You don't know half of it. I have people to hate in my life, for instance, *you.*" Ouch. "And people hate me too, for instance, you." That's true. The print outs were taking forever.

"True." I nodded while sitting down beside him. "You make your life tragic though. You hang out with the wrong crowd outside daily. Find some better people for yourself," I shrugged.

"That's kind of hard to do when you live on your own." He doesn't live with his parents. They're separated but not divorced and both split his funding in half. He ends up earning for himself by working at the diner, the library and the grocery store part-time.

I would know, I've had too many run-ins with him. His grandparents are his legal guardians and the house he lives in is theirs too. They don't live with him, they live two blocks away.

"Doesn't it ever get lonely in the house by yourself? I mean what do you do?" I asked while turning to face him.

"I get my ass up and look into your window. And I see my third-grade girlfriend."

I rolled my eyes but I couldn't help but laugh at that.

I nudged his shoulder with mine, "You're going to have to let that go one day you know." I took a deep breath and stood up, grabbing all the print outs.

"I could never!" he gasped dramatically.

I collected all the copies and turned to give him one last piece of advice.

"Come for English. It's not that bad." I gave him a pointed look before leaving. I went into class and distributed the sheets, leaving one on the seat behind me which has been assigned to Asher but he's never here.

The work was the usual, annotate, analyze, write an essay. I was halfway through my annotations when the door swung open.

"Glad you decided to join us today, Mr. West." Mr. Wayne remarked as Asher came and sat in his seat.

"Happy to be here, sir." He actually listened to me? I turned to him with a small smile.

"You came?" I asked in a little surprise.

He put his bag down and grabbed a pencil from it.

"Of course I did," he answered softly.

I bit back the smile and got back to my work. We still had ten minutes left for class to end and I was finished with the task. I grabbed my phone and began scrolling through social media, looking at Harry Styles, Bella Hadid and god knows who else.

"Riles," I turned in my seat to face him. "How do you summarize a metaphor?" he asked in confusion.

"You don't. You find the meaning and summarize that meaning, linking it together." I explained, "At least that's what I did. You could just quote it." I shrugged before turning back around.

Five minutes went by and I felt him poking me with his pencil. "I'm bored."

I turned to see him resting his chin in his hand.

"Are you done?" I asked, glancing down at his surprisingly decent handwriting.

"Yeah, I finished it a minute ago. Listen, there's a birthday party at the diner tonight and we're short on one staff member. Would you want to help?" he asked while fiddling with the pencil.

"Who's birthday is it? It depends on if I like them." I

shrugged while looking at him.

"It's Mason's little cousin's. He's turning six. We could use another person, please?" he pleaded.

"What time?" I asked, "Because you know our flight is tomorrow at six am," I pointed out.

He nodded, "It's five to seven-thirty. Please?" he requested. "Bring Allison with you," he shrugged.

I thought for a moment before agreeing, "Okay, I'll be there at four-thirty."

He thanked me before we both went back to whatever it was that we were doing.

"Wear something pretty, there's gonna be photographs," he informed me. Why would they take photographs of the people working at the diner?

"Photographs of the people working for the party?" My eyebrows creased in confusion as I turned to him again.

He shook his head before packing his stuff and then explaining.

"You're not just working," he laughed. "You're my date."

I'm his what now?

— CHAPTER NINE —

ASHER

"You didn't tell me I'm your *date!*" she hissed as we walked out of class and to our next one. Free period. Mr. Brown for the second time in the day? Hell yeah!

"I thought you'd guess," I spoke in my defense. I mean come on, I'm asking her to go to a party with me. A birthday party of a soon to be a six-year-old child but a party nonetheless.

"It's a six-year-old's birthday!" she exclaimed while taking a seat in front of me. "You asked me to be there because one staff member wouldn't! Where does that signal date in any way?" She turned in her seat while Mr. Brown watched us in amusement.

"Well, now I told you, okay? And you already said yes." I gave her a pointed look.

"I said yes to helping out, *not* being your date," she argued. Valid point.

"Riles, I'm flattered you're so repulsed by the thought of being my date but suck it up." I had the last words as the class began settling in.

"What if I just don't show up?" she challenged.

Idiot.

"Then you'll just be ruining a soon to be six-year-old's birthday party," I shrugged casually. She clenched her jaw before groaning and turning around.

I usually get things my way.

Mr. Brown took attendance in the class and then left everyone to do their own thing. We were about two minutes into class and Allison and Mason came barging in. "Could we get a moment with Asher and Riley?" They both were panting slightly since they were late but Mr. Brown allowed them anyway.

We looked at each other and them suspiciously before getting up and leaving the room with them. Mason dragged me to one end while Allison dragged Riley to another. I gave him a confused look.

"Listen up buddy, as your friend I'm about to ask you for a favor, and I'm hoping you'll be my friend and agree."

What the fuck?

"I need you and Riley to become friends."

"Absolutely not!" I exclaimed while I heard Riley say the same thing from the other end.

What are Allison and Mason thinking?

"Shut up!" he yelled. "Look, Asher, I really like Allison

okay? And I really like hanging out with her, but every time I do, you and Riley are there and because you two are there, so is your bickering. One day the shit between Riley and you will get to the boiling point and Allison's going to have to pick between her best friend and me who is hopefully her boyfriend by then. I don't want to put her in that position-" he sighed,

"So could you please just try and become friends with her? For the sake of my love life?" he was breathless by the time he finished explaining. I bit the inside of my cheek, contemplating his words while looking in Riley's direction to see her doing the same while looking at me.

She gave me a small nod.

"Fine, I'll try," I told Mason before he fist-bumped the air and silently cheered. "You owe me." I glared at him while he nodded and laughed before fist-bumping me and pulling me into a hug.

"Yeah, yeah now get off of me," I mumbled while pushing him away. Allison and Riley began walking our way and we did too, meeting them in the middle. "Truce?" I took my hand out for Riley.

She rolled her eyes and glanced at Allison. "Truce." She placed her hand in mine.

Now I'm not allowed to annoy her and be a dick. Damnit!

"I'll meet you at the diner," she addressed me and I nodded.

"Are we missing something here?" Allison and Mason question in sync.

They're perfect for each other.

"I'm helping with your cousin's birthday party tonight." Mason blinked in realization.

I cut in,

"And she's my date for it tonight," I smirked at her while she rolled her eyes and balled her hands up into fists.

"I wouldn't have said yes if he had mentioned that before," she spoke through gritted teeth. *"But,* as *his friend,"* she glared at me, "I agreed." She turned and smiled at Mason. After that conversation ended, we headed back into the class.

"So we're friends now? I teased while taking my seat as she took hers.

"Don't push it, Ash, don't push it." She spoke low and warningly.

"Seriously though, who would've thought you'd say yes to that crazy deal?" I chuckled, annoying her even more.

"I'm doing it for Allison, okay? The day your best friend decides to hurt her, I'll never have to speak to you ever again," she spoke demandingly.

She meant that huh?

"Well, it's too bad he's not going to hurt her. He really likes her," I said while she narrowed her eyes down at me.

"For the sake of her happiness, I hope he does like her. But remember, he leaves and you'll leave with him. You will grow no feelings towards me, even of friendship," she ordered.

"And I'll stick to my word and do the same. Deal?" She stuck her hand out at me.

I glanced around the room to see Mr. Brown listening to our conversation, intrigued and amused. His eyes met mine and he shook his head at me.

Is he telling me not to take the deal?

My eyes snapped back to hers that were staring at me impatiently. "Deal." I shook her hand. I looked back at Mr. Brown to see him sighing and shaking his head in disappointment.

What is with that guy?

The rest of the lesson we didn't talk at all, as expected and soon enough, the bell rang. I stood up and waited for the class to leave which automatically left me to be the last one with Mr. Brown behind me.

"You dug yourself a grave, son. Man to man, you're bound to get feelings. But now that you've made her a deal, I'll just wish you luck to keep your end of the bargain," he sighed before leaving.

What the hell is that supposed to mean?

I walked home behind Riley as usual and only spoke to her before she stepped into her house. "Don't be late!" I reminded her. She nodded before flipping me off, probably just because she felt like it, and going into her home.

I walked up to my room and took out a black button-up with a pair of jeans to wear. I placed them out on my bed and caught a glimpse of Riley holding up two dresses in front of her while looking in the mirror. One was peach and one was red.

She better pick the red one, she'd look hot in it.

I shook my head and pushed that thought away before going to take a shower and get ready for the party. I came out of the shower, ran my fingers through my hair after drying it and kept the towel around my waist as I stepped out into my room. I stepped out and grabbed my clothes, throwing them on. I finished closing up the last button of the shirt, leaving the first two undone before turning to see Riley zipping up her dress.

She picked the red one.

Good choice.

I smiled before spraying cologne on and grabbing my car keys, heading to the door. I locked my door and turned to my car at the same time Riley stepped out of her car. "You look hot!" I remarked.

She stopped in her tracks and closed her eyes, taking a deep breath before plastering a smile on her face.

"Thanks! You look average." Damn. She shrugged before beginning to walk.

"Need a ride?" I yelled while unlocking my car and getting it, backing out of my driveway, stopping right in front of hers.

"As your *lovely* date. I'll say yes." Her glare is just something else, I'm telling you. She walked up to my car and sat in the front seat while I opened the door for her. "Look at that! Who knew you'd be such a gentleman. Thank you!" she spoke tauntingly.

"I did that like a real gentleman, huh? Come to my place sometime, I'll show how much of a gentleman I can be."

She rolled her eyes while I chuckled and sat in my seat, driving off to the diner.

We got there and she immediately got down to work. She's worked here before with me as a summer job and she knew how things worked around here.

She refilled the drink containers, set out the plates and took down the orders as kids began coming in. "That's the first list, get to work," she slapped the list onto my chest, going into the kitchen.

I'm impressed.

CHAPTER TEN

RILEY

"Okay, everybody! Get together for the pictures!" Natasha yelled. She's hosting the party and it's Jacob's party.

"Mom, I don't want to take pictures!" he whined. He wanted to cut the cake instead but Natasha wanted to get all the pictures taken first.

"Memories, Jacob!" she scolded. He shrugged before telling all his friends to get ready for the pictures. "You guys too!" she addressed Mason, Ali, Asher and me.

"That's okay," Mason chuckled while waving his hand dismissively.

"I'm not asking, Mason." Natasha deadpanned. I stifled a laugh before standing on one side of the kids with Asher behind me while Ali and Mason did the same on the other side. We were about to click the picture but Jacob spoke up.

"Wait! I want Riley beside me!" he demanded. The boy grew a certain liking towards me.

"Of course." I nodded before going and standing beside him.

"That's *my* date." Asher grabbed my wrist, pulling me back.

I shrugged before taking my wrist out of his grasp.

"And it's *his* birthday," I smirked before kneeling down beside Jacob with all the kids surrounding me.

We got a few with that placement before Natasha said, "Alright now Jacob, let Riley go and stand with her date." Jacob pouted but let go of my hand nonetheless. I kissed his cheek, making him blush before going and standing in front of Asher.

"That sneaky little sh-" I smacked him before he finished that sentence. He rolled his eyes.

"We're taking pictures, so smile." I brushed the creases out of his shirt before turning and facing the camera. We all smiled with the kids beginning to get impatient and running around already.

"Now one kissing on the cheek, come on!" Natasha ordered. We all just froze.

Crickets.

No noise, even the kids stopped moving. "Ew!" they all screamed before covering their eyes.

Asher placed his arms around me from behind and I stiffened.

"Host's orders," he whispered and I just knew he was smirking. I closed my eyes and plastered a fake smile on my face as his lips met my cheek.

"Aw!" Natasha gushed and that's when we knew the picture had been taken.

He pulled away and asked me, "Did you smile?" he smirked.

I rolled my eyes before turning to him.

"So big," I said sarcastically before glancing and Mason and Ali who were holding hands and blushing like crazy before leaving them alone and beginning to clean up.

"Girls, your turn!" Natasha squealed.

This woman likes to make a lot of memories.

I rolled my eyes but stood beside Asher nonetheless. He draped his arm around my waist while I grabbed his face and planted a kiss on his cheek. After the flash went off, I pulled away immediately and caught him *blushing?*

I pinched his cheek with a grin before getting back to cleaning up while Ali and Mason saw everyone out before leaving themselves. I finally finished cleaning the kitchen and got to cleaning the tables.

I got to the table that Asher was on and began cleaning the other side. I grabbed the salt while he grabbed the pepper and placed it on the other table while we cleaned this one. I slid the salt across the table and gave it to him before going to the next table.

This went on till we were done cleaning all the tables and ready to go back home.

I am so tired.

I grabbed my jacket and waited for Asher to turn all the

lights off and leave the keys in the secret spot outside the diner before he led the way to his car and held the door open for me. "Thanks," I gave him a small smile while getting in and putting my seatbelt on.

He drove me home and we said goodnight before I went into my room. I threw my jacket onto my chair and flopped down on my bed. I sighed before getting up and grabbing my pajamas and going to wash my face, take my makeup off, brush my teeth and do all that before coming back into my room and going straight to bed. I stayed fast asleep until my alarm rang.

I was about to snooze it and go straight back to bed but then I remembered... *Paris!!!*

I huffed before getting up and just sitting in bed, staring at the floor for five minutes. I was sitting there when a paper ball hit me in the head.

What the

"What are you doing? Get up we have to leave in twenty minutes!" Asher laughed from his window.

I glared at him before processing what he said and shooting out of bed. I already had my outfit layed out and so I just grabbed it and shot into the bathroom.

I freshened up, took a shower even though I hate morning showers, brushed my teeth, did all that before grabbing a toiletry bag and placing all my toiletries in it. Toothbrush, toothpaste, moisturizer, hairbrush, everything I use for my skin care including sunscreen and a mini container of vaseline.

I grabbed that bag, opened my suitcase, stuffed it in there, grabbed a backpack in which I put my laptop, it's the charger, my phone, it's charger and my airpods before throwing that over my shoulder and getting the fuck out of there.

I went into my parents room and kissed both of their cheeks while they slept before leaving my house, waiting on my porch for Allison to come to pick me up as we planned.

"Hello?" I answered my phone. I heard shuffling before honking, a lot of honking.

"Riley, listen I am so sorry! I cannot pick you up, I'm running late myself, I gotta go!" she hung up before I could say anything.

What the hell am I supposed to do now?

I sighed before standing up to go in and wake up my dad to drive me but Asher opening his front door stopped me. I swallowed my pride and walked over to his house with my suitcase in hand and backpack over my shoulder.

"Hey, Ashy Bashy!" I said sweetly. "So listen, Allison is running late and canceled on me last minute. Will you please be a gentleman like earlier tonight and drive me?" I asked while looking at him with pleading eyes.

"Are you begging?" he smirked.

I need to watch my mouth around him, he tends to use my words against me.

"Yes, I am." I nodded.

He shrugged before opening his car door for me. I did a

little happy dance in my head before putting my suitcase in the trunk and getting in the car. He got in, started the car and we were off to the airport.

"How are you gonna get your car back to yours?" I asked as we left our street.

"Well, I'm having a friend come and pick it up and then drop it at mine," he informed me as he sped up once he looked at the time. He definitely crossed the limit but we pulled into the airport nonetheless.

He got out, grabbed his stuff while I grabbed mine and tossed his keys to a friend. To Jordan Reynolds. He changed schools last year and now goes to a private school in the neighboring town.

He talked shit on me with Asher.

"Have fun," he smirked at Asher. Asher and I rolled our eyes before rushing into the airport, meeting up with our class.

"You two made it," Mr. Walker announced. "Here are your boarding passes, and yours." He handed them to Mason and Ali who came rushing in behind us. "I have news," he addressed the class while anxiety radiated off of us. "The flight was delayed by four hours."

You have got to be fucking kidding me. Are you serious?

"What?" the class exclaimed in sync. "So we crossed the limit for nothing?" Mason and Ali asked.

"Crossed the limit? I ran two red lights!" Asher cut in.

He did not run just two red lights.

"No, you didn't. You actually ran three." I pointed out. The class looked between us in utter shock. "My ride canceled," I announced while glancing at Ali who looked at me innocently.

The class let out a breath in sync.

Even Mr. Walker.

What the hell is going on?

"No, she just wanted to ride with me."

Asshole.

He turned to me with a mischievous look in his eyes and a smirk dancing on his lips.

"Excuse you?" I gaped at him.

What a fucking liar.

I would never have asked if Ali didn't cancel on me last minute.

"You begged," he shrugged with a smirk.

The class gasped.

"I canceled on her last minute. Chill out, find your humanity!" Ali laughed nervously.

— CHAPTER ELEVEN —

RILEY

We were all scattered across an area with a few benches, some asleep, some dead, some in-between. I was one of those in-between that wanted to sleep but the uncomfort-ness of the surroundings weren't letting me.

And there's no way I could sleep on the flight because I'm the type of person that never can.

"I'm going to go and get some coffee, do you want anything?" Asher sighed and walked up to me while glancing at the little coffee machine in the corner of the room.

I looked left, then right, then behind me. "Me?" I asked in shock and surprise.

He rolled his eyes, "Yes *you*. Mr. Walker's paying and I'm getting stuff for Mason and well..." he glanced at Allison who was fast asleep on my shoulder.

"I'll get some tea, thanks," I said hesitantly.

He could poison it for all I know.

He left but not before going up to Mason. I adjusted my shoulder as it began aching from Allison before Mason walked up to me. "My turn," he smiled at me.

"I'm fine," I lied.

He glanced behind me at Asher who I caught giving him 'the look' before Mason spoke again.

"Come on, I'm sure you must be tired too. Please?" he requested.

I sighed and rolled my eyes before slowly standing up and going and sitting in his seat which was across from mine, one seat to the right. I plugged in my earphones and began listening to music.

"Here you go," Asher sighed while sitting beside me with a coffee in his hands while I looked forward to seeing Mason with one in his.

"You didn't poison this?" I narrowed my eyes down at him suspiciously.

He smiled, "No, I didn't." Fair enough then.

I grabbed a cup of tea from him before beginning to walk around and stretch my legs to avoid getting pins and needles.

I got lost in my world and turned the corner as someone exclaimed, "Boo!" I jumped back a little bit but caught myself and the tea before it spilled everywhere and glared at the devil himself that was standing in front of me.

"I stood up from there and came here with my tea for a reason you know," I glared before continuing to look around while he followed.

"I am delighted to hear that you wanted to sit with me," he rolled his eyes. Excuse me? Who the hell told him to be the bigger person and make Mason and me switch?

"Who told you to become oh so great and make Mason and me switch?" I deadpanned before strolling around.

"You are such a bitch," he chuckled.

Surprisingly I'm not offended at all.

"I am," I nodded in agreement, "And I'm sure you would know." I sassed. He looked at me with disbelief before grabbing my wrist, not allowing me to wander off and walk away.

"I'm trying to be friends here like we promised them. So stop being a bitch."

God help me, please.

"I don't see them around us. Just because I said we'll be friends doesn't mean we have to be friends behind their backs. As long as they think we're friends, they should be fine."

I sound like such a bitch. Maybe I really am one.

"Okay look, I know you. Not half, as well as you know me, but I still know you. Why are you acting like such a bitch for no reason?" he asked in confusion.

"Pettiness. Heard of it? You should get used to it. It comes with me." I smiled sweetly before pulling my wrist out of his grip and going back to my seat.

I was about to put my airpods back in but he came and

snatched them from me. "What do you mean I should get used to it? I'm not here to take shit from you, Riles," he huffed while sitting beside me. "I'm here because my best friend asked just like yours did. Do it for her." He gave me that look.

The look that said he had the upper hand whether I liked it or not and he knew he was right.

And it came with his smirk.

I huffed, "Doesn't mean I can't try." I arched an eyebrow at him.

"Well then, I'll be here to remind you every time you try." He smiled at me innocently like he wasn't playing a game too.

I groaned, "Get a life, Ash." I rolled my eyes before snatching my airpods back.

"Make one with me since you are my date." He nudged his shoulder with mine tauntingly.

"I was your date. Party's over." I smiled sarcastically before finally drowning myself in my music.

He tried speaking to me numerous times. Numerous times. I even tried switching seats with people. Especially with girls who were eyeing him like a hawk and glaring at me. They agreed but he managed to shoo them away.

He had just stopped when I threatened to switch with Ashley.

She doesn't take French. She's just booked her own tickets, in the same hotel, for the same dates.

Obsessive much?

Now finally, I was left in peace. I was tired, craving my bed, and craving the peaceful sleep that always came with it.

I woke up to people talking loudly.

What the hell is going on?

I slowly opened my eyes to find my head resting on Asher's shoulder while his head rested on mine. I slowly pulled away and looked around to see everyone staring at us and talking.

"Shoo!" I exclaimed, and everyone got back to doing whatever they were before talking shit. I was about to shake Asher's arm but I decided to let the guy sleep. I looked in front of me to see Mason sleeping with his head in Allison's lap while she was on her phone.

I walked up to her and informed her, "I'm going to go and get some water, okay?" she nodded at me before I headed over and used the water dispenser. I was heading back to my seat, my paper cup in my hand when I saw Asher standing up, looking around for something or someone. I sighed and sat back in my seat.

"What are you looking for?" I asked in confusion while putting my bottle in my backpack.

"I was looking for you! Come on, we're going for the security checkpoint." He grabbed his stuff and I did too and we headed over to the security area.

Are you kidding me? My water will have to go to waste. I don't know why we didn't go through security earlier, we just didn't, it was dumb, we should've waited after security which we will because we still have ages left for our flight. I chugged that water like my life depended on it and I was going to choke on it until Asher took it away from me.

"Will you relax?" he finished the rest of my water as we approached the security checkpoint. I took my laptop and phone out, placing them in a separate tray before getting everything else out and walking through security.

Then I went back to the trays and grabbed all my things. I placed all my things back into my bag only to notice that my passport was missing.

Fuck!

I brought it with me, I know that for a fact and it was with me before I fell asleep because I remember taking my airpods out of the bag and seeing it in there.

"You're holding up the line, please hurry ma'am!" the security yelled.

I frantically gathered the rest of my shit and moved out of the security.

"Where the fuck is it?" I sat down on the floor, on the spot, *yes I really did* and began pouring out the contents of my bag to look for it.

"Riles, what are you doing we have to go, come on!" Allison came up to me and began putting my stuff back in the bag with me.

"I can't find my passport! It had my boarding pass in it!

I had it with me earlier and after I came back from getting water! I just noticed it was gone!" I panicked, still sitting on the floor. "What do I do? *What do I do?* What do I do?" I shrieked while Allison stayed calm.

How is she so calm?

Well, it's not her passport that's lost.

"Why are you sitting on the floor? Come on, we're going to the terminal and waiting there!" Asher came up and looked down at me.

"Shut up Ash-hole I can't find my passport!" Look at that, another nickname for the guy.

"Get up, Ry Ry." I ignored and continued searching. "Give me your hand, get up!" I looked up to see his hand held out, *with my passport in it.*

I glared at him with disbelief before standing up and smacking his arm repeatedly.

"You're going to be dead in a few moments so I suggest you make a run for it," I warned before snatching my passport, putting it back in my bag.

CHAPTER TWELVE

ASHER

I made a run for it. When I woke up and saw her getting the water at the dispenser, I just had to take the opportunity to embarrass and scare her somehow. I might have taken it a little too far by keeping it with me for so long but her reaction was priceless and *definitely* worth it.

"Asher, stop right the fuck there!" she yelled, not giving a shit about the people giving us weird looks as we ran through the crowd.

"Language, Ms. Blakely!" Mr. Wayne shouted. I forgot the guy was here.

"Sorry Mr. Wayne!" she shouted while continuing to chase me. I bumped into a little boy who would've fallen and started crying had I not caught him.

"Hey, you okay?" I asked as he looked up at me cluelessly. Riles used that opportunity and caught up to me, smacking me upside the head while I kneeled to meet the height of the little boy.

"I'm lost." The boy sniffed slightly as his eyes began glossing over and a frown made its way to his face.

She kneeled beside me and looked at the boy.

"I'm Riley, what's your name?" she extended her hand.

"He's lost and you're having an introduction?" I whispered to her in disbelief.

The fuck?

"Every kid is taught not to talk to strangers. If he knows our names, we're not strangers," she explained.

"I'm Asher." I introduced myself.

His eyes stopped glossing over and he began breathing fine again.

"I'm Zack."

I looked around for a parent while Riley held his hand and asked questions, trying to figure out how he got lost.

"How'd you get here Zack?" Riley asked him cautiously.

"With my dad. I don't know where he went,"

Riley stood up while still holding his hand and began looking around with me.

"Do you know what your dad is wearing?" she asked while sitting back down.

"A red jacket. I just went to get candy."

Who knew candy could get you lost?

"Zack, how old are you?" Riley asked while opening the candy that Zack was fidgeting with.

"Eight," he replied while beginning to suck on the sucker. "We were standing right there!" he pointed to the last gate.

"I'll go look okay?" I told her before walking over to the last terminal and looking around. I saw a man looking around frantically while on the phone with someone. "Excuse me, are you looking for someone?" I went up to him and asked and he hung up the phone.

"I'm looking for my son, his name's Zack, he's wearing a navy set of a jacket and joggers and is eight years old. He's blonde with blue eyes!" he exclaimed a little breathlessly.

I take it he's been looking for him for a while and has said this to others.

"I found him with my-" my fucking enemy? "I found him with my friend. He's over by gate twelve." I informed him.

He let out a sigh of relief before following me back to our gate. We walked over there to see Riley tickling Zack, making him laugh before he began talking to her about Hot Wheels cars. I remember playing with those as a kid.

That's nostalgia right there.

"Zack!" the man exclaimed. Zack's eyes shot up to meet mine before looking at the man beside me.

"Dad!" he shouted before running up to him. The man picked him up instantly before planting a kiss on his cheek.

"Thank you so much for taking care of him and keeping

him safe. I appreciate it. Thank you!" he exclaimed before we said goodbye and he went his way while we went ours.

"I guess we're heroes now," I smirked while putting my hand out for her to high-five. She laughed before high-fiving me.

"I guess we are." We got back to the rest of the class to see Mr. Walker and Mr. Brown talking while Mr. Wayne and Mrs. Stevenson were sleeping. Mr. Walker and Brown stopped talking and looked at us with disappointed and angry eyes. "We ran into a child that was lost so we were helping him find his parents," Riley explained quickly. Mr. Brown smiled while Mr. Walker looked at us in shock.

"Bye Riley!" Zack screamed and waved from behind us with his dad while eating gummy bears from the store nearby.

"Bye!" she laughed and waved back. "See." Riley shrugged while turning back to Mr. Brown and Walker. They nodded before we sat down with a sigh. "I'm still pissed at you for stealing my passport. That was clear theft," she huffed while folding her arms across her chest.

"I'm sorry but the opportunity was right there in front of me. I just had to take it," I laughed.

She turned to me with a curious look. She scoffed, "The opportunity to what? Giving me a fu- freaking heart attack?" she caught herself after realizing that Mr. Brown was listening.

"Yeah," I nodded while laughing.

"You should be dead by now. You're only alive because you ran into Zack, I would've killed you."

Well damn.

"Alright guys, come on wake up, we're boarding!" Mr. Walker clapped, waking everyone up.

Those four hours weren't too bad. Or too long.

Everyone grabbed their backpacks and got moving in a line. We went through the passport check before we all got our boarding passes scanned and entered the flight. I read my seat number before opening the cart and keeping my backpack up there. I turned around to see Riley talking to Allison about how she doesn't want to sit in the seat that she has.

"Guys come on, get seated." Mr. Wayne told Riley and Allison.

Riley groaned before turning to me,

"Move," she demanded. I went and sat in my seat. Riley stood on her toes and opened the cart that my bag was in before struggling but managing to get her bag in any way.

It's going to fall on her face.

I quickly stood up while she turned to face Allison and talk to her and pushed her forward, catching her bag before it fell on her head. "You should've just asked for help." I gave her a pointed look before pushing her bag back all the way and closing the cart securely.

"Riley, Asher, take a seat please." Mr. Walker walked passed us and to his seat. Riley sighed before taking her seat. I got an aisle seat, she got the middle seat and Mr. Brown had the window seat.

Poor Mr. Brown, that man will suffer.

"Guys, no chaos please." Mr. Brown pleaded.

I chuckled while Riley awkwardly cleared her throat before smiling at me. A fake one of course.

"Right, no chaos." She arched an eyebrow at me while smirking.

Oh no. She's up to something.

Everyone got into conversation while Riley plugged her earphones in, Mr. Brown started reading and I decided to listen to music as well. The announcements took place and soon enough we were taking off. As the flight began ascending, I turned to see Mr. Brown engrossed in his book while Riley had her eyes closed and was smiling.

"What are you smiling at?" I asked her, pulling her airpod out.

She continued smiling and answered cheerfully. "At the butterflies that I get when flights take off."

That is something a kid would say and feel. Well, she practically is a kid I mean, look at her size. I mean that in the nicest, cutest way possible.

Cutest?

She took her airpod back and got back to listening to music while I did too. I placed my hand on the armrest only to feel hers on top of mine. "Sorry," she quickly uttered before retreating her hand.

Why does she get so awkward after being nice to me?

This is going to be a long-ass flight as it is and it's going to feel even longer because of the way we act with each other.

"Well, goodnight to you two." Mr. Brown said before putting an eye mask on.

Riley slowly turned to me and gave me the 'what the fuck is going on?' look. We suppressed our laughter and acted like we didn't just see that and got back to listening to our music. After five minutes, I hear Riley laugh. *Full-on laughing.*

I turn to her and ask, "What the hell are you laughing like a maniac for?" I asked while laughing myself.

"At that." She pointed to Mr. Brown while struggling to hold the laughter in.

"Shh!" multiple people hissed. She smacked her hand over her mouth and hid behind my shoulder.

I sense the awkwardness coming in a minute.

CHAPTER THIRTEEN

RILEY

We had about an hour left on the flight and I was fucking exhausted. I was tired and sleepy but could not catch the blink of an eye's time to sleep since a baby was crying in the seat behind me. Mr. Brown was fast asleep with his eye mask on, Asher was half asleep, occasionally waking up when his head would fall.

I sighed before deciding to walk around the aisle a few times to stretch my legs. I managed to get up and out of the seat without disturbing Asher and went to the bathroom. I locked the door and leaned against the sink, letting out a sigh. I took a minute to rub the sleep out of my eyes before deciding to go and sit back down.

I walked back over to my seat and began squeezing through the small space. Just my luck, the person sitting in front of Asher's seat, decided it was time to push their seat back. "Fuck!" I hissed as I got pushed forward, landing pretty much on top of Asher.

His eyes snapped open but glimmered with amusement almost instantly. "Hello," he smirked.

So god really is playing with me, huh?

I shook my head, "No." I quickly pushed myself off of him and slid into my seat, cursing the person sitting in front of Asher. Who is sitting in front of Asher? I took a peek and saw *Ashley motherfucking Simpson. Bitch.* I covered my face with my hands, groaning into them. Asher cleared his throat before looking at me with that look. The look he uses to charm girls and teases them.

"Shut up and go back to sleep." I placed my hands over his eyes.

He took my hands off and asked, "Sleep? Okay." He shrugged before resting his head on my shoulder, holding my arm close to himself.

I groaned but let him nonetheless because he would sleep and then I could be left in peace and pull my arm out of his grasp.

To my surprise, he *did* fall asleep and that too peacefully, like a baby just not like the baby sitting behind me. He dropped his phone from his hands and I bent down and got it for him, noticing Mason sleeping on Ali's shoulder while Ali looked at me suggestively.

I shook my head at her before sitting back up, lifting his head and placing it back on my shoulder, keeping his phone with me. Maybe I'll give him a little scare the way he gave me one with my passport.

Traveling is fun but it is damn exhausting.

"Please prepare for landing" were the words that I woke up to. Mr. Brown was back to reading, Ali was sleeping on Mason's shoulder and Asher was still sleeping on mine.

This boy sleeps a lot.

I looked to see if he had his seatbelt on which he did and I decided to let him sleep since he'll be sleepless when he can't find his phone later. He woke up about three minutes later, rubbing his eyes.

"Morning sleepyhead."

He lifted his head off my shoulder and stretched in his seat. "How long do we have left?" he asked while running his hand through his hair while pulling out a pack of gum.

I took a strip before answering his question, "Like ten minutes," I informed him.

"I wanna land!" he huffed while whining and placing his head back on my shoulder. "My legs are completely numb. This is not okay!" he complained continuously.

"Seriously? You're being such a drama queen. Just hold on a little longer," I laughed while putting my phone and airpods in my pocket so all I have to do when we land is grab my bag or well- ask Asher to grab my bag for me.

Everyone was now wide awake and we were landing at roughly eight pm Cali time which meant it was five am in Paris and it was just before the sun rose for Saturday thanks to the nine-hour difference.

I sense jet lag is going to be a whore to this French class.

We landed smoothly and that smile thanks to the butterflies stretched back onto my face. I didn't miss Asher watching me smile at nothing and chuckling to himself. Soon enough, we landed and he instantly stood up and grabbed his bag, my bag and Mr. Brown's too. "Thank you," Mr. Brown and I said in sync. He smiled in response before sitting back down.

We agreed to wait till it was less crowded to get in line and head out and so we waited for people to start filing out. Once it was less crowded, we stood up one by one. He stood up and let me go first before following behind me since Mr. Brown waited to make sure all the students on our side of the plane were out.

We got out of the plane and began heading to collect our luggage. Our flight's luggage was on the opposite side of the airport so we all headed over there. I spotted my suitcase pretty easily thanks to the blue ribbon and swiftly grabbed it.

Asher got his and we moved aside while Mason grabbed his and Ali's suitcase. "Wait here for me, will you? I gotta go call my mom and tell her I landed safely."

He nodded in response and I stepped away. I called my dad since my mom wasn't answering and told him I landed safely.

He wished me luck and fun for the trip before I said bye and hung up. I got back to a frantic Asher. "What happened?" I asked in confusion.

"I can't find my phone!" he asked while looking through his backpack and checking his pockets.

"Didn't you put it in your backpack when we got on the flight?" I pretended to be clueless.

"I took it out to listen to music and then I fell asleep and-" he stopped talking. "Shit! What if I left on the airplane? I have to go get it!" he began heading back to the flight but I grabbed the sleeve of his jacket.

"Check here properly first," I told him.

He looked through his bag once more in frustration. "Can I use your phone to call it?"

I nodded while handing him my phone.

He huffed, "Glad to know my name is still saved under Ashy Bashy," he rolled his eyes.

He never liked that nickname. That's why I use it.

He called his phone and it began ringing, in my back pocket of course.

"It's ringing, I hear it!" I pretended to look through his bag one more time.

"Riles," I ignored him. "Riles," I bit back a laugh. "Riley." Okay, he used my full name so he's mad. He gave me a pointed look, glaring subtly. "Hand it over." He stuck his hand out for me to place the phone in.

I shook my head after snatching mine back, just in case he took mine.

"You took my passport and I spent a long longer than you just did for your phone, not to mention, I went through a lot more humiliation and embarrassment so I think you should-"

He groaned, "Riley, my phone."

Demanding much?

I stood there with my arms folded across my chest and a smile on my face. "Alright then," he shrugged before trapping me between him and the cart that had my suitcase stacked on top of his.

"What are you doing?" I asked in confusion.

He put his right arm behind my back and smoothly pulled his phone out of my back pocket. "Choose a better hiding spot next time, Ry Ry," he smirked before retreating and standing at a normal distance from me.

I rolled my eyes, "Whatever." Soon enough, everyone had their luggage and we were heading out.

"This way everyone!" Mr. Walker leads the way with Mr. Brown walking right behind me since we were in the middle of the line, Mrs. Stevenson was somewhere in between and Mr. Wayne was at the very back. We were pretty much surrounded by teachers like criminals being transferred from one jail to another.

"We're fair and square." I declared as Asher walked beside me.

"Fair and square." He nodded and shrugged.

At least now he won't pull anything on me unless he wants me to bite back.

We split up into two buses since they were minibusses that

were hired by our school. Ali, Mason, Asher and I were on one bus with a few other students staying in hotel 121 and Mr. Brown and Mr. Walker, while the other half was with the other two teachers.

"How long is the drive to the hotel?" someone asked from the back. Tyler asked from the back.

"Roughly thirty to forty minutes." Mr. Walker replied as the bus began moving.

I was seated next to Ali, *thank god.*

"I think I *really* like him, Riles."

My best friend is blushing.

"I can tell," I teased, "The question is, are you going to do something about it?"

CHAPTER FOURTEEN

RILEY

We *finally* got to the hotel. "Hallelujah!" Asher and Mason exclaimed together, being the first ones to grab their bags and get off the bus.

"Alright, now as for the rest of you, can I have all the people sitting on the right side off first." Mr. Walker spoke.

"That's us!" everyone on my side exclaimed. I grabbed my bag, threw it over my shoulder and got off, going to the trunk to grab my suitcase with Ali beside me. I grabbed my suitcase and waited with the rest of the students for one of the teachers to come over and lead us.

"Come on, the others will join us!" Mr. Brown got off, grabbed his suitcase and led us to the lobby of the hotel. We sat down on couches, too many people squeezing on one each, waiting for the others. Once everyone was in, we sat and waited for the instructions.

"Alright, I want everyone to pick the person they're rooming with and I will call out one person's name one by one and they will go and get the room key with their partner. Mr. Brown will be at the counter, helping out with any information that needs to be given." Mr. Walker dictated. "Take two minutes to pick your partners if necessary," he sighed.

No words were spoken. I guess everyone knew their partners.

"Alright then, let's start with Tyler."

Tyler stood up.

"I'll go with Elijah," he shrugged. Both of them stood up and grabbed their keys.

"Veronica?" Mr. Walker said next.

"I'll take Ashley."

She's an option?

"I'm sorry but she's not here with the school. Pick someone else please."

She groaned, "I'll take Kennedy." Now that they're gone.

"Ethan?" he stood up,

"Colby?" he questioned.

"Yeah sure, man."

Next.

"Aria?" I forgot she's here.

"I'll take Bianca." Cheer captain.

This went on for a while until there were only six individuals left. "Justin?"

He thought for a minute. "I'll go with Kian."

Our turn.

"Riley?" I stood up,

"Let's go!" Ali stood up and linked my arm with hers before I got the chance to say her name. I laughed and went to get our room key. Everyone got their room keys and split up, going into their rooms.

We got room seven-eighty. We got into an elevator, pushed to the back with some of the others from our class. "Ow!" I winced as I got pushed further into the wall. "Jesus," I hissed at the man in front of me who was not a student.

"Watch out!" I felt someone grab me and pull me to the other end of the elevator as the man dropped his suitcase. Which would've been on my foot! I looked up to see the hazel-eyed boy.

Asher.

"Thanks." My voice barely came out but I'm sure he got the message. Slowly but surely people began leaving. Now it was just Tyler, Elijah, Asher, Mason, Ali and me.

"Everybody meet in Asher's room in ten," Tyler announced confidently.

"Why my room? Why can't we just meet in yours? It's your idea!" Asher complained.

"Come on, Ashy Bashy!" he spoke tauntingly. Elijah began smirking and I began getting triggered.

That's *my* third-grade nickname.

"Hey!" Ali, Mason, Asher and I snapped.

"Only she gets to call him that!" Ali and Mason spoke for me while Asher smirked at Tyler.

He groaned, "Okay fine. Asher, please? I'll send out a text to everyone," he said before stepping out on his floor. We stood in silence until their floor.

"What's your room number?" Ali asked Mason straight up.

"Room six-six-six." Mason shrugged casually.

How ironic? The devil's number for the devil himself.

The elevator dinged and they got off. "See you in ten!" Mason called out as the doors closed.

"You know what we're going there for, right?" Ali asked me.

I may be dumb sometimes but I'm not stupid.

"Yeah I know, to pick the real roommates," I huffed as the elevator dinged and we got to our room.

"So which one of us gets to keep this room?" Ali asked as she flopped down on one bed and I did on the other.

"It depends on the partners we get, I guess. I can go though if you want?" I offered.

"We'll just see depending on the partners. Plus, I have a feeling of who we'll get," she smiled. We got the text and we headed for his room. We rang the doorbell and stepped in to see the room crowded as fuck.

"Find a seat, ladies." Tyler let us in.

I sat against the door since it was closest and most spacious while Ali went and found a spot next to Mason. The door opened, knocking me over. "Ow!" I shrieked.

Asher appeared and looked at me with guilt and embarrassment. "Sorry, I went to see if there were any teachers," he apologized before sitting down next to me.

It just had to be next to me?

"We're finally done! Boys beginning picking!" Tyler exclaimed after shaking up the fishbowl with chits in it.

Where did he find a fishbowl?

The bowl was set in the middle of the room and one by one, the boys went up and picked a chit. I was in my world until Mason stood up. I watched him carefully as I saw him pull the chit out of his pocket before standing up and walking to the bowl.

Smart.

I guess he genuinely wanted to room with Ali. He pretended to fish around. "Allison." He showed the chit to everyone before going back and sitting next to her. I raised my eyebrows at her teasingly, making her blush.

I'm happy for her.

Asher stood up from beside me and walked over to it. He fished around and pulled one out. He opened it and smirked before reading it out loud and showing it to everyone. "*Riley.*" He stared me dead in the eyes and walked back over to me, sitting down. I saw Allison raising her eyebrows at me the way I was.

"You have got to be kidding me," I groaned under my breath.

"Ready roomie?" he asked while leaning his head on my shoulder while people stared in shock.

"Get off!" I pushed his head off of my shoulder before frowning for the rest of the time people picked. People finished picking and began leaving and that's when I noticed the worst thing possible.

This room had one bed.

"Alright, let's go." I quickly began leaving once it was just Mason, Ali, Asher and me.

"Nah-ah. We're not leaving. They are." Asher quickly grabbed my arm. I glared at him while Ali pulled me in a corner.

"Mason and I aren't ready to share a bed!" she whisper yelled.

"Oh but Asher and I are?" I asked sarcastically. Her eyes softened as she made that stupid puppy face. I sighed, "Is there any chance we can ask for a twin bed?" I turned to Asher while Ali gleamed with joy.

"Teachers will be informed and will get suspicious."

Asshole.

"Were you planning on sharing that bed regardless of who you got?" I asked in shock.

Why am I shocked? I should've known.

"I was planning on doing more than just sharing but I'm with you."

"Oh my god," I chuckled dryly. "I am going to kill someone."
I looked directly at him when I said 'someone'.

"You have all night to do that. Love you, bye!" Ali hugged me before leaving with Mason. I followed them.

"Where are you going, *roomie?*"

Do not blame me if I get arrested for murder.

"To get my luggage, *roomie.* Wanna help?" I asked while glaring not-so-subtly.

He grinned, "Of course!" while following me. "Take the key! We'll get locked out!" he ordered even though he was behind me. I groaned before turning on my heels and grabbing the key.

We went down the elevator with Ali and Mason and surprisingly, Asher did grab my bags for me.

Guess the guy is a gentleman at times.

We came back and he set my bag down beside his before leaving my backpack on my bed. My bad, our bed.

"So, how are we going to do this?" I clapped my hands together.

"What do you mean? What are you talking about?" he asked in confusion.

"I'm not sleeping with you."

He smirked. I walked right into that one. "In the same bed." I clarified.

He smirked, "You're more than welcome to take the

luxuriously carpeted floor?" he arched a brow at me.

"*Or* you can be a gentleman and take the floor?" *I had to try, come on.*

"Nice try," he smiled.

I groaned, "You've got like the biggest room and there's not even a little couch in here?" I whined.

"We'll split the bed but I can promise you, you'll regret it," he smirked.

— CHAPTER FIFTEEN —

ASHER

Since according to our schedule we have tomorrow to ourselves to get rid of the jet lag and just relax, I felt like there was no point in forcing myself to sleep. "Are you sleepy?" I called out. She appeared out of the bathroom with a toothbrush in her mouth.

"Mm-mm." She shook her head before going back into the bathroom.

"Do you want to do something? I'm bored." I called out again.

She appeared once again and did the same thing.

"Mm-mm," before going back inside.

I rolled my eyes before getting off the bed and standing at the bathroom door, leaning on the frame.

"Look, I know us being roommates isn't the most ideal situation," I started as she scoffed, "But we're roommates, okay? So let's just get on with it and find something to do."

She finished brushing her teeth and began washing her face.

"You wanna do something?" she finished washing her face. "Fine then, come up with something to do and whatever it is, I'll agree."

She shouldn't have said that.

"*Whatever* it is?" I gave her a suggestive look while smirking.

She groaned, "I walked into that one. Find something to do." She tied her hair up in a bun before turning the bathroom light off and getting on the bed.

"Do you have charades on your phone?" I asked her curiously.

"I *do*. That idea isn't that bad. I was expecting worse." She pulled her phone off the charge from her nightstand and unlocked it, opening the app. We chose celebrities as the category and she began by placing it on her forehead.

Taylor Swift? I began acting out the music video for You Belong With Me while humming the song.

"Taylor Swift?"

I nodded and she laughed while pushing the phone to the back, saying we got it correct.

Meghan Trainor. Got that one too. *Obama.* That one too. *Leonardo Dicaprio.* Check. *Johnny Depp.* Correct. *Channing Tatum.* Shit, what movie has he done that I can act out? "Crap um-um-" the time ran out before I could do anything.

"What was the last one?" she pulled the phone and took a

look. "Channing Tatum? Are you kidding me? Twenty-one Jump Street, twenty-two Jump Street, She's the man, any one of the Magic Mike movies?"

Damn, guess I should've gotten that one.

I smirked, "Magic Mike huh?"

She closed her eyes tightly and let out a frustrated sigh. "My turn." I took the phone and the game began.

Who the hell is that? "Oh uh- the hunger games! Katniss! Jennifer Lawrence!" I blurted in a rush. She nodded. "Um-um-um- Robert Downey Jr." Correct. "Chris Hemsworth!" That too. "Tom Holland? No? Uh- Andrew Garfield? No?! Toby McGuire!" she laughed and nodded. "Jennifer Aniston!" Ding. "Who the hell is that? Is it an artist?" she nodded. "Justin Bieber?" Nope. "Post Malone?" She looked at me with confusion.

"What? No!" she laughed.

"The fucking uh-uh Harry Styles!" I screamed.

"Yes!" she shouted. Just as we got that right, the timer went off.

"This game is too loud. Most people here aren't jet-lagged you know," she laughed. I got all of them right. "That just proves I'm a better actor than you." She took her phone back and put it on her nightstand.

"Or I'm just better at guessing."

She gave me a pointed look.

"Yeah, maybe you're a better actor," I admitted. She

shrugged before grabbing a water bottle and opening it.

"I just watch more movies. Too many actually," she laughed before drinking.

"Movies like Magic Mike?" I teased.

She choked on the water, gasping for air before gaining composure.

"I could have died!" she coughed, drinking water calmly this time. "I've never watched it you know, I just know about it." She informed me while putting the bottle away.

"Whatever floats your boat." I laughed while plugging my phone on charge on my nightstand.

"Swear! I've never watched it! And even if I had, which I haven't, it's just a movie. Now I know that not all guys have that kind of showing off to do, it's okay Asher, you're not alone." She patted my shoulder sympathetically.

I gaped at her, jaw dropped. "No, I've got more." I laughed.

"Whether I've seen the movie or not, I now know that you certainly have." She smirked before grabbing her book and reading.

"You cannot just give me a snide remark like that and get on with your life. That's not how it works." I snatched her book, placing it on my nightstand and turned back to her.

She was extremely amused.

"I didn't know your ego was that fragile," she smirked. She might be trying to rile me up into switching rooms.

"Bruising my ego won't get you out of the room."

She groaned, "Will breaking your ego get it?" she smiled at me. "I don't like it, I don't want to be here." She twiddled her thumbs in her lap.

"You said it yourself, it's just for the nights." I reminded her.

Am I that bad? Does she hate me that much?

"Yeah but I'm with you, Asher. It's weird. We haven't spoken in almost a year and I made the stupid mistake of helping you and now I'm stuck."

Ouch.

"If you really hate me that much and want to switch rooms then fine, switch with someone." I shrugged. Her head turned to me so fast I swear I heard a crack.

"And you're not going to shoo them away as you did with girls at the airport?" she questioned.

Why was I doing that?

I smiled, "No promises." She rolled her eyes before sighing. "If you hate me enough that you want to-" she cut me off.

"I do hate you. And you know exactly why. Don't try to guilt-trip me," she shook her head to herself.

"I'm not *trying* to guilt-trip you, sorry if I am. I'm here for Mason."

Lie.

"Why can't we be friends again, Riles? What the hell did I do that's so unforgivable?" I turned my body to face hers.

She mumbled something to herself about a 'fucking video'. "Riles?" I asked again.

"You talked shit about me and betrayed me. That's as simple as I can put it for you." She spoke coldly.

"I don't want the simple version, I want details and all the complications," I replied. She can't be so vague.

"I'll tell you when it's the right time. If I'm here with you right now I don't exactly want to relive the fond memory. Go back down memory lane once in a while." She's being so cold towards me.

"Riles, don't use that fucking tone with me. I don't even know what I did wrong and since you refuse to tell me, I'm never going to know. Don't get mad at me," I told her warningly.

"Don't be a dick, I have every right to be mad at you. It's not my fault you don't know where you fucked up. It wasn't that long ago, Asher." She stood up and placed the water bottle in the mini-fridge.

I stood up and cornered her by that table. She turned to face me and stumbled back into the table at the proximity. "What did I do that hurt you so bad?" I spoke in a low voice.

Her eyes softened for a split second but they were gone as soon as they came. She shook her head gently before trying to walk away but I didn't let her.

"Please don't walk away." I grabbed her wrist and pulled her back. "Riley." Her eyes were glossing over.

Why is she crying?

"Please don't let me." Her voice broke off as she wrapped her arms around my neck and hugged me.

What the hell is going on?

I stiffened before hugging her back, wrapping my arms around her waist while she began crying. "I'm not letting you go anywhere," I whispered. We stood there for a moment until she calmed down and then slowly pulled away.

"I'm sorry," she chuckled and wiped the last of her tears away. "That was embarrassing."

I shook my head at her, "It was not embarrassing, Riles. It's okay." I paused. "Now that we've concluded that you're not going anywhere."

She smiled,

"We should probably try and sleep so we can get rid of the jet-lag," I suggested.

She nodded before we got on the bed. We each put one pillow in the middle and since the bed had four we were left with one for ourselves. She turned her back towards me but I faced her.

"Night," she whispered.

I don't know what happened tonight and what she thinks I did, but I intend to find out.

"Night," I whispered back.

CHAPTER SIXTEEN

RILEY

I woke up to hear the shower water running and the room empty. The bell rang and I decided to get it since well- Asher obviously couldn't. "I got your breakyyyy!" Ali exclaimed while handing me a fruit bowl.

"Let's go!" Mason grabbed her arm and they disappeared around the corner.

Okay?

I grabbed the fork and began eating the fruit as I turned around and shut the door. I turned around to see Asher in a towel. Nothing but a towel around his waist while his hair dripped water down his chest. "Are you done gawking?" he smirked at me.

Boy, have you lost your mind?

"What are you doing?!" I spoke through a mouthful of fruits while grabbing the door and closing it.

"You were staring at me and you're asking me what I was

doing?" he laughed as I heard shuffling on the other side of the door.

"Who showers with an open door?" I shrieked from here.

"You were sleeping!" he explained through laughter.

That is the most pathetic excuse for that.

"I'm sure you didn't think I was dead! I could've woken up! What then?" I asked while leaning against the door.

"You would've heard the shower water running!" he replied.

Well, I did hear it.

"The doorbell rang!" I responded.

He laughed as the door opened and I was sent stumbling back but he caught me.

"I don't shower with open doors. I opened it once I got out." He winked before placing me on my feet.

"You don't do that at home!" I argued.

You dumbass bitch, Riley.

He smirked, "You look into my room?" he arched an eyebrow at me. "I thought I would hallucinate," he shrugged.

"I don't look into your room unless I hear something loud which is very often," I scoffed.

"Whatever you say," he teased.

I checked the time on my phone. It was ten am, Paris time.

"You're kind of late for breakfast," I informed him. "I have a lovely best friend who brought it here for me. And you have one that dragged my best friend away." I laughed while sitting at the foot of my bed.

"Go brush your teeth!" he snatched the bowl from me and pulled me up to my feet, sitting in my seat.

"But my food!" I reached out for it as he pushed me into the bathroom.

"Won't disappear completely. I might take some, go!" he pushed me in. I groaned but went in nonetheless and brushed my teeth and washed my face. I came outside to see him eating a pineapple.

My pineapple.

"Excuse me? That is mine!" I reached forward to grab it but he pulled it out of my reach.

"Yeah well you gave it to me so now it's mine!" he popped a grape in his mouth.

"*This* is why I wasn't leaving my lovely fruits with you!" I tried grabbing it again but he just pulled the bowl further away while laughing. "That's the definition of a bully! You take my food and then laugh like that! Like a witch!" I whined while trying to lean forward and grab it.

He fell back on the bed and I fell on top of him. "Hey," he smiled while grabbing both my wrists and holding them to his chest.

"Give me my fruit," I grunted while struggling to pull my wrists out of his grasp.

He gave me a pointed look,

"Ask nicely."

I rolled my eyes before trying to snatch it back one last time before sighing in defeat.

"Can I please get my fruit bowl back?" I asked, my tone flat.

"Nicely." He repeated.

I suppressed a groan and asked 'nicely'. I cleared my throat before saying,

"Can I please get my fruit bowl back, Ashy Bashy?" I raised my voice to the pitch of a sweet one.

"Yes, you can." He handed the now half-empty bowl back to me and let me go.

That position was wrong for us on so many levels.

"Do we have any plans for today?" I asked while grabbing a dress to wear for the day from my suitcase while eating.

"I think everyone's just lounging around the hotel today, most people said they're going swimming," he shrugged.

"When are they going swimming?" I asked while pulling out my swimsuit just in case.

He answered,

"Throughout the day. Mason and Ali are going in five minutes or so."

That's why he dragged her away.

"Why? You wanna go right now?" he asked me, curiosity burning through.

I nodded, "Yeah, I do." I replied sarcastically.

"Let's go then." He got up and walked over to his suitcase, grabbing his trunks.

Oh, he's being serious?

"I was kidding about going right now, but sure. I change first." I quickly tossed the dress back in carelessly before standing up and running into the bathroom. I quickly slipped into my red one-piece and grabbed a towel.

I draped the towel over my arm before going out into the room to see him scrolling through his phone. "Your turn." I huffed while grabbing my sunscreen and applying it on my arms and legs. By the time I was done, he was out and applying some on himself.

"Could you get my back?" he asked with a smirk lingering on his lips.

I just rolled my eyes.

"You are the epitome of cliches, turn around." I put some in my hands and applied it to his back nonetheless.

"Your turn."

Before I could say anything he turned me around and snatched the sunscreen from my hands. He applied it on my back, on however much skin was exposed before I threw my hair up in a bun and threw my flip flops on, heading out the room with him following.

He got the keys with his phone while I decided to leave mine in the room and we headed to the deck. He slipped the key-card into his phone case.

He's probably going to forget he did that.

We got to the elevator and saw a bunch of students from our class waiting for the elevator, all in their bathing suits. "This could take a while. Come on." He grabbed my hand and pulled me to the staircase, speeding down while I kept up.

We got to the pool to see Mason and Ali sitting on the edge with their legs in the water while a few other students swam around.

"I-" he began to talk but the squeaky voice of a mouse cut him off.

"Asher! Hi!" Ashley jogged over to us.

Jogged.

On purpose.

cough *Slut* cough

She should hear that don't you think?

I do.

"Slut," I coughed. Asher looked down at the ground beside me, smiling while biting the inside of his cheek.

"I'm sorry Riley, did you say something? I didn't quite catch that," she dared.

I looked at her then ignored her words.

"Just tell me before you go into the room, I don't have the key," I told Asher before leaving my towel on a pool lounging chair and used the steps to enter the pool. I got into the pool and was approached by Tyler.

"Hey," he smiled while swimming over to me.

"Hey," I replied with a smile. "Are you exploring the city today or just staying in?" I asked him.

"Just staying in. I take it you are too?"

I nodded.

"Sorry about your roommate by the way."

Huh?

"He's not that bad. It's just my hatred for him," I chuckled while looking around to see Ali and Mason flirting, Bianca and Aria were staring at boys passing by and Ashley and Asher were well- they just were.

"So I've heard," he paused, "I see you're not ogling guys like some people." He gave a side-eye to Bianca, Aria and a face of disgust to Ashley.

"I'd rather not," I shrugged.

"Our school came with some fine specimens though, don't you think?" he asked me while looking around at some girls.

Hypocrite.

"That's a little hypocritical of you to say. If you're asking me if I think you're hot then that wasn't a very smooth way of asking." I leaned against the wall of the pool while he did the same beside me.

"Should I be smoother next time?" he arched an eyebrow at me as we turned to face each other.

"I'm flattered that you're hoping for a next time." I smiled.

"Why wouldn't I be? I think you're very attractive," he shrugged.

I raised my eyebrows in surprise.

"You do realize this is like the first proper conversation we're having, right?" I questioned.

He sighed, "You're very hard to impress, Ms. Blakely." He nodded to himself while glancing around, watching people like I was.

"Why are you trying to impress me, Mr. Collins?" I arched an eyebrow while turning to him to see him looking at me.

"Is there a problem?" Asher appeared.

— CHAPTER SEVENTEEN —

RILEY

"There's no problem. Why would you think there's a problem?" Tyler asked. I could hear the nervousness in his voice and I'm sure Asher will take full advantage of that.

"We're just talking," I cut in.

"Sounded like he was trying to flirt and failed miserably." Asher kept intense eye contact with Tyler.

"Well, that's Ashley every day with you, isn't it? What do you want?" I looked back forward instead of looking up since he was standing behind us.

"Scatter, Tyler," he demanded while getting into the pool and standing in front of me.

"Nuh-uh." I grabbed Tyler's arm. "Stay," I said to Tyler before turning to Asher. "What is your deal? I left you alone with Ashley!" I pointed out.

"I'm so glad I'm being compared to Ashley Simpson," Tyler mumbled. It was funny and if I wasn't mad at Asher I would've laughed.

"Yeah you did, thanks for that by the way," he huffed. "Tyler, get going," he turned to Tyler. Tyler began swimming away but my grip on his arm was tight.

"Be smoother next time," I said to him before letting his arm go as I watched Asher's jaw tick.

"So there is a next time?" Tyler asked with a grin.

Asher cleared his throat, "There's not going to be one if you don't leave."

Well damn.

Tyler rolled his eyes but left regardless.

"Do you know my new room number?" I called out, getting a few eyes on me, a few on Tyler and most on a furious Asher who was now standing beside me.

"Six-six-six," he laughed before getting out of the pool and leaving.

"What the hell are you doing?" Asher stood back in front of me with smoke coming out of his ears.

Well not literally but you know what I mean.

"What am I doing? I'm not allowed to flirt back with guys who flirt with me?" I scoffed while trying to walk away but he cornered me against the wall.

"Not *Tyler*," he groaned.

I blinked, "Why not? He hasn't done anything to me!" I argued.

He is being unreasonable and this argument is pointless.

"He's not the right type of person for you. He's not a good guy," he sighed.

"How would you know the right type of person for me, Asher?" I asked while people began watching.

"I know you,"

I rolled my eyes.

"And I know him. And he's not the right guy." He shook his head at me while glancing around at the people.

"Can you tell me someone who is?" I questioned.

"Can you think of someone who is?" he took another step closer, placing his hands on the wall behind me, on either side of me.

"If I could then I would've made a move. Talked to him. I don't like anyone because I haven't met anyone. So I can't think of someone. Can you?" I cocked my head to the side while arching an eyebrow.

"I can think of one," he nodded slowly while inching closer to me.

"Don't even try." I pushed him off and he leaned on the wall beside me.

"Why? You liked me in freshman year." He bumped my shoulder with his.

We're doing this again?

I scoffed.

"Your diary said so." I froze.

Play it cool Riley, play it cool.

I turned to him calmly, "My diary that you stole when you broke into my room?" I smiled at him sweetly.

He shrugged, "Fair enough but yeah, that diary. The one I keep hidden in my room because I know you want it back," he paused, "the one that you can get back," he added.

Another game I'm assuming.

"Why would I want it back now? It's almost been two years, you haven't done anything." I looked forward.

"Yet," he whispered in my ear.

That was his pathetic attempt to get me to play his games?

"What are you going to do? Spread the word? Tell everyone that I wrote in my diary that I liked you in freshman year? Who didn't?" I chuckled dryly. "I did and I lost you then." I breathed.

"You didn't have to," he paused, "Lose me."

I probably should have worded that better.

"Let me rephrase that. I did and then you fucked up and lost me." I propped my elbows up, leaning on them. "But then again, did you ever really want me?" I arched an eyebrow at him.

"What makes you think I didn't? Or I don't?" he questioned.

I can't tell him about the video, I swore never to bring it up.

"Ashley Simpson." I smiled. "Speaking of," I said as Ashley swam over to us or more specifically, Asher.

"No," he shook his head immediately as she approached him.

"But I-" she began.

"Nope." He shut her down instantly. "No." He repeated. He got out of the pool. "Come on, we're going." He grabbed my wrist and pulled me up and out of the pool with ease.

"Don't be rude," I almost pushed him back in the pool but he grabbed my wrists.

"We're leaving. To the room. Now." He said sternly before grabbing my towel and draping it around me while grabbing his, and taking my hand, pulling me to the elevator inside and then up to our room. We got to the elevator and we were the only ones in it.

Crickets.

Awkward silence.

Just to make it more awkward, I whistled a tune. I heard him groan under his breath and I began laughing. "You were so mean to her." I laughed hysterically.

"She needs to back off. It's unbearable." He leaned against the wall of the elevator.

"She won't back off until a girl tells her to. You need to get a girlfriend, Ash-hole." I leaned against it too. I felt his gaze on me. "Mm-mm." I shook my head. "Don't look at me." I glanced at him.

"Just around her, Riles. For one day, please?" he pleaded as the doors opened to our floor.

"No, absolutely not." I shook my head as he leaned against

the door.

Is he not going to open it?

"Why aren't you opening it?" I asked while my eyebrows furrowed in confusion.

"What are you talking about I don't have the- oh!" he nodded as he pulled it out of his phone case and unlocked the door.

I told you he'd forget.

"Riles, just one day? Please?" he begged.

"What do I get out of it? I'll tell you, nothing. I get stuck with you for the day." I took the towel off and walked over to my suitcase. I grabbed that dress and whatever else I needed and stood up only to see him standing right behind me, making me stumble back.

"Please?" he spoke lowly. "You get to live your freshman year fantasies," he smirked.

I pushed his chest before taking my stuff with me into the bathroom so I could shower.

"My answer is no." I smiled before closing the door and locking it. I took a shower, did my thing, got out, got dressed, dried my hair, all that jazz and then stepped out of the bathroom with a sigh to see Asher... sleeping. Still in his trunks.

Guess I took a little too long huh? Oops.

I walked over to him and shook him by the shoulders a little. "Asher," I whispered.

Nope.

"Ash."

Nothing.

"Ashy Bashy."

Nada.

He needs to shower and change. "Ash, wake up."

Still nothing.

"Oh my god, please wake up!" I groaned.

Nope, still nothing.

"I'll help with Ashley," I mumbled under my breath and he instantly shot up in bed.

Knew it.

"You said it, now follow." He smiled before grabbing his clothes and going into the bathroom.

The shower began running followed by his scream, "This water is freezing! You used up all the hot water?" he shrieked while I laughed.

I went on my phone for about five minutes before the bell rang.

"Oh, hi?" I said as Tyler's face popped up in front of mine. "What're you doing here?" I asked.

"You wanna hang out?" he asked with a grin on his face and hope in his eyes.

How do I let him down slowly?

"No, she doesn't." Asher popped up beside me once again, in a towel.

"Maybe another day?" I tried to tell him but it became a question by the time the words poured out.

"Maybe never." Asher grabbed my wrist and pulled me back, slamming the door in Tyler's face.

"That was unnecessary." I looked down at the floor not wanting to look at... him, if you know what I mean.

"Was it really?" he lifted my chin to look at him and that's when I realized how close he was to me.

"You could've done it nicely?" I kept looking into his eyes because that towel was hanging dangerously low.

"I'm supposed to be nice while he flirts with you?"

Well...

CHAPTER EIGHTEEN

ASHER

What the fuck has gotten into me?

Why am I so flirty? And it's just with her too. I suddenly despise Ashley, she's always been annoying but it's now a hatred, I'm not paying attention to any girls, well, except a certain third-grade girlfriend of mine, and I'm now admitting to myself that I find her attractive.

She's fucking beautiful, I can't deny that. She's a passionate person by heart with a wild smile that used to make me feel a certain type of way.

Used to.

In freshman year. I wish I would've done something then because we could have been together still but I didn't make a move and now it's mutual hatred.

Is it really though?

"There's no rule that states you have to be mean to someone who flirts with me..." she trailed off while looking straight at my eyes.

"In my head there is."

Shut up Asher, shut the fuck up.

Am I fucking attracted to her?

There's no way, it's not fucking possible.

She cleared her throat, "Can you please get dressed?" she asked awkwardly.

"Why? Does it bother you?" I smirked while stepping away, trying to push away that feeling of attraction.

"It's public nudity." She gave me a pointed look.

Is it though?

"There's no public here," I chuckled while running a hand through my dripping hair.

Her eyes widened, "I am the public. Put some fucking clothes on." She pushed me into the bathroom and I laughed but got dressed nonetheless.

I came out to see her texting someone on her phone which she quickly put away when I came out. "Good?" I asked while standing in front of her. I was wearing a black v-neck with a pair of jeans.

"Good enough," she shrugged. She grabbed her phone, the key since I'm forgetful, put it in her phone case and put her converse on while I put my shoes on.

"Where are we going?" I asked as we stood up and left our room. She opened the door to reveal Mason and Ali.

"We're exploring the neighborhood," she smiled as we

began walking to the elevator. We got in the elevator and were greeted with... Guess who? Tyler.

"I thought you were staying in for the day?" Riley asked him as we stood at the back, she stood between him and I.

"I thought you were too," he flirted. "Guess not, where are you off to?" he asked her.

"Places." She answered him shortly while subconsciously inching closer to me. I smiled to myself at that, I can't lie.

"Places like? I mean we're in Paris," he chuckled slightly.

"Just the neighborhood." She nodded at him before her arm brushed against mine. I bit back another stupid smile.

"Well, we're going to the Eiffel Tower. You guys wanna join?" he addressed Mason, Ali and me as well.

"We're good. Saving that for later." Riley answered instantly. The elevator dinged and we all stepped out.

"What was that?" Ali asked her as we walked to the entrance of the hotel.

"That was rejection at its finest." I laughed as Riley smacked my arm.

"That was rejection at its finest because someone has an issue with me speaking to boys." She gave me a pointed look as she linked her arm with Ali's and walked with her while Mason walked on the other side of Ali.

"I'm gonna steal her for a moment," Mason took Ali's hand in his and pulled her away. Riley stopped walking and stood in one spot while I stood still with her.

"Shit!" we said in sync. "We're losing our best friends." I huffed.

She nodded while her shoulder bumped mine.

"Guess we just have to suck it up because it's what makes them happy." She shrugged before continuing to walk. "You coming?" she turned to me. I snapped out of it and caught up with her, Mason and Ali walking ahead of us.

"Uber?" Mason called out. Riley and I nodded.

"We'll get two then," Allison said. I ordered one uber while Mason ordered the other. "Bye!" Ali waved as Mason's uber pulled up and they left. Ours pulled up right after and we got in.

We all decided that we were going to meet up at the closest cafe and then go on from there. We got to the cafe and saw Mason and Ali sitting at a table for four. We got there and I sat with Mason while Riley sat with Allison. "I take it we have nothing to do today?" Mason asked.

"Why? We can just walk around, go to some stores, some cafes?" Riley suggested while leaning forward in her seat, her arms resting on the table, the excitement radiating off of her. "Or not?" she asked when no one radiated the same energy as her.

"I mean we could?" I replied when I saw her eyes dulling down.

"Wait, really?" she asked in surprise with a smile forming its way to her face. I caught Ali giving Mason a look.

"We don't really feel like walking around today though, we're still a little uh- a little jet-lagged." Ali tried explaining. "Get what I'm saying?"

Riley nodded slowly.

"Yeah..." she said slowly. "I can go around by myself," she shrugged as our drinks came in.

"No!" Allison screamed, getting horrified glances from people.

Mason winced beside me, "Asher doesn't have anything to do either. He can hang out with you?" he suggested while rubbing his leg.

That kick must have been awfully hard.

"We'll murder each other," Riles snorted.

"Do you have a say in this?" Allison turned to me with a knowing smirk and amused eyes.

What the-

"Riley, can you help me grab some tissues, I don't know where they are." Mason grabbed her hand and pulled her aside.

"You like her." Allison leaned over the table while glaring at me.

"Are you kidding me? I hate her. We hate each other. Quit dreaming." I sipped on my milkshake.

"Liar," she snorted, "You have to find her attractive she's fucking hot," Allison countered. I narrowed my eyes at her.

"She's my best friend. I have to call her hot, come on."

Fair enough.

"She is attractive but that doesn't mean I find her attractive."

Lies, Asher. Lies.

"You're such a liar. You did not want to walk around the city today. You and Mason were planning on staying in today but I convinced Mason to walk around with me, then we convinced

Riles who didn't even try to convince you but here you are. Now you're willing to walk around because her eyes just lost all fucking sparkle when we didn't want to walk around. You're starting to like her. Admit it." She sipped on her smoothie as Mason and Riles sat back down.

What the fuck was that conversation? Can that even be classified as a conversation? I did close to no talking.

"So am I walking around by myself today or what?" Riley asked while sipping on her milkshake.

"No, Asher's going with you, right?" Allison turned to me with the most terrifying look I've ever seen in someone's eyes.

"Right," I nodded. "I'm going with you."

She looked at me with surprise.

"You're going to torture yourself with my company?" she arched an eyebrow at me.

"Nope. I'm going to torture you with mine," I smiled while she bit hers back.

Mason stood up.

"Right then, we'll get going. We're just gonna get back to the hotel I guess," he shrugged while Ali stood up and left with him after we said goodbye. We finished our milkshakes and headed out.

We got out onto the street and she looked left, then she looked right. "Where to, Miss?" I put my arm for her to link hers in.

"To the left!" she linked it while pulling me to the left, and we began wandering into the little shops, stores, and whatnot aimlessly.

It was now lunchtime and we had found a little fast food restaurant nearby and decided to eat there. We got in and ordered a burger with fries each.

"Sorry, you got dragged here with me today, I know Ali made you come," she apologized while taking a sip of her iced tea.

Honesty hour in three... two... one.

"She did make me but I'm glad I came. Surprisingly, I'm having fun with you Ry Ry," I smiled.

"Surprisingly I'm having fun with you too." She smiled back. We talked about trivial things while we ate and then we paid and left.

"Where to now, Miss?" I repeated my actions.

"To the right!" she pulled me to the right as we laughed.

I guess walking around is fun... with her.

— CHAPTER NINETEEN —

ASHER

"I'm tired," she whined as we sat on the bench.

"There's no uber available nearby," I sighed while taking a seat beside her.

"I don't want to walk! Maybe walking around was a- nope, it wasn't a mistake. I had fun today," she sighed while leaning her head back and looking at the sky now filled with stars.

"We have to go before curfew, come on." The curfew was eleven pm, it was currently ten-thirty.

Yes, we've been out that long.

"My feet cannot carry me any further," she sighed. I stood up with a huff and reached my hand out.

"Get up, come on." Her eyebrows creased as she pouted. "Come on."

She grabbed my hand and stood up with a huff.

I bent over and she asked, "What the absolute fuck are you doing?" she laughed while pushing my back, knocking me over.

"Get on if you don't want to walk!" I laughed while standing up and hunching over again.

"You'll die. There's no way I'm getting on you," she laughed before sighing.

I clicked my tongue in frustration.

"Have fun walking to the hotel by yourself then," I shrugged before beginning to walk.

"You're walking the opposite direction, idiot."

That would have been so smooth had I not walked the wrong way.

"That could've been really smooth, huh?" I bit my lip while turning to her. She laughed in her spot. "Come on, let's go!" I stretched out my words while giving her a pointed look.

"Only half-way cause I'm not that cruel, even to you." She sighed in defeat before getting on my back.

She's not gonna want to get off later.

We began walking well- I began walking while she hummed and looked around. "The city's lights are beautiful at night," she whispered to herself.

"You sound mesmerized," I chuckled.

It was adorable.

Asher, your conscience needs to shut up.

"Shut up!" she whacked my head as I continued walking. We talked throughout the walk and soon enough we were pulling up on the street that our hotel was on. That walk wasn't as tiring as I thought it would be, maybe her company had something to do with it. I don't know, so let's ignore it.

"Okay, you can put me down now," she lifted her head from my back and patted my chest.

"We're pretty much there, just hold on," I shrugged as we pulled into the hotel.

"Um- no thank you. Put me down now, please." She cleared her throat awkwardly as I walked to the elevator with weird glances from people. From Tyler, who was sitting in the lobby with his friends. "Ash," she said sternly.

"Okay, okay," I set her down as the elevator doors closed.

"Did I break your back?" she asked before pressing the button to the sixth floor and then leaning on the walls of the elevator.

"I'm still as good as new," I smiled as the elevator opened and a few people stepped in. It opened on the next floor and they stepped out while an old couple stepped in.

"This is going up, correct?" the man asked and we simply nodded. I heard the rooftop was open to people staying in the hotel to get a view of the city at night, so I assumed that's where the couple was heading.

"John, we must've interrupted something, I feel..." the lady whispered to the man who's name I found out is John. The couple seems great. Two people, that have been in love for- forever? The grey hair they have symbolizes that time.

"You're not interrupting anything ma'am, trust me." I

laughed slightly. She turned and gave me a 'are you kidding me?' look. I put my hands up in surrender while biting back a smile.

"Excuse us," Riley said, cutting in as the elevator opened and we slipped through. "Is it just me or are people slowly getting more and more delusional? What the hell could she be interrupting between *us?*" she huffed while opening the door to our room.

"Well, she's not aware of our hateful romance," I teased while taking my phone out and putting it on my bedside table.

"It's not a romance!" she argued.

"Is it not?" I arched an eyebrow at her.

"Come on you have to admit, we flirt with each other a lot, even if it's just to taunt and rile up the other. Flirting is flirting," I shrugged. She opened her mouth but no words came out so she closed it back up.

Got her speechless huh?

"We don't flirt!" She didn't exactly sound convinced at her own words. "We- we taunt and tease!" she countered.

"Because that is just so much better?" I gave her a pointed look, making her huff.

"Well then, we should stop teasing each other, in your words, flirting. Even if it's just to rile up the other." She folded her arms across her chest.

"You sure about that?" I lied down while she did too beside me.

"Hmm, seeing you riled up is fun," she thought out loud. "Yeah, no. We should stop." She shook her head before getting up, grabbing her pajamas and heading to the bathroom.

Do I want to stop?

No.

Do I want her to stop?

Absolutely not.

Why is that 'absolutely' there? Asher!

She came out in her pajamas and placed her dress back in her suitcase neatly. "Are you going to change now or can I brush my teeth?" she asked while standing up. I just shrugged. "I'm going then," she walked back into the bathroom. I changed in the room itself by the time she was out.

"You seriously need to learn when to ask for privacy. You could've just gone to change first, I even offered," she huffed while I went into the bathroom to brush my teeth. I chuckled to myself before brushing my teeth and washing my face with water before I went back into the room. She was lying on the bed with her phone in her hands.

"I'm bored."

Is she not tired?

"Yes, I'm tired. But I'm not sleepy just yet, so I'm bored."

Can she read my mind?

"No, I cannot read your mind. Just your expressions," she smiled at me.

I let out a breath that I didn't realize I was holding and went and lied down on the bed.

"Well, I'm tired and sleepy." I turned to see her looking at me already.

"So we can't go for another round?" she asked while grabbing her phone and going on it again.

"Riley, you are..." I trailed off while looking at her in disbelief.

"Mm-mm. I meant of charades!" she argued, her cheeks turning crimson as she blushed.

"You want to get sleepy? This is how. You lie down and blink rapidly for thirty seconds." I closed my eyes while hugging my pillow as I lay flat on my stomach. She hummed in response before I opened my eyes to see her turning the lights off. "Night," I mumbled into my pillow.

"Night," she laughed slightly before I dozed off.

Time Jump

"What the fuck is wrong with you people? You know some of us sleep at night like normal people and don't drink alcohol." I heard her whisper while light peered in from the door.

What the hell is going on?

I stood up while rubbing my eyes and walked over to the door to see Mason, Ali, Bianca, Aria, Tyler, and Elijah standing there. With a bottle of vodka.

"What the hell are you guys doing?" I asked, my voice

hoarse while I squinted at the brightness of the lights. "What time is it?" I asked.

Before someone could answer, everyone's gaze dropped to Riley who just sat down on the floor, crossing her legs, leaning her head against the doorframe. "Oh, I'm just tired, keep it going, don't mind me." She waved her hand dismissively. I contemplated doing that but no, a bed would be comfier.

"Guys come on, we're having a little game night in my room. Let's go!" Tyler explained in hushed tones.

"You guys are going to drink when we're supposed to wake up at nine tomorrow and leave because we're going to the Louvre Museum? Yeah, that sounds like a *little* game night," I scoffed.

I looked at Mason and Ali who were practically sleeping while standing. "Night guys," Mason huffed before grabbing Ali's hand and going into the elevator.

"Goodbye," I said before picking Riley up and beginning to take her back in.

"Wait, wait, wait!" Tyler grabbed her wrist. "You can't answer for her!"

I really fucking hate this guy.

"Watch me," I answered him flatly while Riley clung onto me, arms around my neck.

"We're tired, buddy. Not tonight. Leave." I said before slamming the door in his face and getting Riley and myself back to bed.

"Your morning voice is hot," she mumbled.

She said what?

── CHAPTER TWENTY ──

RILEY

I woke up snuggled into my pillow when an alarm rang. It was Asher's so I decided to stay asleep until he woke me up. He just wasn't turning the alarm off. "Turn it off!" I groaned into my pillow.

"I will if you let me go."

What?

I opened my eyes to see myself snuggled into Asher. I almost fell off the bed when I pushed myself away from him while he cackled. "How the hell-" he cut me off.

"Do you remember everyone waking us up in the middle of the night?" I nodded while rubbing the sleep out of my eyes. "You basically sat on the floor and fell asleep, so after kicking everyone out I had to carry you to the bed, then you wouldn't get off of me and I was too sleepy to care. In conclusion, you fell asleep on me." He smiled while standing up and stretching.

He was not shirtless when we fell asleep, I would've remembered that.

"And how'd you wake up shirtless?" I threw my hair up.

He opened his mouth to answer but no words came out.

"Maybe you took it off in you-"

I didn't let him finish.

"No. Hell no. Hurry up and get ready so then I can and we can get breakfast." I grabbed my phone and went on social media while he grabbed his clothes and went into the bathroom. I picked my outfit, a pair of denim shorts with a navy-blue cami.

He came out as usual, in a towel, and I kept my eyes sealed shut while he laughed before going into the bathroom, locking the door, brushing my teeth, and taking a shower. I didn't wash my hair because I did that yesterday so I came out, all dressed while he was lying in bed, *shirtless*, with his jeans on while he scrolled through his phone. I plucked my phone off charge and looked at the time. Nine-forty-five.

I grabbed his shirt which was on my side of the bed and threw it at his face. "Hurry up, we're late! Everyone's leaving in fifteen!" I quickly threw my converse on before grabbing the key which I slipped into my phone case, putting my phone in my back pocket and running out of there.

We ran into the dining room where our class was scattered. I grabbed a bowl and put some fruits in there while Asher decided we were going to share, don't know how that happened.

"We're leaving in ten minutes, everybody!" Mr. Walker announced while I went and sat opposite to Ali since Mason was sitting next to her.

"Hey," I said a little breathless. Asher came and sat next to me, taking fruit from my bowl. "We still have ten minutes, go get your own!" I pushed him away from my elbow.

"Sharing is caring, Ry Ry." He continued anyway.

I rolled my eyes and turned to see an amused Ali.

"What?" I asked her while my brows creased in confusion.

She bit back a smile, "Nothing. Why were you two so late?" she asked as she ate her hashbrown.

I cleared my throat, "Our little princess here took too long to shower. I only took fifteen minutes. This guy took thirty," I shrugged nonchalantly while eating a piece of pineapple. Everyone including me turned to Asher to hear his argument.

"Okay, so?" he asked with a mouthful.

"Ew, clean up." I threw a napkin at his face. Ali and Mason gave each other pointed looks. "I'm getting weird vibes from you two today," I said while stabbing a piece of mango with my fork.

Asher nodded beside me in agreement, "Yeah, did you two have sex or something?"

Mason choked. I burst out laughing while Ali patted his back, biting back a laugh.

"You okay?" she stifled a laugh.

He drank some water and was back to normal.

"Dude, what the fuck?" he groaned while addressing Asher.

He shrugged, "Just saying," he mumbled.

"Alright, everybody! The bus is here, come on!" Mr. Brown announced and everyone stood up and walked out and back to the lobby. From there, onto the bus. "It's a twenty-one-minute ride according to maps and we'll be meeting the other students there. Any questions?" Mr. Walker asked while we all got seated.

No one asked anything and before Mr. Walker could say anything else and before everyone even got seated, the bus started moving, sending everyone to the floor. I screamed along with a few others and prepared to fall face-first on the floor but managed to get a cushioned landing, on *Asher*.

"You fucking idiot!" Mr. Walker yelled at the bus driver while fixing his glasses and lifting himself off the seat he fell face first on.

Before I could even get up I started laughing like a maniac at Mr. Walker's reaction. "Mr. Walker, I love you!" I screamed while slowly standing up. "I-" I began but the bus jerked forward, sending me straight back down to the floor.

"Somebody get us a new bus driver! Joshua!" Mr. Walker yelled while grabbing a seat tightly.

I was about to stand up but it happened again.

Okay, I'm getting sick of this. It was funny at first but not anymore.

"Holy Mary mother of God! Joshua, learn to drive your damn bus!" Mr. Walker walked over to where the driver was, leaving us all here.

"Can everyone please stay where they are until Joshua learns how to drive his bus," Mr. Brown laughed with the rest of us. I'm going to take this time to explain why Mr. Walker's reaction was so amusing.

He's from Texas.

He has that yee-haw cowboy accent.

He's our countryman.

"Hey," Asher smirked from under me.

"Hey, sorry about the whole..." I trailed off while looking between us.

"Totally cool," he shook his head with a smirk before winking.

"I'm going to poke your eye out," I warned.

He feigned a horrified expression. "Hostile much?" he asked.

"Sorry, I'm late everybody! What the-" Joshua, our bus driver for this whole trip came running into the bus.

"Get out of here!" Mr. Walker literally kicked a homeless person's ass out of our bus. "Did you forget to lock the damn bus last night?" Mr. Walker asked him.

"No sir, I-" Mr. Walker cut him off.

"Whatever, let's get driving. Settle down, everyone!"

I pushed myself off of Asher before taking the closest seat to where I was currently standing. Ali was now sitting ahead of me with Mason beside her which pretty much meant I'm with Asher.

"This is gonna be a long twenty-one minutes," I groaned while he smirked and bumped my shoulder with his.

"Well, I'm glad we're sitting together too," he said sarcastically.

"Sorry!" Joshua yelled and the bus jerked forward again. I was going to hit my head but Asher's arm went across my chest, firmly pushing me back into my seat.

"You're welcome," he smiled.

"Thanks," I mumbled.

Joshua is twenty-one and from what I know, this is his first time running a tour bus. I leaned my head on the window as the bus ride finally began smoothly. We were about five minutes in and I was *still* admiring the city.

It was so beautiful out here.

We had a speed breaker and with how hard my head hit the window, I was afraid I cracked my head open. "Ow!" I rubbed my temple before leaning my head on Asher's shoulder, still looking out of the window.

"Well damn Riles, I didn't know I was signing up to be your pillow," he chuckled.

"Please. Shut. Up." I said word for word before continuing to sightsee while we drove to the museum.

Finally, we got there after the whole bus ordeal. We all walked out to see the other half of our class already there at the entrance waiting for us. "Alright, file on out everybody!" Mr. Brown stepped out first, everyone following while Mr.

Walker made sure everyone grabbed everything and got out.

"Alrighty, we're pretty much going to explore the whole museum. We're going to go for a lunch break at one pm and we'll come back after that to finish off. Now, to cover more areas we're going to split the class with the four teachers! Mr. Brown, please pick." Mr. Brown cleared his throat.

"I'll take Tyler, Aria, Kennedy, Elijah, Justin, Kian, Riley and..."

God, this group fucking sucks, please give me some good company.

"Asher."

Fuck me.

Asher smirked, "Shall we?" he offered his arm for me to link mine with.

Well, I kind of speak to Kian.

Occasionally.

I rolled my eyes before following our group with Asher behind me. I saw Kian walking by himself while Justin flirted with Aria. I took the moment to jog up to him.

"Hey."

"Hey."

CHAPTER TWENTY ONE

ASHER

If I'm being honest, Kian's already gotten too close to her for my liking, but she's hanging out with him so I don't get much of a choice, instead, it's just rubbed in my face.

"Wait, for real?" she asked.

"Swear," he laughed while putting a hand on his heart.

"Cross your heart and?" she asked while raising her eyebrows at him challengingly.

"Hope you'll be mine," he winked at her.

"Shut your face," she laughed while pushing at his shoulder.

"Weren't you and Kennedy..." she trailed off questioningly.

"We were. She uh- she dumped me." He scratched the back of his neck awkwardly as we continued walking.

We had currently finished the part we were supposed to see but the next group hadn't finished theirs so we were just roaming around freely.

"Did she?" she asked him in shock.

"No, she cheated, actually," he confessed.

"With who?" she interrogated, stunned.

Shit, shit, shit, shit, shit.

It's not me, don't think for a second it is.

I can't let him answer that.

"Mason Sparks," he cleared his throat hesitantly.

Fuck.

"M-Mason? Wait, when was this?" she asked while her eyebrows furrowed in confusion.

"A couple um- a couple of months ago. It's- it's been a while." He looked down at the floor.

"How many months?" she asked but he didn't answer. "Kian."

He's gonna blurt it all out.

"Like, one," he mumbled.

*Let me just tell you guys how I can hear the conversation. I'm walking right behind them. Like **right** behind them.*

"H-hey guys!" I exclaimed while walking up to them and placing both arms, one around each.

She abruptly stopped walking and placed a hand on my chest.

"You knew, didn't you?" she looked at me with disappointment in his eyes.

"Riley, hear me out." I sighed.

"Okay, enlighten me." She grabbed my wrist and pulled me aside.

Hey, at least I got her away from Kian.

"I gave him my word. I had to keep it. You know you would've done the same for Ali." I huffed as we stood in an isolated corner.

"She wouldn't be flirting with other guys while talking to Mason, Ash." She gave me a pointed look while her hands resting in her back pockets.

"He wasn't sure then," I tried explaining.

"You know that's not a valid excuse. You know it." She looked at me with the disappointment in her eyes. "And if Ali did it, I *would* tell you to tell Mase. Or tell him myself." She sighed before walking away and back to Kian, with her arms folded across her chest.

Should I warn him?

As much as I want to let him learn his lesson the hard way, I have to help him out as his friend. I pulled out my phone and texted him. *'You're fucked. Riley knows about Kennedy.'* I finished typing out the text and was about to send it when Riley came and snatched my phone.

"Hey I was-"

She deleted everything I had typed and put my phone in her back pocket.

"I'm not going to tell her. I want to give him a chance at

coming clean. One chance. Do not warn him, or tell him to confess and admit or give him any fucking clues. I mean it." She glared at me before handing my phone back to me "And if he doesn't tell her then I will!" she shouted before linking her arm with Kian's and strutting away with him.

I groaned and stared at the blank phone screen.

Loyalty to him or her?

I turned my phone off and placed it in my back pocket.

To her.

Always to her.

Not to mention, she's absolutely right. Ali deserves to know and it's about time Mase learned his lessons; player ways aren't the way to go.

"Can my group please follow me? We're heading on to the other side of the museum now!" Mr. Brown clapped and got our attention before we all walked over to where he was and began following.

Riley was walking a few steps ahead of me with Kian while Bianca was making her way up to me. We turned a corner and Riley abruptly stopped walking and turned to look at me.

Ashley.

She raised her eyebrows at me, asking me what to do. I shrugged with my hands in my pockets, not knowing how this was going to down. "I do not like him. Don't misread it," she quickly said to Kian before letting go of his arm and running up to me, linking her arm with mine.

"You fucking owe me big time Ash, big time." She huffed as she walked by my side, while I saw Bianca groaning and going back to Aria.

Two birds with one stone? Um- yes!

"Oh wow, Asher what a coincidence seeing you here! What are you doing here?" Ashley feigned confusion while walking up to us and walking beside me.

Riley cleared her throat before switching places with me so I was walking against the wall and Ashley wasn't beside me anymore.

She plays a damn good girlfriend.

"We're here with our planned school trip. Why are you here?" she asked Ashley with a smile plastered on her face.

"The better question is why are you hanging out with him?" Ashley asked her while narrowing her eyes down at our linked arms.

"I'm hanging out with him because- oh wait, it's none of your business. Leave us alone, Ashley." She rolled her eyes before nudging my ribs with her elbow gently.

"Goodbye," I waved as we reached the opposite side of the museum, where it was reserved for our class.

No more Ashley.

She tried to get past security but they escorted her away while informing her this area was reserved for us. "Goodbye," she waved at me mockingly before beginning to walk back to

Kian but I grabbed her wrist and pulled her back.

"You can't tell Allison. Riley please,"

I agreed to support her argument but that doesn't mean I'm not going to try and save my best friend's ass.

"I'm not telling her," she said. I let out a sigh of relief. "Until the day after tomorrow."

Are you kidding me?

"If he hasn't told her by then, tough luck. He needs to own up and realize his mistakes, you know that too," she shrugged with her hands in her back pockets as we continued walking with our class.

I sighed, "I do. But that's my best friend, Riley. He'll hate himself and he'll be heart broken."

Does their romance and chemistry hold no importance to her?

"She'll be heartbroken too, and she'll hate herself for ever trusting him. But this is his chance to come clean. I don't want to see either of them hurt and I know you don't either, but it's the right thing to do. Whether you warn him or not is up to you, I can only hope you'll do the right thing."

With those words, she walked off, *back to Kian.*

Okay, that's it. I'm not spending any more time letting this thought feed off of my brain and energy. It's Mason's problem and as much as I want to help, this one's on him.

She can't be trying to separate them just to get rid of me, can she?

No, she wouldn't do that, Ali's her best friend and that

would hurt too much for Riley to just sit and watch. I was looking at one of the art pieces very absentmindedly when I felt someone come and stand next to me.

I slowly turned and saw Riley.

"I left him with Justin, they are rekindling their bromance," she said while staring at the work of art that was ahead of us. "I don't want to tell her." I turned to her. "But if he doesn't then I have to."

I nodded, "I understand where you're coming from just- I don't have anything to do with your actions, do I?" I blurted it out before I knew it.

She chuckled slightly, "I'm not going to break my best friend's heart just because I want to get rid of you." I sighed in relief. "I don't want to get rid of you," she said softly.

"Are you sure about that? I've already made this trip hell for you," I chuckled slightly.

"Give yourself more credit. You stayed out with me the whole day when no one else was willing to. I know you weren't either but you did anyway," she bumped my shoulder with hers. "You're not that bad," she looked at me.

"I already lost you though. A while ago." I turned my eyes to meet hers.

"I didn't go anywhere. I'm right here, I'll always be here."

"You don't like me anymore though. I lost that." I spoke.

She cleared her throat, "It's bad to like someone who doesn't like you back anyway."

"Who said I never liked you back, Riley?"

Asher, listen to yourself sometimes and

shut.

the.

fuck.

up.

— CHAPTER TWENTY TWO —

RILEY

I snorted.

Gee, that's so attractive, Ry.

Then again, why do I need to be attractive? I mean it's Asher. "You did not like me back, Ash. There's no fucking way," I laughed as I saw the class began moving but I didn't exactly bother to follow.

"Why?" he chuckled awkwardly.

Why is he embarrassed?

"There's just- there's no way. In what world? It just doesn't happen," I laughed while turning my gaze back to The Coronation of Napoleon.

"What doesn't happen?" he began laughing with me.

"Crushes don't like you back. It only happens in movies. That's why they are called 'crushes'. They crush you." I shrugged nonchalantly. I turned to see him looking at me with wide eyes.

"You said that so nonchalantly. That's not normal, that sounded..." he trailed off, not being able to find the right words.

"Hold on, don't change the subject. *Did you?*" I asked him accusingly with wide eyes. He remained silent. "Oh my God, you did! Didn't you?" I pushed him teasingly. "This is unbelievable. *The* Asher West used to have a crush on me!" I laughed.

He scoffed, "Don't act like you had no role in this. And why do you say my name like that?" he questioned.

"It's for the effect." I shrugged. We remained in silence while staring at the artwork. "How come you never asked? Never made a move? No hints? No flirting?" I asked, staring straight ahead.

"We stopped talking when I finally grew the balls to ask."

He did not like me when he talked shit, that doesn't make any sense.

"You liked me when you talked shit about me?" I asked him skeptically.

"When did I ever talk shit about you, Riley?" he chuckled dryly.

But Jordan and Ashley said...

Even the video sounded like Asher...

Mr. Brown's voice cut my thoughts off. "You two, come on! We're going to see the Mona Lisa, let's go!" he waved us over.

I sighed and began walking with Asher by my side. I silently began smiling and giggling to myself.

"What?" Asher chuckled.

"*You liked me!* You liked me!" I stopped walking and he did too. "You-" he cut me off.

"Liked you, yes I did! I liked you! Now can we please move on?" he laughed as we resumed walking.

"Awe, is someone embarrassed by their little crush?" I teased as we met with the rest of our group.

"It's not a crush. Not anymore." He said quickly before taking a step back and away from me. I looked at him in confusion until Kian came and took his place.

Oh.

"Hey," he smiled at me.

"Hey," I smiled back, my mind now stuck on possible outcomes of our freshman year.

"You okay?" he asked me.

Where is all this concern coming from?

"Yeah? Why wouldn't I be?" I asked.

He shrugged, "I don't know, you seem dazed," he explained. I turned briefly to see Asher looking down at the ground, smirking to himself at my words.

"I'm not dazed, just scheming." I smiled.

"Scheming?" Kian questioned.

"Scheming." I nodded. He let it go while I smirked to myself. He is going to be thinking of possible things I could be up to for the rest of eternity.

Exaggeration guys, exaggeration.

We stood there as Mr. Brown began explaining the history and story of the Mona Lisa with our guide. Boring.

Let's take this time to explain Kian, shall we?

Kian and I briefly became friends from a group project in biology. He had to come over to my house a few times with the others in our group and the others were, unfortunately, Elijah and Bianca so we were the only ones working. We finished the project and talked a little bit after but it faded out.

He's a nice guy. Charming, handsome, sweet, but there's no spark there. I won't lie, I thought for a second somewhere in between that I had a tiny crush on him, but those thoughts were pushed away when I was happy for him and Kennedy. But as we found out, that didn't exactly work out.

Anyway.

"Can I steal her for a minute?" Asher came up to us and asked, already grabbing my wrist.

"Uh-yeah, sure." Kian stepped away and stood with Justin while Asher stood beside me.

"Can I help you?" I turned to him with my arms folded across my chest.

"Scheming?" he questioned.

Knew it.

"Were you eavesdropping on my conversation?" I arched an eyebrow at him, amused.

"Yes, I was. What are you planning on doing?" he narrowed his eyes down at me. I laughed, dropping the act.

"Nothing," I sighed after laughing, "I was just saying that because I knew you were listening and I wanted to confuse you."

He gave me a 'are you serious?' look.

"Oh really?" he deadpanned before poking my sides, tickling me, resulting in me shrieking, loud. Everyone in the area stopped doing what they were doing and stared at me in disbelief. I turned pink in embarrassment before slapping his arm.

"You are going to be in a lot of trouble once we get back to the hotel room, I'm not letting you get any sleep tonight," I huffed while watching some people from our group take pictures.

"Yeah right," he scoffed, "You'll be asleep by the time we get back there," he chuckled.

"Riley, come on we're taking pictures!" Kian called me over. I turned to Asher with a smirk and arched eyebrow before walking over and standing beside Kian. He wrapped an arm around my waist as we all smiled and held poses for the camera.

"Wait, get one more!" I exclaimed when Elijah was about to put his phone back in his pocket. I got away and went and dragged Asher over to the rest of us. "Come on, it's not every day that we get to see the Mona Lisa," I had him stand beside Kian before jumping on his back.

"Cheese!" some of us screamed while everyone smiled at the camera.

"Mr. Brown, could you?" Elijah asked hesitantly.

"Of course," he laughed as Elijah came into the picture. Once we were done with taking pictures, we headed off to the next area. I walked beside Asher since Kian was talking to Tyler and I'm trying to stay clear from there.

"Tyler's a dick," Asher said out of nowhere.

"Geez okay," I laughed, "Where did that come from?" I asked as we continued walking behind the class.

"Look at him corrupting Kian like that. He tried to drag you to his room for the party you know, you got lucky I got you back into the room."

Corrupting?

I watched him glare at Tyler before turning to me, blushing slightly in embarrassment. "What if he thought I wanted to go?" I questioned.

"You were sleeping, Riley. Literally sleeping on the floor and even when I carried you, you did not flutter your eyes open once," he scoffed, "He knew you didn't want to go."

I know he knew but what I didn't know was that Asher was still so mad at that.

"Why are you fuming at that?" I pressed.

"Of course it makes me mad that he tried to drag you away, why did he even touch you?" he ran a hand through his hair in frustration.

"Since when are you so possessive?" I asked, my brows creasing.

"I'm not possessive, I'm protective. There's a difference."

I rolled my eyes, "Oh yeah, a huge difference that must be," I said sarcastically. "Let's talk about something else before you blow up," I bumped his shoulder with mine before linking my arm with his. "I'm hungry, what time is it?" I asked.

He pulled his phone out and checked the time.

"It's time for the lunch break," he replied.

"We're going for lunch, let's head out this way!" Mr. Brown raised his hand so we all knew what direction he was heading in before following him out. We met up with everyone on our bus and everyone filed in.

"Can you please take us to the nearest fast-food restaurant?" Mr. Walker asked Joshua. He nodded and soon enough we were off. I zoned out for a little bit but the argument between Ali and Asher snapped me out of it.

"The Mona Lisa is *creepy!*" Asher yelled.

"No, it is not! It is a beautiful and smooth work of art!" Ali countered.

"Riley"! they both shouted in sync, turning to me.

I find it extremely creepy, to be honest.

"It's pretty creepy if you ask me," I mumbled uneasily. Asher cheered while Ali groaned.

I didn't mean to take his side, I swear.

CHAPTER TWENTY THREE

RILEY

"Come on everybody! Get going." Mr. Walker tiredly ushered everyone back into the bus. We were all tired as hell and were pretty much sleepwalking. We got out of the museum hours ago but everyone decided to split up and meet back at ten-thirty.

And somehow they managed to convince Mr. Brown who honestly didn't need much convincing but Mr. Walker too who got irritated and allowed it.

The teachers took this opportunity to explore and now we were all meeting back at our bus point, dead. Asher, Ali, Mase and I all hung out together at the closest restaurant for a while and then we walked around, got lost for an hour and then found the same restaurant and decided to sit in the park near it until ten-thirty to kill time.

I was at the back of the line with Ali and Mase in front of me and Asher beside me when Asher decided to grab Ali's arm. "Has Mason told you anything important?" he asked her out of nowhere.

"Asher!" I pulled his arm away from hers.

"Allison, has he told you anything, yes or no?" he asked her again.

This is about Kennedy. It has to be.

"Anything about himself?" he pressed further.

"What the hell are you doing?" I asked while turning him to face me.

"I have to. I'm not hinting him. You never said I can't hint her."

No, no, no.

"Ali, are you coming?" Mason asked her from inside the bus.

"In a minute," she replied.

"Has he?" Asher asked again.

"What the hell are you talking about?" she questioned.

"Just answer the question. Just answer." I said when Asher didn't reply. "Did he?" I asked.

"No?" she responded. "Should he?" she was freaking out. I knew it.

Asher opened his mouth to say something but I didn't let him.

"No! We were just messing with you," I faked a smile.

She sighed, "You scared the living fuck out of me," she breathed while placing her hand on her chest as she got into the bus and we followed.

"Now what the hell are you going to do? Tell her and lose him? Or let me tell her?" I whispered to Asher as we sat down. He sighed while running his hands over his face. Before he could say anything, Ali stood up and walked over to us as the bus slowly began moving.

"Is there something I should know? Or ask Mason?" she asked in confusion. Asher and I looked at each other.

"Please sit down Ms. Jones!" Mr. Walker ordered.

"Sorry," she replied but didn't move. "Is there something I should know, guys?" she sighed in exasperation.

I was still looking at Asher while panicking and my breathing quickening.

"He's a player," I stated.

"Riley," Asher whispered.

"Just- just ask him how he feels about you and uh- and if he's loyal. I'm just worried about you. Asher doesn't know anything I just asked him to mess around with you." That last bit was a lie but...

"Riley," she sighed knowingly. She knew what was coming.

Oh my god, this is my fault.

"Just ask him," I breathed, "And let him explain."

She sighed while slowly nodding, "Okay," she went back to her seat.

I turned to Asher, panicking.

"Ask me what the hell I was talking about and ask me loud. Do it," I demanded.

He huffed, "What the hell were you talking about?" he asked loud enough for them to hear.

"I can't tell you," I replied. I watched as Ali looked at us from the corner of her eyes before turning to Mason, losing interest in our conversation. "This is all my fault," Asher and I whisper to ourselves in sync. "I never should have threatened to tell her." I ran a hand through my hair while sighing.

"I never should have asked her before we got onto the bus."

Is he kidding?

"If I never told you, you wouldn't have asked her." I pointed out.

"And if I never asked her then she would never have known." He countered.

"I should never have asked Kian," I mumbled to myself.

"I should have never eavesdropped."

Before I could reply to him, Ali showed up.

"Asher, get up."

She was going to cry.

"Get up."

She knew.

He told her.

"Get the fuck up."

Shit.

"I'll get up." I stood up.

"No. No, you won't." She shook her head at me while sniffling.

"I'm sorry," I whispered to her. Asher stood up to leave but I grabbed his arm. "Wait." He sat back down as I slid out of my seat and into Ali's, beside Mason. "It's my fault." I sighed.

He turned to me.

"No, it's not. I should have told her earlier."

What the hell are we going to do now? Fuck!

I ruined them.

"It was none of my business, I never should have interfered." I leaned my head on the seat ahead of mine.

"You did it out of concern, Riles. It's okay," he sighed while running a hand through his hair.

"I'm so sorry," I whispered. "What are you going to do now?" I turned to him. We stayed in silence until he broke it.

"I'm gonna need you to do me a favor."

Please tell me I can fix this.

"She's going to ask to switch rooms with Asher or call you back and kick me out."

That's right, she will.

"I need you to say no," he paused, "And I know you want to say yes but-"

"I'll do it," I said immediately. "I'll do it if it helps." I nodded eagerly.

God, why did I open my mouth and hint her so obviously?

He nodded while giving me a small smile.

"I'll get Asher." I stood up and went to my seat. I gestured to Mason with my eyes and Asher took the hint and went and sat with him. I sat down beside her as she leaned her head on my shoulder.

"He lied," she whispered.

"He didn't exactly lie. He just didn't tell you the complete truth."

I'm trying to defend him now, okay? Cut me some slack.

"What do I do?" she looked up at me. I sighed before answering.

"If he means that much to you, then you find it in your heart to give him a chance. Don't just hand it to him, make him work for it. But you'll have to trust him."

I'm guessing.

"I'm scared," she sniffed.

"I know," I nodded, "But you'll figure it out. Trust me." After that, we fell into silence until we reached the hotel. I sighed and linked my arm with Ali's as we stepped out at our turn with Asher and Mase behind us.

"Shall we head to our rooms?" Asher asked awkwardly.

Awe.

Not.

The.

Time.

"Can I please switch rooms with you, Asher?" Ali asked him. He glanced at Mase then at me.

"I um- I actually wanted to room with Riley. If you know what I mean. But if you want then I can-" Ali cut him off.

"It's fine," she waved her hand dismissively before walking off with Mason following her guiltily.

"Was that part of the plan?" I asked in confusion as we made our way to the elevator.

"Was what part of the plan?" he asked as we stepped in.

"You saying that," I stated. "Cause she was supposed to ask me and I was-" he cut me off.

"It wasn't part of the plan and it wasn't a lie either," he said while staring straight ahead at the closing elevator doors.

"What do you mean it wasn't a lie? All you said was 'if you know what I mean?'" I pressed.

"I said it to her and she understood what I meant. Nothing for you to know," he said as the elevator dinged at our floor and we stepped out.

"Everything for me to know because it was about me!" I argued while opening the door to our room.

"If you have common sense and instinct, then you'll understand even if you don't want to admit it." He spoke while sitting at the foot of the bed and taking his shoes off.

What is there that I would understand but do not want to admit?

"Figure it out, Riles. You're smarter than that," he smirked while grabbing his pajamas and going into the bathroom.

It can't be what I thought it was because he can't genuinely want to room with me since that would mean he and I are civil which we're not. We hate each other. He has no reason to want to room with me.

"I'm not telling you, so might as well change and get ready for bed." He opened the door with his toothbrush in his hand and set his clothes back in his suitcase.

"Do you want to room with me?" I asked while grabbing my pajamas and placing them in the bathroom while he brushed his teeth.

No answer is an answer, people.

"Why the hell would I want to room with you? I hate you, Riles. We hate *each other.*" He rolled his eyes.

Something didn't seem right.

He's acting off.

"Do we?" I asked. "Or well- do you?"

CHAPTER TWENTY FOUR

RILEY

Answering that question with honesty is a hazard to my ego and her reaction is probably a hazard to my health and safety.

"Of course I do, what kind of question is that?" I replied brushing my teeth. Her expression faltered while a wave of hurt washed her eyes.

Her reaction is probably a hazard to her happiness.

Damnit!

"Not like that," I spoke through the toothpaste. "Wait." I finished brushing my teeth and rinsed my mouth before turning to her. I sighed, "I don't hate you."

True.

"But I don't like you either."

Lie.

"You're Riley so..." I trailed off while shrugging.

"That's not convincing enough for me. Why would you

get so protective?" she mumbled to herself while grabbing her toothbrush.

"Cause we're pretending to be friends for Mase and Ali," I replied.

"Mase and Ali weren't in our group today, they were nowhere near us," she looked at me in the mirror. She rinsed her mouth, "They had nothing to see." She turned to me with a smirk tugging at her lips.

"So what if I cared about you and got protective? Which I don't."

Lie.

"Then you have a feeling for me which is deeper and stronger than hate, that's all." She shrugged before pushing me out and locking the door to change.

I don't have any feelings for her, let alone one stronger than hate.

She opened the door and I was still standing in my spot. "Why are you rooted in one spot?" she asked while walking past me and placing her clothes in her suitcase.

"You need to stop thinking I have any feelings for you, Riles." I went and sat on the bed while scoffing, feigning arrogance.

"Why?" she asked while sitting beside me.

I shrugged, "Because you'll break your own heart."

She's not wrong about my feelings though.

"You don't want to see me heartbroken?" she arched an amused eyebrow at me.

"I'm not that cruel," I replied.

"*Or* you just like me," she shrugged while grabbing her phone and going on social media.

"As a person? Sure yeah, you're not bad. Romantically? You're dreaming. And you wish," I scoffed.

"*No, you wish.*"

Do I?

No, there's no way.

"You had to think about it, didn't you?" I turned to see her looking at my face with a scrutinizing gaze. "Think about it," she said, "You can give me your answer whenever you want."

Answer to what question?

What is she playing at?

"What exactly is your question?" I asked, my brows creasing.

"Do you like me?" she asked straightforwardly.

"You're asking me if I like you romantically?" I inquired. She simply nodded. "If you're hoping for a yes, then please prepare yourself to be let down." I grabbed my phone and opened social media.

"I think I can take it," she replied. "And either way, I don't think I'll be let down. If you say yes, then it works in my favor, if you say no, it also works in my favor," she shrugged.

"If I say no then you won't have to think otherwise and deal with me, but how exactly does me saying yes work in your favor?" I asked.

"In ways that you'll never think," she said smugly.

"Should I be prepared for possible humiliation?" I questioned.

"If I should be prepared for hearing a yes, then possibly."

Since when is she so sly and cunning?

"You're playing games," I stated.

"All learned from you," she smiled at me. "I was friends with you through your player phase." She shrugged before turning her lamp off which turned mine off too but I turned it back on.

"Can we change the topic?" I asked.

"Are you not tired?" she asked, turning it back off.

"Nope, I'm bored." I turned it back on.

"Well, I'm tired. It's almost midnight anyway." Back off.

"Well, I'm not." I countered, turning it back on.

"So blink rapidly for thirty seconds," she turned it back off with a groan.

"Or you can stay up with me and talk?" I suggested, turning it back on.

"Talk about what? We don't have civil conversations that don't lead to arguments. Ever."

True.

"No. But we can tease and make each other laugh." I pointed out.

"You've barely made me laugh," she scoffed.

"Bet I can." I arched an eyebrow at her.

"Bet you can't." She challenged me. I poked her sides in an attempt to tickle her and make her laugh but she smacked my hand away. "No touching," she glared at me. I nodded slowly.

"Fine, no touching." I grabbed my phone and opened Google.

She forgets that I know how to make her laugh very well.

"Are you a magician? Because when I look at you, everyone else disappears."

She turned to me with a bored expression.

I can do this all night.

"I'm not a photographer, but I can picture you and me together."

Still nothing.

"Do I know you? You look a lot like my next girlfriend."

Damn.

"They say Disneyland is the happiest place on earth. Well, apparently no one's ever been lying next to you."

She bit the inside of her cheek.

Almost there.

"For some reason, I was feeling a little off today, but then you came along and turned me on."

She turned her head the other way, smiling. "I'm lost. Can you give me the directions to your heart?"

Come on, Riles.

"Was your dad a boxer because damn you're a knockout!" I heard her breathe shakily. She was laughing.

"There's only one thing I want to change about you, your last name. Would you take mine?"

"Aside from being sexy, what do you do for a living?"

She was losing all composure. "I'd say God bless you, but it looks like he already did."

Come on, Ry Ry.

"I must be in a museum because you truly are a work of art."

She snickered. "You don't need keys to drive me crazy."

That one's not too bad.

"Can you please take me to the hospital? I think I broke my leg falling for you."

She lost it and she burst out laughing. She got her shit together and looked at me while panting slightly and breathing heavily.

"You cheated. That's not fair, you used google! You couldn't even think of them yourself." She ran her hand through her hair before tying it in a low ponytail.

"Hello. Cupid called. He wants to tell you that he needs my heart back." I said the last one on that list before turning my phone off and putting it on my nightstand.

"You made me laugh already, aren't you done?" she chuckled while putting her phone on her nightstand.

"Would you still say I've barely made you laugh?" I smirked as she turned the lamp off.

"Since you made me laugh using google, yes. You've barely made me laugh."

You've got to be kidding me.

"I'm afraid I'm going to have to touch you." I sighed while sitting up and getting closer to her.

"No!" she gasped in horror while already sliding off the bed. "Asher, don't!" she warned.

"I'm sorry but I have to make you laugh now, I take it as a challenge," I snorted while crawling over as she stood at the edge of the bed.

"Asher don't. Please don't!" She began backing up but ended up crashing into the wall. Once I made it to the edge of her side of the bed, I stood up in front of her, only mere inches away.

"Please don't do it," she whispered while already laughing when my hands hovered above her waist. "I'm gonna get an asthma attack," she squirmed as I simply placed my hands on her waist.

"I haven't even done anything yet," I chuckled.

"Asher please don't!" she began giggling as my grip tightened. "You made me laugh already!" she shrieked.

"Well, I wanna make you laugh more."

I have never been so blatantly honest.

I began poking her sides and tickling her while she struggled to throw my hands off of her. "Don't! Please, I-" she tried talking but it didn't exactly work since she began laughing like a maniac. "Asher, please! Please!" she sighed while catching her breath since I gave her a break.

"I'm the person that's made you laugh most, admit it!" I smiled as she began taking deep breaths.

"No you're-" I began tickling her again. "Okay, okay!" she screamed and I stopped.

"You're the funniest person I know!" I smiled at her.

"That's not what I asked you to say," I smirked.

"Please don't-" I tickled her again. "Wait!" she sighed.

"You're the person that's made me laugh most. You make me laugh more than anyone ever has and you make me laugh like crazy and I smile when I'm with you! But please, please, please don't tickle me."

I wish all those words were true.

Could they be?

Could I do something to make them true?

CHAPTER TWENTY FIVE

RILEY

"There, I said it! Happy?" I asked a little breathlessly.

"Very," he whispered with his hands still planted on my waist.

What is happening to me?

We were only a few inches apart and were both breathing softly. "Asher," I whispered gently, "We should sleep."

There's a strange feeling in my stomach and I'm quoting Chuck Bass here, it's like something fluttering.

And I'll ask myself what Blair asked him, butterflies?

Can it be- no. No, it can't. I can't begin to like him. There's no fucking way. He- he's been a player, he's betrayed me, hurt me, my feelings to the point where I would dread waking up and seeing his face.

On the other hand,

he's been nice to me ever since we started talking again even if it was for Ali and Mase, he truly has made me laugh more than anyone else, he teases me to the point where I smile to myself like an idiot every day, he cares about me, or so I think, he's protective of me and worries about me.

Is he that bad?

The better question is, *would it be that bad for me to like him?*

I guess I just have to breathe and wait for a sign.

"I really did like you, Riley."

Where is he going with this?

"And maybe I-" he was whispering but banging on our door cut us off. I jumped while his grip on my waist tightened. We sighed in sync before I went to answer the door, pushing him off gently.

"Can I help you?" I asked Tyler.

"Uh- can I speak to you for a moment?" I didn't answer. "Alone," he added. I looked at him weirdly while Asher came up behind me.

"Is something wrong?" I questioned.

He shook his head,

"No, I just- there's something I need to tell you."

Okay then.

"I'll be back," I turned to Asher before stepping out into the hallway with Tyler. I leaned against the wall while folding my arms across my chest, waiting for him to talk.

"I think I know why Asher doesn't like you talking to me."

Interesting.

Let's see where this goes.

"And why is that?" I asked, my eyes narrowing in confusion.

"I was talking to some of the guys today, Kian, Justin, Elijah, everyone here with us and uh-"

Spit it out already.

"Asher's kind of told everybody to stay away from you."

He what now?

"He's told pretty much every guy in our grade to stay away from you, and not try with you." I'm so lost.

"He's instructed, well- demanded actually, that no one asks you out, takes you on a date, comes over to your house, do anything with you basically."

Huh, has he now?

Tyler could be lying.

"Did he say anything to you personally?" I inquired.

He scoffed, "He threatened to punch me in the face after that day at the pool. Otherwise don't you think I would've come to your room?" he asked me.

"Why would you come to my room? You do know I wasn't being serious, right?" I asked.

I even joked around with him about it afterward.

"Yes, I know but we could've hung out with everyone else. It could've been fun," he shrugged, "But Asher..." he trailed off.

I bit my lip in thought.

"Well, thank you for telling me. I'll figure it out."

Will I?

"Riley," he called me before I could go back inside, "Please don't tell him I told you, he'll kill me."

I nodded, "Will do." With that, I headed back inside.

Is that my sign?

Let's just ignore it until Asher gives me a sign- or a few.

I closed the door and turned around to see Asher leaning against the wall, staring at me. I turned to see him and jumped, stumbling into the door. "Jesus, you scared me." I laughed slightly while beginning to walk to the bed.

"What did he tell you?" he pushed himself off the wall and stood in my way. "What'd he tell you, Riles?" he pressed further.

I cleared my throat while tilting my chin up, "That you've told all the guys to stay away from me and not take me out or date me. Is it true or is he just talking?"" I asked bluntly.

Sorry, Tyler.

"It's possibly true."

I scoffed, "So it's true." I stated. "Why?" I asked.

He shrugged, "I didn't want anyone else to have you."

Ugh, so fucking cliche.

"Quit playing around, Asher," I groaned while walking past him and sitting on the bed.

"I'm not playing around," he scoffed.

I simply rolled my eyes.

"Whatever, can I go to sleep now?" I asked while reaching out for the lamp switch.

"Of course you can. My only mission was to make you laugh," he shrugged while getting in bed beside me.

I don't think I can go to sleep tonight without answering my question.

Do I like him?

Like romantically like him?

To be honest, he's the first and only person to ever give me butterflies and I think that's vital.

"Something on your mind?" he whispered to me in the dark. I just shook my head.

He can't see you, dumbass.

"No, not really," I replied. We stayed in silence for some time before he cleared his throat.

"I said it to protect you, Riley." *He did?* "Most guys would just want you for the hookup. And the ones who genuinely like or liked you still made an effort. Kian did. He's cool."

I sighed, "Kian and I never liked each other. We were just friends," I explained truthfully.

He scoffed, "He liked you, Riley. You just never saw it and then his feelings faded out. He told me," he explained.

"I thought I liked him too, but then I realized I didn't. I was too busy missing someone else." I chuckled coldly. I was referring to him, he better know that.

"Do you still miss me?" he asked after a moment of silence.

"Every second of every day. Every moment that I'm without you," I admitted.

"You don't have to anymore," he whispered as I felt his hand hold mine.

"It's not that easy," I whispered, retracting my hand.

"It could be." He held mine again. "Can you find it in your heart to forgive me?" he pleaded.

I felt my eyes tear up before I sniffed slightly.

"I forgave you the second you spent the day in my room and we sat on the floor reading," I admitted. "I forgave you when we argued that day," I whispered while he intertwined our fingers.

"Thank you," he whispered while squeezing my hand.

I inhaled a deep breath, "I'm forgiving you once, don't mess it up twice," I sighed. It took a lot for me to forgive him and it just took a lot more to tell him that.

"Thank you for being there for me when no one was. I never thanked you for it all. You were there when my parents left, when my grandparents moved out, you were there through it all. Thank you."

Of course, I was there for him. Then, I'd do anything for him.

"I'll always be here," I whispered. He squeezed my hand three times and I couldn't breathe. I was surprised he remembered.

It was a little thing we did. Whenever one squeezed the other's hand thrice, it meant we'd be there for each other. We made it up in third grade and then it meant I love you. Once we grew older, we mutually understood it just meant that we had each other.

Kind of like in times of hardship.

I shakily whispered, "Night."

He breathed, "Night." I closed my eyes and let my mind wander until I fell asleep, the anticipation of tomorrow, already killing me.

"Riley, you have to wake up. Come on, we're going to Musée d'Orsay." I heard his voice while his hand brushed against my cheek.

"What time is it?" I questioned tiredly. I heard shuffling before he answered.

"It's eight forty-five."

I groaned, "We're supposed to wake up at nine. You take longer than me. Fifteen minutes." I snuggled deeper into my pillow.

"Riley," he sighed.

"Asher, please?" I whined. I was greeted with silence.

"Fine, just fifteen," he sighed by the time I was already back asleep.

"Okay come on, fifteen minutes are up." I felt him grab my shoulder and turn me to face him.

"No." I pouted as he grabbed my arms and made me sit up.

"Riley, we don't want to be late again," he huffed while I just sat there with my eyes still closed, talking to him.

"No," I said bluntly.

He sighed in exhaustion.

"Riley please," he softly chuckled while I scooted forward so I could lie back down but before I could, his hand went to the small of my back, holding me up. "You're not getting back in bed," he stated.

I opened my eyes, squinting.

"I hate you."

"Great, can I get a good morning hug now?" I shrugged but hugged him nonetheless, and boy did it feel good.

That's a good start to my morning, I guess.

CHAPTER TWENTY SIX

RILEY

Asher had already taken a shower but once again, we were on a time crunch. So I decided to shower later tonight and just got dressed and put a little makeup on before grabbing everything and heading to the dining hall with him. We walked in earlier than yesterday but still later than everyone else and looked around to find Mason and Ali.

"They're going to kill us when we get there if they haven't killed each other first," he huffed as we spotted the table and began making our way to it.

I rolled my eyes and we got to the table.

"Hey guys," I said while sitting beside Ali since she wasn't sitting with Mason.

Yikes.

"Can we go? I already ate. Let's go. Can we go?" Ali blurted out quickly.

"Whoa chill," I chuckled, "We just got here, let us grab a bite."

She opened her mouth but Mase cut her off.

"She hasn't eaten anything. I tried," he shrugged.

I turned to her.

"Well my little lady, come with me." I linked my arm with hers and pulled her with me. "We can grab a different table if you want, Ali. You don't have to sit with him." I said to her while we grabbed our plates and began getting whatever we wanted from the buffet.

She sighed while I grabbed hashbrowns for her and myself. "But I do. I don't want to drag you away from Asher."

What?

"Are you serious? Why not? He wouldn't care." I explained.

"Who says?" his voice spoke up from behind us. I gave him a pointed look and he sighed and walked away to a different area.

"See." Ali gave me a look that read 'I told you so.'

I sighed, "Ali if you don't want to hang around with him then we don't have to. Out of curiosity and concern, did you let him explain?" I questioned as we grabbed glasses of apple juice.

"Um- about that... Not exactly," she mumbled.

"What do you mean?" I asked as we began walking back to the table.

"I've uh- kind of been ignoring him and giving him the silent treatment since I found out."

You're kidding, right?

I looked at her wide-eyed. "You didn't talk about it at all? You didn't let him explain?" I asked, stunned while she shook her head in response. "Ali," I sighed, "I think you're making a mistake. Just let him explain, that's all I'm saying." I whispered as we sat in our seats. As expected, she completely ignored Mason's existence and acted like he wasn't even sitting at the table with us and only talked to me.

She was talking to me about some model's photoshoot and I wasn't paying attention when I felt someone's leg nudge mine under the table. I looked up to meet Asher, of course. I raised my eyebrows at him and he just shrugged. I rolled my eyes and got back to eating when he did it again.

I looked up, glaring at him to see him smirking while drinking his apple juice. I began ignoring him when he spoke up. "I don't mean to make this awkward but uh- how exactly are we sitting on the bus?" he asked as we all finished up.

"I'm sitting with Ali," I replied immediately.

It'll help her and I'm kind of planning on avoiding Asher and the conversation we need to have about last night.

"I need to talk to you," he looked at me while speaking slowly.

"About what?" I asked, feigning confusion.

"About last night," he replied.

"I'll sit with Mason," Ali huffed beside me.

"Are you sure?" I whispered as I turned to her.

"Yeah," she inhaled. "He can explain," she said while looking him dead in the eyes.

Geez.

"Come on, let's go!" Mr. Brown and Walker called out from the entrance. We all grabbed our stuff and headed out. We got into the bus and Ali and Mase sat at the very back while Asher and I found seats somewhere in between, as usual, I was in the window seat.

"You wanted to talk?" I asked while setting my little backpack down and turning to him.

"Where exactly do we go from where we left off last night?" he sighed while leaning his head on the headrest.

I pulled the armrest between our seats down while answering.

"Back to where we started," I huffed.

"Riley," he pushed the armrest back up.

"Back to after third-grade? I don't know. Back to friends?" I thought out loud.

"Are you willing to go back to being friends?" he asked me with surprise laced in his voice.

"Yes, but I doubt our best friends' situation would allow that," I sighed while leaning my head back as the ride started. "Plus, we've already been pretending to be friends in front of them, it's not like they see a difference. We've been acting like friends too." I shrugged.

"Are you willing to be more?" he asked.

"Don't push." I turned to him, deadpanning.

"Geez okay, I had to try." He put his hands up in surrender.

"I really hope they work it out," I huffed.

"I do too because if they don't, then I'll have to say goodbye to you too."

Is that his first thought?

"I was thinking more because if they don't, then my best friend will be devastated but that too," I mumbled.

"Did we have to tell?" he asked.

"My loyalty lies with her," I explained.

"And mine lies with you so..." he trailed off casually.

Are we just going to act like he never said that?

I think not.

"It shouldn't though. He's your best friend." I pointed out.

"Yeah, but you were first," he reasoned.

"I left you," I stated.

He shook his head, "No, I lost you."

After that, we fell into one of those moments where you're just staring into each other's eyes.

Yeah, that happened.

"You're giving me too much importance," I chuckled awkwardly.

"I'm making up for the lost time. Plus, you deserve it." He

said as the bus stopped and everyone filed out.

"Asher," I sighed as we got off. "You have to take his side. You have to be loyal to him because for the past year we've hated each other. Please?" I pleaded.

"Riley," he sighed.

"Please?" I begged. "That doesn't mean you have to think what he did was right, it just means you have to defend him, support him, help him think of ways to get her back?" I suggested.

"For him?"

He seemed unsure.

"For them?"

Still unsure.

"For me?"

Got him.

He sighed in defeat, "Okay fine, but just so you know, in my heart I'm on your side, always."

Is anyone else trying desperately hard not to swoon?

"Now if you haven't noticed, we are behind everyone else. Shall we get going?" he looked forward and I did too to see everyone already heading inside.

"Yeah, let's go." I sighed as we began walking in a comfortable silence.

Yeah, surprisingly it was comfortable.

We caught up with the class to find them all circling something while Mr. Brown and Walker were gone getting entry tickets. Asher grabbed my hand and pushed through the crowd and we stumbled upon Mase and Ali, shouting their lungs out at each other. I began to step in but Asher held me back.

"They have to let it all out."

He was right.

So I kept shut and watched with everyone else. "I'm not saying that you weren't allowed to hook up with her! I'm not mad at that! I'm mad that you didn't tell me! We're not dating, Mason! I know you are free to have sex with whoever you want!" Ali screamed.

I turned to Asher before sighing in exhaustion.

"If you would let me explain why I did it then you'd understand!" he shouted.

"You're not explaining anything to me! All you're doing is asking me to forgive you! How can I do that when you aren't telling me why you did it in the first place?" Ali yelled. Asher and I looked at each other in confusion.

Why won't he tell her?

"Well, I didn't think this was a public matter, this is exactly what I was trying to prevent! A scene!"

They are both so furious. "I'm the one who's creating a scene? A scene?" she shouted.

"Yes! You're the one who started yelling!" he replied.

"Because I'm getting frustrated with your pathetic excuses. Just admit you were trying to hide it!" she demanded.

"I was going to tell you after this fucking trip, Allison. I didn't want to ruin it!" he screamed.

"Tell me now! Tell me why you did it!" she ordered.

"She wanted to and I wasn't obligated to say no. We aren't dating!"

That indeed is a pathetic excuse.

"So I was right? You couldn't keep your dick in your pants? I can't believe I like you!"

She just confessed. Wow.

CHAPTER TWENTY SEVEN

ASHER

"What the hell is wrong with you? Why would you say that? Is that seriously the reason?" I asked.

After Allison confessed on impulse, we were told that something was wrong and the booking was actually for tomorrow so we all split up around the city and decided to meet at the bus point like yesterday.

Currently, Riley had pulled Ali away and I had Mason so we could talk to them.

"Of course it's not the reason!" he shouted in frustration. "I never even slept with Kennedy!"

Say that again.

"I just went along with it because she was trying to break up with Kian!" he exclaimed. I stopped walking abruptly and he did too, turning to face me. I punched him square in the jaw. "You son of a bitch! What was that for?" he asked while rubbing his jaw.

"Me son of a bitch? You son of a bitch! You're breaking

her heart because she thinks you cheated on her and yeah you're not dating but you two are a thing! She thinks you cheated and you didn't! You fucking asshole! Go and tell her the truth!" I shouted.

He shook his head while looking at the ground. "There's no point. She already hates me."

Damn right she does.

"She has every right to. You fucking idiot, you said you slept with Kennedy to keep her name in the clear with Kian, but now who's paying for it? You're saving Kennedy's ass but breaking Allison's heart!"

Can someone give this guy a reality check?

"Doesn't she mean more to you than that?"

He fell into thought.

That's right, think you fucking idiot.

"On top of that, Riley is fucking worried out of her mind that you two won't work and she'll have to take care of Ali! She thinks all your excuses are pathetic which they fucking are and she hates what you did, yet, she's fucking defending your name! Go!" I shoved him back.

"I don't know where they are!" he shouted in frustration. I groaned before pulling my phone out and calling Riley.

"Hey," she sighed.

She sounds tired.

"Hey listen, could you come to the cafe, please? With Ali?"

I asked into the phone.

"The closest one?" she asked.

"Yeah," I replied.

"I'll be right there." With that, she hung up.

I turned to see Mason looking at me, amused while chuckling. "What?" I questioned, frustrated.

"You like her, don't you?"

Come on.

"What?" I groaned.

"You like her. Oh my-" he snorted. "You like Riley. You don't like that Allison's upset because it's making Riley upset. You're out here punching me because Riley's worried. You're doing it for Riley. You like her."

I am so done with this world.

"I don't have time for you stupid shit right now," I pinched the bridge of my nose. "They're getting here, I'm taking Riley and by the time we come back, you better have fucking made it up to Allison." I huffed as Riley and Ali walked up to us.

"Hey," she whispered while standing beside me.

"We're gonna head out. Fix it." I glared at Mason before taking Riley's hand and pulling her away.

"Whoa wait, what's going on?" she asked while walking with me.

"He never actually slept with Kennedy," I sighed.

"Wait, what?" she shrieked.

"Kennedy asked him to lie so she could find a reason to break up with Kian," I explained.

"Why would she do that to him?" she thought out loud.

"That's fucked up but it's between them. Now, what the fuck is Mason going to do?" I asked as we walked into an ice cream parlor.

She shrugged as we sat down.

"Whatever it takes to make it up to Ali."

That's a fair answer.

"Oh my god Asher, your best friend is so stupid!" she groaned while rubbing her temples.

"Hi there, what can I get for you?" a girl asked with a slight French accent.

"Two chocolate ice creams please," I dictated.

"Any toppings?"

Riley replied, "One with brownie pieces and one with chocolate chips please."

The waitress smiled,

"A few minutes and your order will be here."

I turned to Riley with a smile.

"You remember my ice cream order," I pointed out.

"So? You remember mine," she stated.

Touche.

"Yours is an easy order."

She snorted, "Yours is literally chocolate ice cream with chocolate chips," she laughed.

"What can I say? I like my chocolate." I shrugged while playing with the menu card.

"You're telling me?" she chuckled. We fell into silence and that's when I realized how stressed she was.

"Relax," I sighed, "They'll make it work." I nudged her hand with mine as our ice creams were delivered. "Thank you," Riley and I said in sync as the waitress walked away with a smile.

"I'm honestly curious now, is he plain fucking stupid?" she asked while digging into her ice cream.

"Yes," I answered bluntly before eating.

She nodded while shrugging before pulling her phone out and going on social media and texting someone. She was in the middle of typing out her text when her phone rang. "Hey dad," she answered. "I'm fine, what about you?" She laughed, "Dad, it's only been like three days." She went silent for a moment while a smile danced on her lips.

"Did he really?" she chuckled, "Well, please tell him he will be the first to see me once I'm back."

Who are they talking about?

"Okay dad, love you bye." And with that, she hung up.

I cleared my throat awkwardly, "Who will be the first to see you once you're back?" I asked hesitantly.

"Jacob." She answered nonchalantly.

"Mason's six-year-old cousin Jacob?" I asked in surprise while she nodded. "Why?" I questioned.

"He came to my house with his mom with roses," she laughed. "He wanted to see me."

Did he bring her roses?

I heard that right?

He is very smooth for a six-year-old.

"That little sh-" she cut me off.

"Why is that what you always say about him? He's a kid," she shrugged.

"He flirts with you a lot for being a six-year-old," I scoffed while rolling my eyes.

"He just likes me. What can I say? I'm a likable person," she flipped her hair with attitude.

I sighed, "Well that you are but seriously, that kid knows no bounds. He just showed up with roses?" I asked while we finished up our ice creams.

"Jesus Christ Asher, drop it," she laughed as we stood up and went to the counter where we paid and then left. "Why so hard on him? What did you do for the first girl you ever liked?" she asked as we walked the streets.

I placed my wallet back in my pocket and answered her.

"Well, the first girl I liked was my age and not eleven years older than me." I laughed as we walked past the shops. "But you know what I did. I did it for you. The teddy bear with glued on roses, multiple times, gummy bears, more gummy bears, sour patch kids, more roses on teddy bears, that drawing, oh god." I facepalmed while she began laughing.

"I think I still have that somewhere in a box."

Oh no!

"Why?" I asked while laughing with her.

"It's a memory," she shrugged. "You took a long time to draw it too." It was a drawing of us sitting at the beach with the sun setting. Our third-grade teacher, Mrs. McCall helped me draw it and by that I mean she gave me the idea and kept encouraging me even though I thought it looked like shit which it kind of did.

"I took four hours for that hideous thing," I laughed.

"Hey!" she smacked my arm. "It's not hideous! It's beautiful. I loved it then and I still love it," she smiled as we continued walking. We make conversation until we got to the spot where we left Ali and Mase and saw them *making out.*

"Yeah um- no. I love my best friend but I have no interest in watching her make out with him." She linked her arm with mine and we walked back in the direction we came from. We were walking when our phones dinged simultaneously. We opened them and saw the same text.

From Tyler.

'Party in my room tonight. Tomorrow's day has been canceled. Room number three-two-eight.'

We kind of ignored it but it was an unspoken understanding that we were going. "I'm not eleven years older than him yet, we have to wait till June for that," she chuckled.

"It's like three months away, come on." I deadpanned.

"Hmm, what about you? It's in two months. May second." She bumped my shoulder with hers.

Well then...

CHAPTER TWENTY EIGHT

RILEY

"Okay, now shoo you two!" Ali pushed the boys out of mine and Asher's room before grabbing my suitcase and throwing it on the bed, pouring all it's contents out.

"Hey!" I exclaimed, "Now I'm going to have to clean it all up," I groaned while plopping down on the bed as she shuffled through my clothes.

"Wear this," she said as she threw a dress at my face. "With this jacket," that too. "With these shoes." Was she honestly going to throw that at my face?

"Bitch, wait!" I exclaimed moving out of the way and taking the shoes from her hands.

Let's assess.

It was a baby blue sundress with a denim jacket. That's more of a day outfit. "How about this," I grabbed a pair of skinny ripped jeans. "With this," and a red halter top, "This jacket?" I held up the same denim one. "With these shoes?" I held up my Adidas shoes.

"No dress?" she groaned.

I sighed, "I'm not feeling the dress. Let's go with this, okay?" she shrugged while I went to change. I stepped back out so I could sit and do my makeup.

"Don't move,"

She demanded while pulling all my hair behind my shoulder.

"What are you doing?" I asked as I began applying my makeup.

"Double dutch braids." She parted my hair down the middle, it's probably not down the middle at the back and began with my right side. I put a little bit of makeup on, until it was satisfactory for me, and just sat still, going on my phone till she was done. "So, tell me about Asher," she asked while her eyes focused on my hair.

"What about him?" My eyebrows furrowed as I kept my gaze on my phone.

"How's everything going between you two?" she pried.

Where is this conversation heading?

"Um- it's going?" I said but of course, it was more of a question. "We're roommates," I stated the obvious.

"Well no shit, but are you two planning on becoming friends or just pretending in front of Mason and me?" she asked nonchalantly while I froze up at her words.

"Who told you we were pretending?" I played dumb.

"Bitch, please."

Alright then.

I sighed, "We're becoming friends, I guess. I mean, we kind of have to because if we don't then all we'll do is argue. And uh- obviously there are issues from the past but I think we're moving forward," I explained.

"After a year? Finally!" she huffed as she finished up my hair. "Do you think you like him?" she asked as she loosened my braids a bit, giving them a more effortless look. I gave her a pointed look from the mirror. "What? Don't act like its not a possibility." She stepped away as we threw our shoes on.

I huffed and turned to her while she zipped up her ankle boots. "I'm trying not to think about it," I paused, "Or admit it."

Fuck me.

Her eyes snapped up to mine in shock. "I don't wanna say it," I huffed.

"Say it," she smirked.

"Please don't make me say it."

She shrugged like it was no big deal, "Say it."

I groaned, "I like him."

God really fucked me over with that one.

"I know." She shrugged before linking her arm with mine and leading me out the door once I grabbed my phone and the keys.

"You're a bitch," I mumbled to her.

"I know," she smiled cheekily. "Do you think he likes you back?" she asked me as the elevator doors opened.

"Do you think who likes you back?" Asher's voice pulled my gaze to the front and to my surprise, Mason and him were there.

"Kian," Ali shrugged.

"What?" I snapped my head in her direction.

I think I'm feeling a little whiplash.

"No- not Kian," I stated as we stepped in and pressed the button to the second floor, where Tyler was staying.

"Then who?" Asher interrogated.

"Nobody," I said quickly as the elevator went down excruciatingly slowly. We fell into an awkward silence and then finally the doors opened. Ali and Mason walked ahead of us since they knew where the room was.

"You look pretty," Asher whispered as we walked.

"Thanks, you too."

You dumb bitch.

"Not pretty but uh- you know what I meant." I laughed awkwardly.

"I think," he chuckled. "Are you okay?" he asked.

"I'm perfectly okay, why wouldn't I be?"

Breathe. Breathe. Breathe.

He shrugged as we made it to the room. "I don't know you seem a little worried and stressed," he explained casually. "If it's about Ali and Mase then don't worry, they're back where they started," he said as Ali and Mase locked hands.

"I can see that," I mumbled absentmindedly.

"Hey!" Bianca greeted.

"What can I get you guys?" Tyler asked as we walked into the area by the mini-fridge. "Room service? We have pizza and some fries on the way, anything specific?" he asked.

"A drink," I said. Both their eyes widened.

"What?" they asked in sync.

"A drink," I repeated.

"Uh- sure, which one?" he questioned.

"What do you have?" I asked.

"Just uh- vodka." He scratched the back of his neck. "Everyone's kind of just doing shots tonight."

That's a no for me.

"Can I get some vodka and coke?" I asked.

"Sure thing." He nodded before grabbing a glass, pouring coke out and adding a lot of vodka.

"You're drinking tonight?" Asher asked.

"I haven't had it in a while," I shrugged.

It's just one drink.

"Thank you," I took the glass before he wandered off somewhere else.

He also had one of the biggest rooms out of everyone staying here. Asher and him. "Truth or dare!" someone shouted and everyone settled down in a circle.

"Elijah, truth or dare?" Kennedy asked.

"Dare," he replied confidently.

"Go ding dong ditch the room at the end of the hall."

Boring.

He shrugged and did the oh so difficult dare he was given.

Sarcasm.

"Aria, truth or dare?"

She replied, "Truth."

He thought for a moment.

"Who do you like?"

So original, Elijah.

"Justin," she answered nonchalantly.

Props to her.

"Kian, truth or dare?"

He shrugged, "Truth."

I guess everyone's playing it safe tonight.

"Out of all the girls in this room, who do you think is the prettiest?"

Not too bad of a question but very cliche.

Sorry, I'm in a mood.

"Probably Riley."

Bitch what?

"Thanks," I said, a little surprised at his answer. He just smiled at me.

"Asher, truth or dare?" he asked him.

"Dare."

Let's see where this goes.

"State the name of the one girl you'd never date."

That's basically a truth but alright.

"We're not including Allison for obvious reasons," he announced and everyone agreed. "Kennedy." He answered bluntly.

"Why?" she asked.

"It's not my turn," he smirked. "Riley, truth or dare?"

Great.

"Truth," I shrugged.

"Who are your top three guys, most to least attractive that are present in this room?"

I rolled my eyes before thinking about my answer and then spitting it out.

"What if I can't decide between one and two?" I questioned.

Lie.

"Then we'll call it a tie," Tyler said.

Works for me.

"Asher, Kian, Ethan." I pretended to glance around the room to catch Asher's reaction and to my surprise, he was smiling. "Mason, truth or dare?" He picked dare.

"Makeout with someone for fifteen seconds," Bianca said.

Wonder who he's going to pick.

Once that was done, the game continued. For a while. A long while. "I'm gonna go get some air," I mumbled to Asher before getting up and going over into the balcony. And then finally, I let the thought process take over.

Why did he react like that?

Why did he smile?

It was a tie!

Well, not really but still!

Also, I'm just saying, Ali got all the information on Asher and me but she has yet to tell me what happened between her and Mason and how they sorted it out and came to a conclusion.

I need to ask her about that.

"Hey," I got startled and jumped a little to see Asher beside me. "Sorry," he smiled.

"It's okay." I waved my hand dismissively.

"So you kept your word. Just one drink I see." He began making conversation.

"Yes, I did What about you? Nothing?" I asked while looking out at the view.

"Nothing," he shook his head, "I'm good getting drunk on how beautiful the view is."

That it is.

"Very true," I laughed while turning to see him already looking at me.

That didn't mean what I think it did, right? Yeah no, don't get ahead of yourself, Riles.

"Very true," I mumbled again.

CHAPTER TWENTY NINE

RILEY

"No get this, get this," I laughed hysterically, "I fell down the hill!" I was telling Asher the story of how last year for spring break my parents and I went camping in the mountains and I got lost and fell down the hill six times after talking to the trees to keep myself company for hours.

"Are you sure you're not drunk? You're finding this a lot funnier than it is," he laughed. I was wheezing as I rested my head on his shoulder. I was laughing at the memory and well- I guess he was laughing at me. "What is so funny?" he asked as a slight breeze blew across us.

"I have no idea," I laughed.

"Where the hell did they- there you guys are!" Ali sighed in relief as she approached us with Mason and grabbed my arm. "Come on, new game." They dragged us back inside with me pouting and whining and Asher laughing at me.

"We're going to play suck and blow," Bianca smirked while she dangled a card from a deck.

Where did she find that?

Some people began complaining and beginning to leave the room but Tyler was quick to usher everyone back in, demanding this was played as the last game for tonight and then the party would be over. I highly doubt that.

We decided to stand in the pattern of a boy, girl, boy, girl, girl, boy, boy, girl and then the pattern repeats. I didn't care who I was standing with so at first, I just stood next to Ali since our arms were linked until Tyler came between us, changing the pattern to Mason, Ali, him, and me. I didn't care. Then Kian came and stood between Tyler and me, thank god. I gave him a grateful smile and he smiled back in return. Ethan was on my left until Asher came and took the spot.

This should be interesting.

"What happens when someone loses?" Aria asked.

"They both take a shot."

I groaned.

They're still going on with the shots? Some people are barely awake and alive right now?

Just to clarify, this is my immediate circle, Mason, Ali, Tyler, Kian, me, Asher, Bianca, Aria, Justin, Elijah and then everyone else is too far. I guess we're starting then.

"I'll start as the host and we'll start to the right then switch directions when someone drops the card." He put the card to his lips and passed it over to Ali. I didn't miss how Mason's grip on her hand tightened but the game kept going nonetheless. Until Veronica dropped it, failing to pass it onto Colby.

She huffed while they both passed on the card back to Kennedy who was on Veronica's left and we re-started after deciding no shots. The card was coming closer to me and I couldn't care any less. The card reached Mason and Kian turned to wiggle his brows at me suggestively while I nudged him.

He smoothly passed it to Ali who passed to Tyler before shrieking, "I'm getting sick of this!"

Tyler struggled but Kian got it, he then passed it to me smoothly and I kept it until I turned to face Asher.

Next thing I know, I see him pull the card away with his hand before pressing his lips to mine. Gasps spread like wildfire across the room but that was the last thing on my mind.

Asher West was kissing me.

I heard someone ask, "What the hell is going on?" before Ali and Mason shush them. I was about to kiss back but he pulled away.

"It slipped," he whispered against my lips.

"I bet," I whispered shakily.

He pressed the card to his lips before passing it back to me and then I passed it back to Kian. This time, no one dropped it and we managed to keep it going smoothly. It was now back to Asher, he passed it back to me and we finished the game once Tyler got it back.

Everyone cleaned up a little, it was currently one in the morning, we could wake up late tomorrow since plans were canceled because for tomorrow, both classes, the one in this hotel and the other were going separately and the other group was going tomorrow. "Night," I said to Mason while Ali walked back with me.

Mason and Asher decided to stay back for a few more minutes.

"He kissed you," she stated the obvious.

"Shut up. We don't talk about it," I said quickly as we made it to the elevator.

"I think he really likes you, Riles. Ask him," she shrugged.

"If I can ever look him in the eyes again then I will," I groaned as she pressed the buttons for us and I leaned against the elevator walls. Once my floor was there I got out and headed straight to the room.

I opened the door with a sigh and changed straight away.

I just finished putting my clothes back in my suitcase after changing and taking my makeup off when the doorbell rang. I inhaled before walking up to it and opening it to see Asher.

Well, I couldn't avoid him forever, he's staying in the same room as me.

A solid minute or two went by and he wasn't saying anything, he wasn't moving, he wasn't coming inside or leaving, he was just standing there, staring at me.

"Are you going to come in?" I asked, chuckling awkward

and shyly while I fidgeted with my earring.

His eyes flickered from my eyes down to my lips before coming back up to my eyes. He bit his bottom lip, almost in thought before impulsively grabbing the back of my neck and smashing his lips on mine, hard.

So hard that I stumbled back and if it wasn't for his grip on my waist, then I would've tumbled down to the floor. I didn't hesitate or wait to kiss back this time. I wrapped my arms around his neck and kissed back while I kept walking backward with each step he took forward.

I didn't just start liking him today and then god snapped his fingers like Thanos and he kissed me, nope.

I liked him for a while. Since way before I helped him by giving him my English notes. I don't know if I ever really stopped liking him since freshman year. He was like that one crush that never goes away but does it have to?

My back hit the wall and a few seconds after that we broke away, both breathing heavily, and panting slightly for air.

"I like you," he whispered bluntly.

"I'd hope so, you're kissing me for the second time tonight," I chuckled.

"Riley," he sighed, "I've liked you since freshman fucking year."

Oh wow. Whoa, I genuinely didn't see that one coming.

"You have?" I asked.

"Yes," he huffed, "And I tried to get rid of it, I tried to

move past it but tonight- tonight with you and Kian flirting and rumors spreading that he liked you and was planning on asking you out I just- I couldn't keep it anymore. I'm sorry for kissing you like that."

I'm sure he's sorry since he isn't moving away or letting me go.

"Kissing me down there or up here?" I asked curiously.

"Down there because there was no warning but not up here, definitely not up here."

I sighed, "Why didn't you tell me before?" I questioned.

"You always said you hated me."

I never hated him, just said it.

I inhaled and let that go. "Kian and I weren't flirting, Asher. He doesn't like me, as far as I know, and I don't like him. I like someone else." I spoke lowly, looking down at the ground.

"You do?"

I nodded.

"Who is it?" he took a step back.

"You."

His eyes snapped up and met mine with surprise and relief swirling in them.

"Are you just saying that because I did?" he asked.

"No!" I grabbed his shirt and pulled him closer. I found myself saying, "I'm saying that because I've wanted to since freshman year. And I'd regret it if I didn't say it now," I whispered softly.

He kissed me again, softer, more gentle, slower and shorter but kissed me nonetheless.

"You have no idea how long I've wanted to do that for," he sighed after pulling away.

"Actually, I do." I smiled to myself. Next thing I know, he's hugging me and I'm hugging him back.

Look at how much of an emotional wreck and fucking fool he makes me. I don't crack like this in front of people, I have a bad bitch front, even though I am a cry baby.

"You should probably change," I whispered before pulling away slowly. He held my face in his hands before kissing my cheek and then going to change.

I took that time to get in bed and fangirl.

Asher West kissed me.

Thrice.

I don't know what's going to happen tomorrow, and I'm terrified, to say the least, but I also can't wait.

I'm fucked, aren't I?

CHAPTER THIRTY

ASHER

What the hell are we going to do now?

I don't regret kissing her, not one bit, but now the thought of being awkward with her is haunting me. Well, I think I should start by stepping out of the bathroom. I got out, placed my clothes back in my suitcase and got in bed beside her.

"So..." she mumbled, making it even more awkward. She could be doing it on purpose, she tends to enjoy watching me squirm.

"Please don't," I chuckled while scratching the back of my neck.

"Look at you! You're blushing," she pinched my cheek.

"Riley," I gave her a pointed look.

"What?" she feigned innocence.

"I'm pretty sure I can make you blush a lot harder, okay?" I sighed.

"Yeah, yeah whatever..." she trailed off. Then the awkward

silence dawned upon us, again. "Okay, can we like, I don't know, talk?" she chuckled awkwardly.

Not a good feeling, is it?

"Let's talk." I turned to her. "About what though?" I questioned.

She shrugged, "I don't know. The past? Present? Future?" she suggested. "Let's talk about what made you kiss me," she teasingly traced my jaw before laughing when I pulled back and almost fell off the bed. "I'll stop, I'll stop. Seriously though, why did you do it?" she asked while tying her hair in a braid which she threw over her shoulder.

"Because I like you and my jealousy and feelings got the better of me," I shrugged.

"I still don't get what you were so jealous over." She snorted while plugging her phone on charge.

"You two were *flirting*," I stated the facts. "He stood next to you to pass the card to you specifically."

She rolled her eyes, "He stood there and saved me from having to do that with Tyler. Who would you rather it be?" she arched an eyebrow at me.

I sighed, "Kian, obviously, but what if he did what I did before I could do it? What if he kissed you?" I questioned.

"Then I would've pushed him off."

I scoffed, "You took so long to process that we were kissing when I kissed you, there's no way you would realize it in time," I shook my head.

She smacked my shoulder, "That's because I was processing that it was you who kissed me."

In that case...

"And then you pulled away before I could kiss back so I didn't get a chance, then you kissed me up here, thanks for the warning up here by the way, so much better than downstairs. After that, we had the detailed confessions of our feelings which to be honest only helped confess, it didn't really bring us anywhere and now we're here with me ranting because we have absolutely nothing to talk about so I'm blabbering whatever comes to mind so that at least one of us is talking because you're not talking. Are you talking? No, you're not, so I-"

Oh my lord.

"Riley shut the fuck up!" I placed my hand over her mouth. She stared at my hand, then into my eyes. "Will you let me talk?" I asked.

She nodded slowly and I pulled my hand away.

"I'm sorry I pulled away before you could kiss back, I thought you didn't like me and didn't want to kiss me back, you're welcome for the kiss up here, a lot better, I know, the detailed confession might not get us anywhere now but at least we know how we feel about each other and we can figure out where to go from here, and now that I've shut you up and stopped your rant and started talking myself, we can talk or we can sleep because it's currently past two in the fucking morning," I replied to each bit of her rant before sighing.

"Right, where do we go from here?"

Is that all she got from that?

"Well, I'm sure neither of us is ready to date,"

I'm not.

"Yeah," she agreed.

Thank god she agreed, that could've gone really wrong.

"But I'm sure we don't exactly want to leave each other alone either."

She nodded, "Absolutely not."

Absolutely huh?

"And we don't want each other talking to any other guys,"

"Or girls," she glared.

"Or girls," I nodded with a smile.

"So let's settle on this. We're a thing." I paused to think and gather my thoughts before continuing. "We're a thing which means we can hang out all we want, we can act however we want with each other without a commitment but that doesn't mean we can talk to other people so we're still loyal to each other. We can do some things a couple would do, I guess, but we're not taking any titles, we're not dating, we're not single," I huffed.

"So we're in that complicated/talking zone?" she asked and I nodded. "We're basically where Mason and Ali are," she shrugged.

"Yeah, pretty much just uh- more confused with where to go from here. I mean, they know they want to date eventually."

I don't think we know that one for sure.

"And we don't. We're just seeing where this goes. It's a mutual attraction with a lot of confusion. Correct?" she asked.

"Correct," I nodded in agreement. "One question though," I turned to her while she looked at me with anticipation.

"How much and how often do I get to kiss you?" She just gave a bored, deadpanned look. "What? It's a genuine concern of mine!" I exaggerated, making her blush just a tad bit. It's very hard to make her blush with words.

Not really but, she likes to think it is.

"How am I supposed to answer that question?" she chuckled while tilting her head up, looking at the ceiling.

"You give me an answer?" I suggested.

"So helpful," she rolled her eyes. "I don't know. I mean as long as it's not in front of a large audience, as much as you want, I guess? I'm not sure, let's just leave it up to the moments?" she began smiling and blushing like crazy, looking all giddy.

"Do we have a large audience right now?" I smirked while inching closer to her.

"I doubt it," she smiled while inching closer too, taking me by surprise. "However," she pushed me away, "It is two-thirty in the morning and I have to sleep." She turned the lamp off and got under the covers.

I chuckled before grabbing her arm and turning her to face me.

"Do you want to go somewhere tomorrow night?" I asked her with a plan already forming in my mind.

"Why tomorrow *night?*" she questioned skeptically, her eyes narrowing slightly.

"Just answer," I clicked my tongue.

"I mean yeah sure," she shrugged casually. "Why though?" she asked.

"I have a surprise in mind," I whispered.

Her eyebrows shot up as her eyes widened.

"What do you mean? What surprise?" she interrogated.

I smirked and didn't give her a straight answer,

"You'll find out soon enough."

She began whining, "You can't leave me hanging like that, tell me!" she demanded.

"I thought you had to sleep?" I smirked.

She pouted with the covers in her hand, under her chin.

"Please?"

It takes a lot to not give in to that, believe me.

"Sorry," I shrugged. She huffed and turned over, her back facing me with an annoyed look spread across her face. "Riley," I chuckled.

Ignored.

"Riley," I grabbed her arm, only for her to jerk it away. "Riles," I turned her to face me again.

"What?" she huffed.

"You'll like it, I swear." I laughed slightly.

"And if I don't?" She arched an eyebrow at me daringly.

"Then you get another teddy bear with roses and my head on a platter." I smiled.

"That's a good deal, I'll take it." She smiled ear to ear. "Okay, night." She turned her back to face me once again and turned the lamp off.

"I don't get a goodnight kiss?" I feigned hurt while lying on my side, facing her back.

She turned to face me with raised eyebrows.

"I didn't exactly get one either so..." she looked at me smugly.

"Would you like one?" I smirked.

"Frankly, I'd like to sleep." She smirked and began to turn back around but I grabbed her and turned in time, planting my lips on hers for a short moment.

"My turn?" I asked once I pulled away.

"Sure," she smiled before kissing my cheek.

Way to let me down.

I gave her pout but she just tapped my cheek twice before

turning to lie down on her stomach, slowly dozing off while I did too.

Neither of us were exactly asleep, almost asleep when I felt her rest her head on my chest with her arm draped around my torso.

"Shut up. Don't say a word," she mumbled, making me smile before we eventually dozed off.

CHAPTER THIRTY ONE

RILEY

I woke up to Asher still fast asleep beside me, with his arm loosely draped around my waist. I checked the time on my phone, careful to not wake him up and saw that it was eleven in the morning.

Wow.

Hell did we sleep in!

He was sleeping like a baby and disturbing him seemed like it would send me to hell, so I let him stay asleep and decided to go and shower. I did everything I had to do to wake myself up, I washed my hair thoroughly before stepping out of the shower, shivering slightly before swiftly wrapping the towel around my body.

I grabbed another towel, a hand towel, and began towel drying my hair, only to realize I left all my clothes in my freaking suitcase.

You've got to be fucking kidding me.

Great job, Riles. You dumb bitch.

It's okay, it's okay Riley. He's asleep anyway.

I took a deep breath before slowly opening the bathroom door, peeping my head to see him still asleep. I slowly stepped out and tiptoed to my suitcase. I bent down, swiftly grabbing the baby blue sundress that Ali picked for me to wear last night, with that I grabbed my bra and underwear and stood up to see Asher looking at me, lying on his side with his head resting in his hand which was supported by his propped up elbow.

I jumped and stumbled back, crashing into the wall while gripping onto the towel for dear life. "Jesus," I mumbled to myself. "You scared me," I chuckled awkwardly while tucking my hair behind my ear as I began to slowly shuffle backward, heading to the bathroom.

"I love waking up in Paris," he laughed while looking up at the ceiling, lying flat on his back. I grabbed the closest pillow and flung it at his face, making him laugh. I was about to turn and run into the bathroom and lock it but he rolled over to my side and off the bed, right up to me.

I, of course, ran my back straight into the wall that I was gliding along with heat rushing up to my cheeks. "What were you doing?" he chuckled.

I rolled my eyes before dangling my dress in his face, "Grabbing my clothes," I answered.

He looked at my clothes before smirking, "Nice bra," he snickered while looking at my black lace bra.

"Asshole," I pushed him off and ran to the bathroom, locking it shut while turning red. I came back out with my hair dried and two strands tied at the back with the dress on. I stepped out to see him lying in bed, shirtless, with one hand under his head and the other scrolling through his phone.

"Do you wanna go somewhere during the day?" I lied on my stomach beside him, while turning to look at him.

"Do you have somewhere in mind?" he asked, putting his phone down. I thought before shrugging,

"We could go swimming. I know I just showered but I won't dunk my head in," I shrugged.

"Just let me get changed and brush my teeth," he hopped out of bed and went into the bathroom with his swimming trunks in his hand. He came out after a minute and I had managed to change in the room before he came out with his hair still a mess.

"Can you like, I don't know, brush your hair or something?" I chuckled while going into the bathroom, grabbing my towel and applying sunscreen. "Get my back please," I turned to him while throwing my hair up in a bun. He got my back then I got his and we were off. The pool once again had a bunch of people from our french class and were all in their worlds, with their friends.

And then I spotted Veronica with Ashley.

Oh boy.

Ashley quickly said something to her before making her way up to Asher. "Hi," she smiled while batting her lashes.

"Bye," Asher replied before taking my hand and walking past her to a lounging chair where we left our towels before getting in the pool. "What time do you wanna head out tonight?" he asked as I leaned against the wall with him mirroring my actions beside me.

"You tell me, you made the plans." I smiled.

"Alright," he sighed. "How about we leave at eight? We can have dinner?" he suggested.

Isn't that a little late?

"Curfew is eleven. You do know that right? Why so late?" I asked as I saw Mase and Ali entering the deck.

"Just trust me. We're gonna have to break the curfew but just trust me," he shrugged slightly.

"You acting a little suspicious. Don't you think?" I turned to him, narrowing my eyes.

"Very. I'm acting very suspicious but just trust me, it'll be worth it." Before I could respond, Mason cut me off.

"Hey guys, what's up?" he said helping Ali in the pool before they walked up to us.

"Nothing much, how about you two?" I asked, squinting a little at the sun while looking at them.

"Same," Ali replied. "Do you guys have any plans for today or tonight?" Ali asked. I was about to answer that but Asher didn't let me.

"Nope. We're just chilling." I locked eyes with him and took the hint. It was a secret.

Why?

I don't know. "Us too. There's no fun in leaving if we're tied down by the curfew anyway," Mase groaned. My eyes automatically lifted to meet Asher's while I bit back a smile.

"What are you smiling about?" Ali turned to me.

"N-nothing," I replied quickly.

Too quickly.

"Oh my god you two totally kissed last night!" she exclaimed, squealing a little.

"Um- yeah they did. We were there," Mason deadpanned.

"You idiot, after the party. They kissed again. Isn't that right?" she arched an eyebrow at me.

Look, usually, I have a silver tongue and I'm good at playing with words to get out an undesired situation. But lying to your best friend is a whole different type of sin.

"Possibly."

That's not a lie, is it?

"We did," Asher replied.

Nevermind then.

"And?" Ali pried.

"It's complicated," I answered. She huffed before shaking her head and letting out a humorless laugh.

"It's always complicated between you two. Why am I surprised?" she shrugged before going off into another area of the pool with Mason.

"It's always complicated between you two. Why am I surprised?" Asher mimicked with a high pitched voice. I smacked his arm while laughing.

"That is my best friend! A very accurate impression though," I laughed with him. We swam around for another thirty minutes or so before Asher asked,

"You want to head back?" I nodded and we stepped out, grabbed our towels and dried ourselves off before heading upstairs. We got into the elevator with Tyler and Elijah heading downstairs in their trunks.

"Hey," Elijah smirked while checking me out.

"Shove it," I rolled my eyes while standing beside Asher as Tyler began laughing.

"I wouldn't be laughing that was you a day or two ago," Asher mumbled more to himself but everyone heard and then Elijah began laughing as they stepped out.

"Was that necessary?" I asked as the doors closed and the elevator began moving up.

"I don't know, was it?" he deadpanned. I huffed before the elevator jerked and fell still while a red light instantly turned on inside. I fell back, my back colliding into the wall with a strong force making me hiss in pain.

"Are you okay?" Asher grabbed my hand while looking at me head to toe for any injuries I suppose.

"I'm fine. What's going on?" I asked while looking around.

"I think the power's out," he sighed while trying to press

the emergency bell button but nothing happened.

"This is a hotel! How is their power out?" I groaned while sitting down with my back against the wall. "It should be back in a minute or two, right?" I asked as he sat beside me.

He nodded, "It should. Let's just wait and see," he sighed.

"I feel like taking a nap." I huffed while resting my head on his shoulder.

"You could. This might take a while," he replied while holding my hand in his.

"Don't try to flirt with me while we're stuck in an elevator." I pushed him and stood up with a smile on my face.

"Why not? I've got you all alone," he smirked while pinning me against the wall.

"Oh really?" I raised an amused eyebrow at him.

He didn't answer. Just kissed me.

I mean, that's an answer on its own, isn't it?

Yeah, it is.

I kissed him back as the elevator jerked again and started moving once again.

"Might take a while my ass," I laughed with a smile.

CHAPTER THIRTY TWO

RILEY

The rest of the day went by very slowly, probably because I wanted it to go by faster. Anyway, it was currently eight and we were heading out for dinner. We decided to go to a hotel called Chez Sam. By car, it was one minute away so of course, we decided to walk. "Ready?" Asher called out from the room on the bed.

I was in the bathroom putting my hair up in a half up half down while I had a red sundress on. He was wearing a white button-up and blacked ripped jeans. "Just to be sure, is this a date?" I asked while turning the light off and stepping out.

"Holy shit," he whispered to himself.

"What was that?" I smirked.

"Holy shit." He repeated himself while checking me out with admiration in his eyes.

"Hey!" I snapped him out of it. "Is this date or what?" I asked curiously while slipping my converse on.

Comfort first, baby.

"Love those shoes, really go with the look," he said in a high pitched voice while walking up to me.

I laughed, "You can avoid the question all you want." I shrugged as we left while I slid the key card into my phone case.

"You look gorgeous." He smiled down at me. "It is a date."

I feigned surprise, "Oh, is it? I had no clue." I gasped dramatically. He chuckled as we got to the elevator. I stepped in with a little hesitation which got me an amused look from Ash before we got down to the lobby and left.

"So, where to after dinner?" I asked while linking my arm with his as we approached the restaurant. It was on one hundred-eighteen avenue and our hotel was on one-twenty-one, hence we made it here so fast.

"Well, the restaurant closes at midnight, and I plan to keep us there until then. After that, we'll walk around till it's time." He smiled down at me while my cheeks began heating up under his gaze.

"Should I be expecting this surprise to blow my mind?" I asked as we were led to a table for two.

"Possibly," he smirked. I rolled my eyes and we ordered. I just stuck to spaghetti and Ash didn't understand most of the menu so he stuck to it too.

"Didn't you take French classes for a year?" I laughed while propping my arms up on the table.

"What makes you think that helped?" he asked in complete seriousness before I watched as his lips bit back a smile.

"It could've if you wanted it to." I gave him a pointed look.

He shrugged, "I don't really care that much."

Everyone is already stressed about what to do in life later and he isn't?

"You aren't worried about the future?" I asked him curiously, waiting for his response.

"I care, I just don't let it ruin the present. Whatever happens, happens and I can deal with it when it happens."

Finally, someone with the same logic as me.

"Everyone's already so stressed in our grade, it stresses me out." I huffed while sipping my water.

"You're good though," he thought.

"Not in math though, don't even get me started," I rolled my eyes. "Let's talk about something else, why did you never make a move on me earlier?" I questioned while tapping my fingers on the table.

"Didn't I tell you? I thought you hated me."

I'm not convinced.

"Hmm, that's not it. What's the real reason? Spit it out." His tongue rolled over his bottom lip before he bit it in thought.

"You can tell me," my hand slipped over his before I could think about it.

I gave him three squeezes and his eyes came up to meet mine.

"I was scared," he admitted, "Scared that we would hurt each other and then lose each other again. Scared that I'd hurt you."

That's not right.

"Scared that you'd hurt me or that I'd hurt you?" I questioned cautiously.

It's a sensitive subject.

He's been hurt.

Multiple times.

I wouldn't blame him.

"It's just scary to let someone in after... you know your own family leaves you." He chuckled dryly with a sad smile.

"Hey," I squeezed his hand to make him look up at me. "I wouldn't hurt you, ever. And I'd never leave," I told him what I always had.

"Even if I hurt you?" his voice was just above a whisper.

Would it be worth it? Would he be worth getting hurt?

"Even if you hurt me," I nodded.

Holy shit.

I cared about him a lot more than I thought I did.

"Why would you do that to yourself?" he questioned.

"Sometimes, you have to get hurt to help the ones you care about," I shrugged slightly.

He smiled, "You care about me?" he asked with a smile dancing on his lips.

That's a sight to see.

"A lot more than you think," I said as our waiter approached with our food and drinks. I pulled my hand away as he set our plates down in front of us. "Merci," Asher and I said in sync.

"De rien," he smiled before walking away.

"I guess we can be posh and French when needed," he mumbled, making me laugh before we began eating while making conversation. Soon enough, we were done with our dinner and were waiting for the bill. It was brought, Asher suggested to pay and I didn't argue.

Before the waiter could go away I spoke up, "Excusez-Moi?"

He turned to me, "Oui?"

I asked if we could stay for a while. "Pouvons-nous rester un peu?"

He smiled at us, "Oui!…"

"Oui! Bien Sur!" he smiled before walking away.

"Yes! Of course!" I translated with a British accent.

"I don't know why you did a British accent but you're pretty good at it," Asher laughed as his change was brought back.

"I don't know why I did it either. I've always been able to do it, might as well put it to use." I shrugged.

"What is that supposed to mean?" he questioned in confusion.

"That means, whoever we talk to tonight, stranger or not, we have to talk in an accent. Do you accept the challenge?" I asked, once again in a British accent.

"I do," he replied in a British one too.

He just got ten times hotter..

We kept the conversation going, pretending to be posh, role-playing weird character voices in accents and saying famous dialogues and quotes in them too and before we knew it, it was midnight.

The same waiter walked up to us. "Désolé, nous fermons." He gave us a small smile. That translates to, sorry, we're closing.

"D'accord, merci." Asher and I said okay with a thanks before grabbing everything and heading out. "Now what?" I asked in the accent as we strolled around.

"I don't know, we've got some time so where do you want to go?" he asked while checking the time on his phone before slipping it in his back pocket, also in the accent. I began laughing but answered nonetheless.

"Someplace we can have fun," I smiled.

"Where do you suppose I find a bedroom?" he smirked cockily. I gasped and smacked his shoulder.

"How about we go to a park nearby?" I asked.

"We could also just walk the streets of the city of lights and relish the moment?" he spoke as if it were the most obvious thing.

"The city of lights indeed, alright then," I sighed exaggeratedly.

"I believe it's also referred to as the city of love." He emphasized as we kept walking aimlessly.

"I believe it is," I smirked as we kept walking.

After thirty minutes, my feet got tired so he was piggybacking me around. It was now twelve-forty-five and we were sitting on the bench. "I'll call an uber." He pulled his phone out and successfully called one.

Once it was here, we got in and began the drive. "To the-" the driver began asking but Ash cut him off.

"It's kind of a surprise for her," he said quickly, still talking in the accent.

"Oh, I see. Are you from England?" the driver asked as he began taking us to the destination.

"Yes, we are," Ash said through gritted teeth while I bit back a laugh. We got there and I was told to keep my eyes shut.

"How will I get out?" I asked, keeping up the accent still.

"You will hold my hand and trust me, come on," he said as we stepped out after thanking the driver. We walked around and soon I felt the ground beneath me soften.

It's grass.

"Where are we going?" I grunted while Asher caught me as I slipped.

"We're not going. We're already here." He took his hands off my eyes and revealed *The Eiffel Tower.*

"Five..." people counted down. "Four, three, two, one!" and the final show began where the tower twinkles and sparkles for ten minutes instead of five like it does between sunset and one am.

I gasped while looking at the beautiful sight in front of me.

It was more than I had ever imagined it to be.

"Do you like it?" he whispered.

"I love it!" I squealed before going up on my toes and kissing him with everything in me.

This boy has me falling.

"Thank you," I whispered as we sat down slowly on the grass, looking up at the glimmering lights.

"For you? Anytime."

Paris, the city of love.

CHAPTER THIRTY THREE

ASHER

"It looks beautiful," she whispered, completely mesmerized at the sight in front of us.

"I know," I whispered while looking at her.

"Stop it," she spoke warningly while looking up at me and shoving my face away, making me look at the dazzling tower.

"What?" I asked while chuckling.

"Look at it, Asher. It's glimmering."

She really wanted to be here.

She really wanted to see it.

"I see it," I laughed while she turned to me with disbelief.

"How are you not mesmerized in the least?" she gaped at me.

"I'm looking at you, I am mesmerized," I leaned in teasingly.

"Asher-" she began talking but I kissed her. She pulled away with flushed cheeks and a smile before turning to the tower as it glimmered for the last time tonight. Riley was lying between my legs, her head resting on my chest while my arms were around her and it truly felt right.

It felt so right.

It glimmered for the last time, the bottom to the top of the tower before it slowly dimmed away. People that were around us began slowly getting up and leaving and so did we. We stood up, dusted ourselves off before getting off the grass, onto the concrete.

"Thank you for tonight," she smiled while holding my hand before pulling me into another kiss.

"Anytime." I smiled after she pulled back before we began walking. We walked for about ten minutes before she got on my back for another five minutes and then we ordered an uber.

We sat through the drive in silence with our hands intertwined as she looked out her window at the lights we flashed by while I looked at her, occasionally looking out of my window as well.

"Merci," we thanked before getting out and getting into the hotel. We were walking to the elevator when Mr. Brown's voice stopped us dead in our tracks.

"Shit," Riley whispered before we saw Mr. Brown walking up to us, coming out of the bar.

"Where are you two coming from?" he asked while glancing at our held hands. I was about to spit out a lie but Riley answered,

"The Eiffel Tower." She cleared her throat awkwardly.

"A date?" he raised his eyebrows in surprise.

"Yeah," I mumbled awkwardly while rubbing the back of my neck. Mr. Brown gave me the 'I told you so' look.

You were right, Mr. Brown.

I accept my defeat.

I gave him a small shrug.

"It's one-forty-five in the morning," he gave us a pointed look. We both looked down at the floor. "Get to bed and tell nobody that I let you two get away," he huffed.

"Night, Mr. Brown." Riley smiled before taking my hand and running, pulling me into the elevator with her. We sighed as the doors closed and the elevator began moving up. "What did he give you that look for?" she asked as the elevator opened on our floor.

I smiled to myself before answering. "He told me I was bound to like you when he heard our conversation at school," I mumbled.

She snorted as we entered our room.

"Why did he- oh my god!" she screamed as we saw Ali just sitting at the foot of our bed. "Jesus fuck! What is wrong with you? How did you get in?" Riley asked while panting slightly with her hand on her chest.

I let out a breath that I didn't realize I was holding since I got a jump scare from Ali just sitting there. "I knew you two went out." She narrowed her eyes down at us like we were criminals. "Mason was too sleepy so I came to play detective myself. And I was right! You two went out on a date!" She pointed a finger at us while circling us.

"And?" I asked. Riley smacked me upside the head.

"Jesus," I mumbled while rubbing the back of my head.

"You lied to me," she folded her arms across her chest and looked at Riley.

"Actually, I did," I interrupted while putting my finger up in the air.

"I will break that finger, shut up," Riley whispered to me.

"Why didn't you tell me?" she questioned Riley like a mom.

Is this how friendships work between girls?

"Well, to be completely honest, I didn't know we were going for a date until before we left and I asked him and I didn't know we'd be out so late. I just knew we'd break curfew," Riley admitted.

"Where did you two go?"

Oh no. Oh, dear. Oh boy.

Riley looked at her with confused eyes.

I mean, I wanted it to be our moment but I guess it won't work with the interrogation Riley's being put through.

"Just around the city, the neighborhood, actually." Riley tried to play it off but Ali wasn't budging. "The rooftop." Riley said quickly.

Huh?

"We were upstairs on the rooftop. We were looking at the view and just talking. We were on a date. We sat together at a table and talked on and on for hours and kissed. Multiple times, in fact, anything else you'd like to know?" Riley huffed, lying through the skin of her teeth.

She was upset.

No, she was mad.

Allison straightened up and dropped the act. "I was just curious." She shrugged slightly.

Riley sighed, "How is it that you get to ask all about my life but you never answer me?"

I can't help but feel like I shouldn't be here.

"I asked you at the pool when Mason and Asher were together. You just changed the subject," Riley reasoned. I don't know if this is important, but Mase did that too. He doesn't exactly interrogate me like Allison interrogates Riley though.

"I didn't want to tell you! It's none of your business!" Allison snapped.

Riley blinked in surprise.

"Then what makes you think I would want to tell you?" Riley countered.

"Fine, don't tell me! I was just worried about you, what if he breaks your heart? He was a player!"

Okay then.

"Excuse me?" I raised my eyebrows.

"Don't go there, Allison. Mason isn't any better," Riley said quietly.

"Riley!" Allison yelled. "What is your issue with Mason? First, you lied and said that he slept with Kennedy-"

Whoa hold on.

"I did not lie! I told you what I was told!" Riley defended. Her hand dropped out of mine as she began making fists.

"She didn't lie, Allison. Even I didn't know! There's no way she could've known and I told Mason to tell you the second I found out." I defended her.

"Then get off my case!" Allison shouted.

"What the hell are you talking about? You're the one who is talking to me about how I don't want Mason and you together!" Riley argued.

"I have to go," Allison mumbled quickly, trying to get away.

"Allison!" Riley stopped her while grabbing her wrist. "What has gotten into you?" Ali didn't respond. She jerked her arm away before leaving the room, running off.

"What the hell just happened?" she whispered while turning to me with wide eyes.

"I have no idea," I mumbled, confused as hell myself.

"I-" she opened her mouth but no words came out. "Did I do something wrong?" her voice was barely coming out. "Was it something I said? Should I not have told her everything? Maybe I-" I cut her off.

"Riley, you didn't do anything wrong. She'll come around," I sighed.

She threw her arms up in disbelief.

"I mean," she scoffed, "What the hell is she so mad at me for? She even said all that shit about you and she's the one who always told me that you and I were great together, and..." she trailed off.

"It's okay, Riles. Maybe she doesn't trust Mase and she's still hung up on it. She forgave him too easily," I tried explaining my thoughts. It wasn't exactly working.

"That's not an excuse though, is it?" she chuckled dryly.

"Of course not, you'll be fine, you two will talk it out." I put my arms around her while she wrapped hers around me. "Relax." I rubbed her back while sighing.

"Did I fuck it up?" she whispered.

I pulled away to look her in the eyes,

"No! Absolutely not! Riley, you did not fuck this or anything else up. You didn't do anything wrong." I shook my head at her.

She sighed and rolled her eyes before throwing her arms around my neck.

"I'm going to kill myself," she groaned.

I pulled away looking at her with furrowed brows.

"I dare you to say that again." I glared at her. She chuckled before leaning her head back with a sigh.

I wrapped my arms around her waist while hers were loosely draped around my neck. "Tired?" I asked while my lips hovered over hers.

"Hmm," she agreed.

"Sleepy?" I asked while kissing her jaw. She blushed and laughed before humming in response again.

"Well then, go change." I kissed her for a moment.

CHAPTER THIRTY FOUR

RILEY

I facepalmed myself while laughing. "What are you high on?" I laughed as he got back on the bed.

He fell off the bed for the third time in the last five minutes.

"I don't know what's wrong with me!" he laughed while groaning into a pillow.

"Asher, we have to sleep! We're going to Musée d'Orsay and we have to wake up at nine, come on." I nudged his arm as he lay beside me. He was trying so hard to fall asleep but just couldn't. He kept shuffling beside me and it was extremely difficult to go to sleep with that happening beside me.

"Stop. Moving." I groaned into the pillow.

"I can't sleep," he groaned.

How exactly can I help with that?

I sighed and opened my eyes. "Come here," I huffed.

"What?" he looked at with confusion.

"Put your head in my lap," I demanded while he just looked at me in confusion. "Just trust me," I huffed and he listened and rested his head in my lap. "Now close your eyes." And he did. "Now try sleeping," I said as I began running my hand through his hair.

It helps me, why couldn't it help him?

I saw him smiling to himself while he slightly hummed in content. "Is that okay?" I asked, my voice just a whisper as my eyes began drooping.

"Mm-hmm," he hummed. I did that for a few minutes before stopping. I felt him grab my hand and place it back in his hair. I smiled to myself and kept going until his breathing steadied and he fell asleep, not too long before I did as well.

I groaned as his alarm began ringing. He got off of me and turned it off. "Time check?" I groaned.

"Eight-thirty," he huffed.

"Have fun," I laughed before going back to sleep.

"Mm-mm." He shook his head. "I don't take that long and I don't need to wake up early." With that, we both went back to bed.

My alarm rang, sharp at nine, and I woke up groggily. I sighed and threw my hair up blindly in a bun before getting up and opening the curtains, making Ash groan and hide his face in the pillow.

"Wakey, wakey!" I laughed. I walked over and kissed his cheek before grabbing my clothes and taking a quick shower, getting dressed and stepping out. He had his clothes laid out and went into the bathroom as soon as I came out, kissing me on the cheek as he went in.

I smiled as I tied my hair in a high ponytail and tied a knot at the end of my t-shirt before buttoning up my high-waisted black denim shorts and throwing my Adidas shoes on. I slapped my cheeks a little to make them blush naturally and took a final look in the mirror as Asher came out with damp hair and no shirt.

He threw a white v-neck on carelessly, making parts of it see-through from the water. I went into the bathroom and grabbed a hand towel, throwing it on his head. "Dry it," I demanded while plucking my phone off charge. He ruffled his hair and ran his fingers through it carelessly before ruffling it again and throwing his shoes on. I checked the time and we were perfectly on time.

"Nine-thirty. Not bad." I smiled at him as I grabbed the key card, slipping it into my phone case and heading for the dining room with him. Asher and I talked while walking through the buffet, grabbing whatever we wanted, putting it onto our plates before going and sitting at our usual table.

We were here before Allison and Mase.

Allison.

Oh no.

I forgot that we weren't exactly on speaking terms after insulting each other and our boyfriends? No. Our roommates that we share more than kisses with? Yeah, that sounds about right.

We sat there with Asher beside me and we began talking as Mase and Ali walked in. They walked through the buffet together, got whatever they needed and then walked up to the table. Well, Mase did.

Allison just stomped. She put her plate down on the table with a bang, directly in front of me before giving me a bitchy smile. I gave her a small smile before waving as a bitch would.

Trust me, pissing her off is a bad idea, but I like to play with fire.

Her jaw clenched before she sat down with a huff.

"Can't you guys talk this out?" Mason groaned. I opened my mouth to tell her that I was willing to if she was but she snapped first.

"Who's side are you on?" she slammed her hands on the table.

Geez.

"Yours!" Mason put his hands up in surrender out of fear.

I snickered but obviously, she heard.

"I don't want to sit here!" she shrieked as people began watching. I rolled my eyes.

I'm not taking her shit.

"Allison come on," I huffed.

"Not until you apologize." She folded her arms across her chest.

"Apologize? For what? Going on a date and not telling you?" I asked with wide eyes. "Allison, you haven't told me anything about you and Mason, do you see me throwing a fit? No! So suck it up and deal with it, I'm not always going to tell you everything!" I snapped. People stared and my breath got caught in my throat. I realized that I too was now standing and I was furious.

"Riley," Asher whispered from beside me as his hand found mine.

"I don't interrogate you, that's the difference. Because I know that if there was something you wanted me to know, you would tell me yourself. And if you don't, then it's none of my business and I take that hint. You need to learn to take that fucking hint." I got my hand out of Asher's and left the dining room.

I went to the lobby and sat on one of the couches. I closed my eyes and took deep breaths before I felt the couch dip beside me. "Hey," Asher said softly with two plates in his hands. I looked at him struggling to not drop one and began laughing while taking my plate from him.

"You should eat. We have to leave in fifteen." He said while placing his plate on the glass table in front of us.

"I'm not that hungry anymore." I sighed while leaning forward to put my plate there too but he grabbed it before I could.

"Just have a little bit. I'll even feed it to you," he pleaded while holding up a piece of hash browns in front of my mouth. I sighed before eating nonetheless and taking my plate from him with a smile. He did too and we began talking about trivial things.

Then the class filed out with Mr. Brown and Walker

leading them. Asher and I quickly went back to the dining room and left our plates on the closest table before joining the back of the line. We all got to the bus and got seated before the drive began. Asher leaned his head on my shoulder while tracing circles on the back of my hand with his thumb while our fingers stayed entwined.

"She hates me, Ash," I whispered while glancing at Ali who was sitting one seat ahead of me in the left aisle.

"No, she doesn't." He kissed the back of my hand before the bus stopped and we reached.

"I don't hate her, but I don't exactly like her, mainly for saying what she said about you," I pouted as we got off and stood with the rest of the students.

"We're going to start with Van Gogh's self-portrait and then go to see a Starry Night and figure out the rest." Mr. Walker announced before leading as we all followed.

"She said it about me, what are you so mad about?" he asked me while chuckling as we walked side by side.

"You're *my*-" I stopped when I didn't know how to word. "You're my roommate who I have a complicated, more than kisses relationship with. Of course, I'm mad!" I huffed as he grinned at me.

He kissed the side of my head as we made our way in and walked over to Van Gogh's self-portrait. "This isn't as creepy as the Mona Lisa but it's still very creepy," Ash whispered as Mr. Walker and Brown began explaining the story behind the portrait.

I find Van Gogh very intriguing. He was successful yet shot himself and his artworks are impeccable.

"Very creepy indeed," I whispered while looking at the painting carefully. "In a good way though, I like it," I said softly as we began moving forward, walking away from the painting.

I managed to take a picture of it since photography was now allowed, just no selfie sticks.

"Van Gogh would've been a cool guy," Elijah said while walking past us.

He would've been so cool.

Smoking god knows what with them and grinding on every girl he sees at a party.

Right, Elijah?

He's so annoying and immature, he gets on my last nerve.

We made our way to A Starry Night when Allison came up to me.

"Hey,"

CHAPTER THIRTY FIVE

RILEY

"What do you want?" I asked with a bored tone and expression, not looking at her just looking at the painting.

"I'll be right back," Asher whispered in my ear before leaving me alone with Ali.

Traitor.

"Listen, Riles, I didn't know you'd get so mad at me for asking you about your date, okay? I just wanted to know, as your friend. Asher's not a player, I know that. I just..." she trailed off.

"You were just looking for excuses," I stated.

"Yeah," she admitted with guilt. She huffed and continued. "I didn't tell you anything about Mason and me for a reason," she sighed.

"And that was?" I questioned.

"Don't you think it's a little embarrassing that the guy you've been talking to for a while lies about sleeping with another girl to save her and doesn't give one shit about how you feel?" she laughed humorlessly.

So Asher was right.

"Do you think you forgave him too easily? For lying to you?" I asked while turning to her.

"I don't know," she shrugged. "What if he lies again? What if he does it again because I forgave him so easily the first time and he thinks he can get away with it again?" she questioned.

"From what I know, he really likes you. And I don't think he would do that. As much as I hate that he's a player, I don't think he's playing you," I explained. "That doesn't mean you should forgive him so easily though. As for now, you two are sorted and doing good so don't do anything just- just think about it if it ever happens again," I sighed.

"I'm sorry for being a bitch," she apologized.

"It's okay, you were confused." I shrugged it off.

"Are we good?" she asked hesitantly.

"Yeah, we're good." I gave her a small smile.

"We're moving to another area, come on." Mason and Asher approached us. I snapped a picture of the painting before we moved forward.

"Everything okay?" Asher asked while I linked my arm with his.

I nodded, "Everything's okay."

We had pretty much seen the entire museum and it was

currently noon. We had seen all the highlights there were to see and now had the rest of the day off. "Where are we going now?" Justin asked from the back of the bus as the bus began moving.

"Back to the hotel. There's an activity for you all." Mr. Walker announced suspiciously. Everyone began talking about what this activity must be and after about twenty-five minutes, we were back at the hotel.

"Can everyone please meet us at the pool deck after freshening up." Everyone dispersed. We entered the room and I immediately flopped down on the bed.

"What do you think the activity is?" I asked while standing up and grabbing a cami and a pair of running shorts from Nike.

"I think some partner work or something?" Asher guessed while I went to change. I came out to see him throwing a black tank top for men over his head. My phone dinged as I was about to throw my converse on.

Ali texted. 'Wear flip flops. It's some water activity.'

I sighed, "We have to wear flip flops or sandals. It's a pool activity." I threw my flip flops on and he slipped into Adidas slides. We got down to the deck to see everyone assembled in straight line squinting slightly at the blinding sun.

"What is going on?" I mumbled to myself as we were pushed into line by Bianca and Elijah.

"We're volunteers," Bianca smirked.

I rolled my eyes before standing there waiting for Mr.

Brown or Walker to tell us what the hell we were doing.

"If anyone has their phones in their pockets please leave them on the table." Mr. Walker announced. I huffed and placed my phone with Asher's. We all stood there with our arms folded across our chests, waiting to be told what the fuck to do. "Can everyone please pick a partner. *Not your roommate.*"

Everyone picked their roommates since the teachers didn't know who our real roommates were.

"If possible of the opposite gender."

Great.

Asher's shoulder bumped mine and I turned to see him smirking at me. I rolled my eyes but couldn't suppress the smile that formed on my lips. "Nobody here is paired up with their roommate, correct?" Mr. Brown asked while looking directly at Asher and me.

I looked everywhere but at Mr. Brown and Asher and he let it go once again. Clearly, he knew.

Why didn't he point it out?

That means he knows that about everyone. He seems to know that Asher and I have something going on even when there are people in our class who are clueless about it. And that is very confusing.

"Today we're going to do a little getting to know and trusting each other activity!" Mr. Walker clapped his hands together, catching everyone's attention. Some people got curious and some groaned. I didn't exactly know how to react so I waited till he explained further.

"You and your partner will do various activities to get to know each other and trust each other more. It will consist of asking each other questions, guessing answers, seeing how compatible you two are, trust falls-"

"Trust falls?!" Aria asked in shock.

"Into the pool." Mr. Walker smiled. "Bianca and Elijah, you two can be partners. No more volunteering needed." I watched as Bianca's face morphed into horror and surprise before huffing at having to work with Elijah.

"We'll start with questions. Every time your partner gets an answer wrong..." he paused for dramatic effect. "You get to pie them in the face with whipped cream."

Are we seriously doing this at the pool deck of a hotel in Paris while we're on a school trip?

"We've rented out the deck for the remainder of today."

Oh great.

"Everyone grab two plates and a can of whipped cream."

Seriously, what the fuck is wrong with our teachers?

"Also, I would like to thank Tyler for giving us this idea!"

Son of a bitch.

Everyone turned to glare at Tyler and I mean everyone.

"Geez, chill," Tyler mumbled while walking over to Veronica. Guess they're partners. Wait. That leaves... I turned to see Kian sighing while Kennedy walked over to him. I tapped Asher's arm, still watching as Kian tried to back out of the activity but he couldn't convince Mr. Walker.

"I'll be your partner!" Everyone turned to me.

"It wasn't me." I put my hands up in surrender. I looked beside me to see Ali stepping forward.

Oh no.

"Um- no you won't." Mason grabbed her arm. "Riley can do it."

Bitch, what did I do to you?

"Can't you, Riles?" he asked me.

"Um- no?!" Asher answered, already grabbing my wrist.

"Then I'll do it." Ali strutted off to Kian while Kennedy walked over to Mason.

"Just a sec," I walked over to Ali and pulled her aside for a minute.

"Are you sure?" I asked with concern.

"He needs to learn his lesson somehow," she shrugged.

"Okay," I said, still unsure before walking back over to Asher.

"Couldn't you have just done it?!" Mason yelled at me, making me jump.

"Mason, chill!" Asher pulled me closer to him.

"Ali wanted to do it!" Kian shouted, stepping in.

Shouldn't a teacher break everyone apart at this point?

"Kian shut the-" Mr. Brown cut Mason off.

"Guys!"

Pin drop silence.

"Figure it out! I don't want any fights here!" and then he walked away.

"I don't want you working with him!" Mason said to Ali.

She inhaled, "You should have thought of that before lying to me and saving Kennedy's ass. Now work with her," she said sassily before standing beside me, pulling Kian with her while Ethan and Colby pulled Mason to the other end of our line up.

"I know you wanted to work with her, I'm sorry," I faintly heard Ali whisper to Kian.

What is that supposed to mean?

"I'll get the whipped cream," Asher sighed before going and grabbing our paper plates and a can.

"You guys have five minutes! The pair with the least questions answered wrong wins! Time starts now!"

Okay, I guess we're just going to pretend like that never happened.

"What's my full name?" Asher asked while putting whipped cream on a plate.

I snorted, "Asher Robert West." I smiled as he handed the

plate to me. "What was the name of my dog I had when I was five?"

He knows it.

He smiled, "Danny Devito," he laughed.

"Asher!" I looked at him wide-eyed.

"Danny! Danny!"

Told you he knew it.

Asher teased me and called him Danny Devito.

"How many teddy bears with roses have I given you?"

Oh crap.

"Um- four?" I guessed, already preparing myself to get pied.

"Riley!" he gaped at me.

"Did I get it wrong? Please don't say I got it wrong! Don't pie me too hard!" I began pleading.

"You got it right!"

Phew.

CHAPTER THIRTY SIX

ASHER

"What is my full name?" she asked me.

That one's easy.

"Riley-" What is her middle name? Oh my god, do I actually not know this? Jesus. "Riley Wilson Blakely?" I guessed, using her mom's maiden name. She shook her head before pieing me in the face. "What was it?" I asked while cleaning myself up.

"It was Rose." She put the plate down.

"Your middle name is your nan's name?!" I asked while licking some cream off my finger. I've met her grandma. Rose is her mom's mom. "What is my mom's maiden name?" I questioned.

"You've never told me this!" she whined.

"Yes, I have." I countered.

"Cooper?" she guessed.

Damnit.

She got it right.

I sighed and gave her the plate. "Where was the first place I went to, outside the United States?"

We went together with our grandparents.

"Bali, Indonesia." She nodded and handed it back over to me. "What was our first date? Third-grade time?" I questioned while adding more whipped cream because I knew she'd get this one wrong. There's no way she remembers.

"Stop it!" she pulled the can out of my hand and put it back on the table. "Um- game night?" she guessed.

"How did you know that?!" I asked wide-eyed.

"I didn't, I guessed." She laughed while taking the plate. "If I could get a tattoo, what would I get?" she questioned.

"Just the word 'love', right here." I pointed to the side of my index finger while holding it up. "How old was I when I got my tattoo?" People notice it but no one ever says anything. It's my nan's birthday in roman numerals, right under my ear on the side of my neck.

VIII • XXIV • MCMLVI.

That's the tattoo.

"That one, right? I mean you don't have any other." She lightly brushed her finger over my tattoo, giving me goosebumps. I'm almost seventeen so that means I needed a permit to get it. My grandpa allowed it. I still think it's only because it's his wife's birthday that I got.

I'm very close to her. She never wanted to move out but

my grandpa did. She's all I really have in my family.

"Fourteen?" she guessed with uncertainty.

"Nope, fifteen," I said before pieing her. She gasped while cleaning up her face.

"Times up! Line up, everybody!" We laughed and stood where we were standing earlier. "We'll go down from your left to right in order, each pair stating how many they got wrong. We'll start at the end, Colby and Megan?"

Oh yeah, Megan was here too.

"Twelve."

Yikes.

Did we even ask twelve questions total?

"Eight."

"Fourteen."

Jesus!

Tyler and Veronica.

How amusing.

"Twelve," Mason announced for Kennedy and him.

If he didn't really know her that well then why help her dump Kian?

"Six," Kian announced.

"Two," I said. Everyone's jaws dropped as they turned to us in shock. Even Mr. Walker. Not Mr. Brown though, he just smiled. "One each," I added, just to rub it in everyone's faces.

"Alright, winners get free snacks tonight!" Mr. Brown declared. Riley and I high-fived before we moved on to the next game.

"Alright, can every pair stand one behind the other along the edge of the pool." And we all did. Riley stood in front of me while I put my arms around her and rested my chin on her head as whispering already began.

"I need you to pick person A and person B."

Riley looked up at me, "I'm A." I just smiled before we listened further.

"I'm gonna need person A at the front, facing their partners." Riley turned to face me with confusion written all over her face. "Alright, hold your partner's hand." I held her right hand in my right.

"Now person A, continue leaning back until I say stop." I saw some of the girls already beginning to whine, not wanting to take a dunk but here I have Riley, gladly beginning to lean back.

"Riley, did you curl your hair?" Ali asked while tightening her grip on Kian's hand.

"No? I slept in a braid," she shrugged while continuing.

"Stop."

And she did.

"Girls, follow along, please. You have to trust your partners. Keep going." She began leaning further back, having me hold on tighter. "Keep going, keep going." She began laughing while I held onto her, making sure she didn't fall.

Her hair *did* look curlier today and it looked really pretty, that work shouldn't have to go to waste, even though she doesn't care if it does.

"Mr. Walker I-" Kennedy began speaking before we all heard a loud splash. He let go of her hand. She reached the surface, gasping for air, "Mason!" she shrieked. He just shrugged and stepped back, not apologetic in the slightest.

She may be a bitch but he doesn't have to be a dick about it.

"Keep it going." Mr. Walker rolled his eyes. "Stop!" he shouted right as the ends of Riley's hair were about to touch the water. "Switch." He demanded and I instantly pulled Riley up.

"Don't drop me," I said warningly.

"I'll try my hardest," she smiled while holding my left hand.

"Start." I began leaning back extremely slowly to kill time and so she wouldn't have to put so much effort.

"Put your feet right in front of mine. Mirror them. Touching toes." She whispered demandingly. "It improves stability." She added.

I shifted my feet slowly until my slides and her flip flops were touching edges. "Keep going." We heard multiple splashes, suggesting that the majority of the guys since guys were mostly person B, had fallen.

"Come on, keep going." Riley began closing her eyes while holding on tight so she wouldn't drop me.

"You can let go, it's fine. I'll jump." I told her as Kian fell in beside me.

"You jump, I jump, Jack." She laughed while quoting Titanic.

"Come on, just a little longer."

She began grunting while tightening her grip. "We still have Tyler and Asher left. Veronica, Riley keep it going." She bit her lip.

"God! You have too much muscle," she groaned.

There was another splash and I was now the only one up. "Stop!"

She immediately pulled me up and let out a breath she was holding. She smiled up at me while shaking her hand.

"You're welcome," she smiled cheekily. I smiled back at her before sneaking in a kiss on her cheek as we began the next activity.

"Since Tyler has decided the last activity which we don't know, we'll let him explain."

This is going to be great.

Note the sarcasm.

"Couples yoga, everybody!"

How is this allowed?

Who gave him the right to choose?

Literally who the fuck asked him?

Who said he could talk?

Who?

"I can't even touch my toes," Riley groaned. Everyone groaned and began protesting. "Either that or a treasure hunt. Kind of." he said, confused himself.

Amazing.

"Or we can get back to our rooms and shower and relax until dinner?" I suggested while holding my hand up in front of Riley's face as she began squinting at the sun. I heard Ali squeal beside me before Riley and turned to her in confusion.

"What?" we asked in sync.

"Are we missing something?" more than half the class mumbled at the same time. She pushed herself off of me and straightened up but I pulled her back, wrapping an arm around her. I just glared at everyone and they sobered up.

"What about our prize for winning both activities?" Riley questioned out loud.

"We have tomorrow off as well since the other hotel group is going to Arc de Triomphe and we want to break that into two classes as well since we have too many. You could choose the place or we can stay in?" Mr. Brown suggested. Riley looked up at me with confusion.

"Let's go to Champs Elysees!" Aria suggested.

"That's already scheduled on the second last day we have planned," Riley replied with a huff.

"Stay in!" Bianca shouted. And then people agreed.

"We should ask for the rooftop rented out for tomorrow's dinner. Everyone can bring a date?" Riley suggested while turning to me.

"As long as you're my date," I smirked. She shook her head while smiling before suggesting the idea.

"Is everyone okay with that?"

Pretty much everyone agreed.

"Alright, that's the plan. Everyone can go now, we'll see you at dinner!" And with that, we were all off to head back to our rooms.

Riley was grabbing our phones when I snuck up to her and pied her again. She screamed before grabbing tissues while groaning and cleaning herself up.

"I am going to kill you," she threatened while narrowing her eyes at me.

"Yeah, yeah." I smiled as we began walking with held hands. We got into the crowded elevator before it began moving up. We got off at our floor and headed straight for our rooms. We sighed simultaneously as we walked in.

"I'm showering first!" she shrieked, already grabbing her pajamas.

"You have whipped cream on your face," I laughed while pulling her against my chest, pointing at her cheek.

"Oh, do I? That's funny, I wonder how that happened?" she asked sarcastically. I grabbed her chin before licking it off of her.

"Asher! Ew!" she pushed me away as I laughed and wiped her cheek frantically. "I'm definitely showering first!" she ran into the bathroom.

The door locked with a click and the shower water began running. I looked around the room while sitting on the bed before I began laughing.

She forgot her clothes outside.

Again.

CHAPTER THIRTY SEVEN

RILEY

"Asher, could you pass me my clothes, please?" I stuck my head out of the bathroom, hoping he would give me the clothes that I left on the bed.

No response.

"Asher?" I called out.

Nothing.

I tightened the towel around me and stepped out to see the room empty. I huffed and walked over to the bed, grabbing my clothes and turning to go back into the bathroom when the door opened.

The bedroom door.

"You guys seriously need to figure this out. Did you really have to come to get me, Mason? I mean this is between you two and-" Asher stopped talking when he saw me.

He was talking to Mason and Ali.

And they were all looking at me.

While I was in a towel.

Asher stood in between while Mason and Allison kept yelling at each other.

They both also abruptly stopped talking when they saw me.

"Oh hey," Ali shrugged. She's not who I'm worried about, she's seen me in a towel before. Asher's eyes were still wide open while his jaw dropped slightly.

He closed his mouth and put his right hand over Mason's eyes and his left hand over Ali's.

"Bitch, I've seen her before!" Ali smacked his hand off before plopping down on the bed. "You on the other hand," she gave him a pointed look. He cleared his throat before putting his hand in front of his mouth. "Eyes," Ali said.

He then put his hand in front of his eyes.

"I'll take that as my cue," I mumbled before slipping past Asher and back into the bathroom. I quickly got dressed and towel-dried my hair, not before groaning into my hands. I finally gathered the courage and opened the door to step out when I saw Mason and Ali both being pushed out the door.

Asher turned to me with a sigh.

"Why?" he huffed. "Why did you have to do that to me?" he leaned against the door.

"Are you taking her side?" Mason opened the door, having Asher topple over.

"Later," I said quickly before closing the door in his face, making sure to lock it this time. "Need a little help?" I reached my hand out and pulled him up. I leaned against the wall while he stood in front of me, his eyes roaming around my face, lingering at my lips.

He began leaning in but I grabbed his face. "Shower first, please." I pushed him into the bathroom before handing him his clothes and closing the door. He sighed before I heard the shower running and sat down on the bed. In about five to ten minutes, he was out the door.

"You did not have to step out in that towel," he sighed while belly-flopping onto the bed beside my legs.

"How was I supposed to know you weren't in the room? When you didn't answer I stepped out to grab my clothes. You didn't even knock." I pointed out accusingly.

"I have to knock to enter my own room?" he raised his eyebrows at me.

"When you're walking in with friends, yes!" I exclaimed.

"One friend. The other is yours," he stated.

"The other, I'm not bothered about," I countered.

"I covered his eyes."

To be fair he did.

"A good five seconds after you guys saw me," I reasoned with a pointed look.

"I was- processing?" he said but it came out more like a question.

"And by processing you mean you were checking me out."

He gaped at me.

"I saw you." I kicked his leg with mine.

"Can you blame me? I mean you looked-" he rolled his tongue on the inside of his cheek. I smacked his shoulder while biting back a smile.

"You can't say stuff like that," I blushed.

"Why not?" he leaned forward and hovered over me. I began turning my head away as he leaned in, making me blush. "Riley," he whispered while tilting my head to face him. He began leaning in again and just as our lips were about to touch, the bell rang.

I pushed him off out of panic and caused him to fall off the bed. I gasped, "I am so sorry!" I covered my mouth while standing up.

"I can't get you alone for one fucking second," he mumbled while standing up and getting the door.

"That's not how it works! I have to teach you a lesson somehow!" Ali's voice boomed through the room.

Asher groaned while sitting on the bed beside me, resting his head on my shoulder as we watched them argue.

"I already apologized and told you the truth!" Mason argued.

"Yeah and then I realized I forgave you too easily! You lied and I let that go too easily!" Ali reasoned.

"Right, right. You forgive me and then just suddenly

realize that forgiving me was a mistake?" Mason questioned.

To be fair, she doesn't have to act the way she is right now. I told her to teach him a lesson next time. Everything between them was already cleared up.

She turned to me while Mason looked at her impatiently.

I slightly shrugged at her.

"I didn't agree with what you did. That's not fair to him," I told her softly.

"My point exactly, thank you!" Mason turned to me.

"Mason shut the hell up. I still don't like you. You fucking yelled at me for no reason down there." I rolled my eyes at him. "Both of you need to talk this out without dragging us into it." I felt Asher's gaze on me but I continued talking.

"Now I suggest you both sort this out as soon as possible because tomorrow we have a dinner and you're both going to need dates. Now unless you want to go with Kennedy and you want to go with Kian, you two need to make up," I huffed.

"I wouldn't mind going with Kian but since he's like in love with you, I can't!" Ali shrieked in frustration.

"Ali!" I sat up, looking at her wide-eyed.

She smacked her hand over her mouth.

"That's not what I meant!" she said while turning to Asher.

He sat up beside me and looked at me.

"Is it true?" he asked.

How am I supposed to answer a question that I don't know the answer to?

"Not as far as I know," I sighed. He began to stand up but I grabbed his hand. "Please don't," I said softly.

"I'm sorry," Ali said before leading herself out with Mason following.

Was that really necessary?

Did Ali have to say that?

I feel like I should be mad right now but I don't have time for that, instead, I now have to focus on fixing things between me and Asher since looking at him right now doesn't exactly give off the impression that he's happy.

I looked up at him and he was still standing.

"Please sit down."

Nope, didn't listen.

"Please?" He huffed and sat down on the edge of the bed, his back pretty much towards me. I huffed and got off the bed and sat down on the floor in front of him.

"What are you-"

I cut him off. "Shut up."

He huffed.

"I don't know if Kian likes me, Asher. I can't answer that until he tells me if he does or doesn't. And I'm not going to ask him because it is very unnecessary. But you need to know that whatever his answer is, it will change nothing. I like you. It's you that I like," I explained as easily as I could.

He stayed silent while I sat beside him on the bed. I waited for him to say something but he just stared at me. "Hello? Anyone in there?" I knocked on his head jokingly, trying to lighten the mood. He didn't laugh or even smile.

"Can you find it in you to trust me?" I asked.

He sighed before answering.

"I trust you," he said while looking me in the eyes. I smiled and realized that I wanted him to kiss me.

"Now that you've got me alone for one fucking second, can you kiss me?" I asked with a grin on my face. He chuckled before pulling me in for a kiss.

It was short.

And sweet.

And I was not satisfied.

That's what to get me alone for?

Bitch. Nuh-uh.

I got back on my side of the bed while he got on his.

"That's what you wanted to get me alone for? I am disappointed, to say the least." I shook my head, acting exaggeratedly disappointed.

He scoffed. "What do you want me to do?" he asked.

I swear if I had tape I would tape my mouth shut because what came next was not what I wanted.

"Oh, I don't know. Can you maybe bite me in the neck?" I said sarcastically before my eyes widened.

"Oh my gosh," he chuckled. "Sure," he leaned in.

"No wait I was-" I began but then started giggling and blushing when he placed a kiss on my neck while trying to push him off.

"Don't want it anymore?" he asked while pinning my wrists above my head and beginning to tickle me, making me scream and laugh.

He stopped before kissing me again.

Longer.

Harder.

Then down to my jaw, then my neck and stayed there for a while.

Well, that's going to give me a hickey.

CHAPTER THIRTY EIGHT

RILEY

"Asher, we can't just skip dinner, everyone's waiting and I'm sure you're hungry, I know I am." I put my shoes on. Asher was trying to convince me to skip dinner because he had a bad feeling. About Kian. "What's the worst that you think will happen?" I asked while turning to the boy who refused to get out of bed.

"Kian will come and join our table and steal you!" he threw his hands up in frustration. "Look I like the guy and I don't want to hate him, but with the thought that is now lingering in my head, I can't trust him."

I sighed and lied down beside Asher.

"Do you trust me?" I asked.

"I trust you but that doesn't mean I trust him." I want to say he's playing with his words but he's really not.

"If he tries anything we'll sneak away. Promise!" I scooted closer to him while he grabbed my hand and played with my fingers. The small gesture warmed my heart. "Please?" I kissed his cheek.

"Please?"

Then his jaw.

"Asher." When I kissed his neck, he gave in.

He grabbed my face gently and pushed me away. "You really test me," he sighed before getting up at putting his shoes on. I smiled before sitting beside him while he put his shoes on before kissing his cheek a few times.

I was about to kiss it a few more times but he grabbed my face and kissed me. "If we don't get going right now, we'll never be able to get out," he chuckled.

I'm falling for him.

"Okay," I stood up and grabbed the key card, slipping it in my phone case as usual and putting that in the pocket on my sweatpants. I was about to step out but he grabbed my wrist.

I looked at him in confusion. "Put a cardigan or something on, you're not going out like that." He looked at me head to toe. I was wearing my pajamas. My sweatpants with a white cami. I gave him a pointed look. He just gave me one in return.

"I didn't bring my cardigan," I lied.

"Then wear my jacket." He swiftly grabbed his Nike zip-front jacket and handed it to me. I unzipped it and threw it on, leaving the zip down. He grabbed the zip and zipped it up. All the way.

"Nice try," I smiled before unzipping it.

"Please?" he pouted.

"You please?" I pouted back. He sighed in defeat and we headed downstairs. We walked downstairs following some of our classmates while being followed by some as well. We all walked around the buffet, grabbing whatever we wanted and finding our seats. I sat on the sofa side after grabbing my food with Asher beside me, leaving the two chairs in front of us for Mase and Ali.

"Hey," Ali sat down in front of me.

By herself.

"Um- hi. Where's Mason?" I asked in confusion while pouring water into my glass. I got spaghetti and some garlic bread for dinner and that should be enough. Asher got some pasta and Ali seemed to have the same as me.

"I don't know," she shrugged while taking a bite out of her garlic bread.

"What do you mean?" I questioned while crossing my legs.

What? It's comfortable that way.

My knee rested on top of Asher's leg and I noticed he was tapping his foot, causing his leg to shake up and down. I grabbed his left hand and intertwined our fingers, resting it on top of his leg, stopping it from shaking.

"I mean, I don't know. I came here myself," she shrugged casually. I turned to look at Asher before turning back to her.

"Do you know if he's even here?" I raised my eyebrows at

her. She just shook her head no.

Look, she's my best friend and I love her to death, but she's blowing this way out of proportion.

"Ali-" I began but someone's voice cut me off.

"Is this seat taken?" Kian asked.

I slowly looked up at him and turned to Asher when I felt his grip tighten on my hand. I squeezed his hand thrice and he relaxed. I shook my head, "No, it's not taken. I don't think." I wasn't sure if Mason would be joining us tonight.

"It's not," Ali confirmed.

"Mason's not here today?" Kian asked while sitting down. My eyes met with Asher's while Ali answered Kian.

"He didn't come with me so I guess not," she replied. I felt my phone vibrate in my pocket and I took it out to see a text from Asher.

'We should eat and head out. Not because Kian's here. I don't mean to sound rude but I can't really keep hearing her talk about Mason like that. He's my best friend.'

I turned to him and nodded in agreement. We all fell into an awkward silence as we ate.

"Congrats on the win in the activities you guys," Kian addressed us. "By the way, the idea for the dinner date tomorrow was really good, do you all have dates?" he questioned, making conversation.

All three of us answered simultaneously.

"Yeah."

"Yeah."

"No."

We all turned to Ali as she said no.

I'm getting sick of this.

"Ali," I said warningly.

"It's true," she shrugged nonchalantly.

Since when is she so bitchy towards Mason?

Last I checked she was just trying to teach him a lesson.

I'm getting worried.

"Who are you guys going with?" Kian asked.

"Him."

"Her."

We answered while pointing at each other.

I turned to Asher before quickly looking back at my food. "I'm gonna go get a slice of garlic bread," I announced before getting up. I walked over to where it was and saw none.

"Une minute s'il Vous plait," there was a waiter, taking back the empty tray. I nodded and waited for the garlic bread to be brought.

"So, is that his jacket?" A voice startled me. I looked to my right to see Kian.

"Huh?" I voiced my confusion.

"The jacket. Is it Asher's?" he repeated.

"Um- yeah. It's his." I nodded.

Cue the awkward silence.

I took this as my chance and just asked him straight up if he liked me. I know I said it was unnecessary but Asher was getting bothered and when I finally hear Kian say no, I can tell him and he'll be fine.

"Kian, um- you don't by any chance uh- how do I say this?" I stammered. "You don't like me, do you? Like, like like me?" I asked while tucking a loose strand of my hair behind my ear and turning to him.

"I did," he admitted and my heart dropped.

"But not anymore."

I let out a breath I didn't realize I was holding. "You used to like me?" I asked as the garlic bread was brought.

He nodded as we began walking back.

"Yeah, a long time ago. Like when we did the group project thing."

The same time I did.

Now, normally the thought of what we could have been would have crossed my mind but I was surprised, to say the least when it didn't. No, the first thought that crossed my mind when I heard him say that, was that I could finally tell Asher the truth and be one hundred percent sure of it.

"Liking you now would be chaos," he chuckled.

"Yeah," I nodded while laughing. "Chaos."

Speaking of.

We sat back down to see Ali and Asher pretty much in a staring contest. I sat down and didn't bother breaking it. "Guys?" Kian asked and Ali blinked first, breaking away.

"I see you won that one," I mumbled to Asher. "Mason?" I asked. I didn't have to phrase the whole sentence, he knew I was asking if they were arguing about Mason.

"Yeah," he nodded.

"I need to talk to her about that," I sighed while finishing up the slice of garlic bread before drinking my water.

"So talk," Ash shrugged. I gaped at him. "She didn't hesitate."

He wanted to get back at her on behalf of his best friend.

"It's not the right thing," I whispered while shaking my head as Ali and Kian talked about the dinner tomorrow.

"You can't always do the right thing," Asher replied.

"No, but I can try."

He huffed, "Well, I can't." And he turned to her.

"Allison." She looked at him. "You don't have to treat Mason the way you are."

Here we go.

"Asher," Ali said sternly.

"If you can talk shit about him in front of Kian then I can defend him, okay?"

Valid point.

"Him not telling you was wrong, I get that, but he didn't lie."

Also true.

"Yeah well, he wanted to help Kennedy now he can be with her too," she replied.

Very bitter I see.

"If he wanted to be with Kennedy then he would. But look at that table, do you see him there? No. You wanna know where you will see him? Upstairs in your room, beating himself up over hurting you. Get over it, Allison. He apologized," Asher huffed before getting up.

I watched as he filled up a plate with food for Mason and left.

"Your boyfriend is a dick." She narrowed her eyes at me.

"He's not my boyfriend," I said through gritted teeth.

Why is she coming at me? I didn't go down her throat when Mason was a dick to me earlier today.

"He may be a dick but what he said is true. You're hurting Mase a lot more than he hurt you, Allison."

And with that, I left.

—— CHAPTER THIRTY NINE ——

ASHER

Once I left the dining hall, I went straight up to Mason's room with the dinner for him. He's my best friend, I can't leave him hanging like that. I rang the bell and he answered, looking like shit as expected.

"You look like shit," I stated. He just stared at me monotonously. "Have you eaten? I hope not because I brought this up here, you better finish it." I walked in and sat on the edge of his bed. He followed after closing the door and just sat on the bed, staring at the blank TV screen.

"Should I even be with someone who treats me like shit for making one mistake?" he asked me while I handed him the plate.

"I don't mean to make you feel worse but buddy, your mistake was pretty big. Not as big as she thinks but still, pretty big," I explained, "She gets upset and triggered just at the mention of your name. And she's trying to talk shit about you to get herself to hate you, but she knows she doesn't.

Everyone does," I sighed as the bell rang.

I inhaled as I walked up to the door and answered it. It was Riley. She stood there awkwardly, fiddling with the sleeves of my jacket that ran past her arms since it was too big for her. "Am I intruding on a bromance?" she asked hesitantly.

"Come on in," I let her in.

She sighed as she sat beside me.

"How are you holding up?" she asked him.

"You don't even like me, why are you here?" he asked her bluntly.

"Because my best friend likes you but she's being incredibly stupid about everything. She's being very blind-sighted right now. I'm sorry for the way she's treating you. I'm trying to get through to her but she's kind of blocked everyone out and is just doing what she thinks is right." Riley sighed while explaining.

That.

The accurate description of what is happening with Allison. That is it.

"Don't you think she's pushing it too far. I mean she-" Mason began but the bell rang, again.

"I'll get it," Riley sighed and went to get the door, coming back with Ali.

"Um- hi," she said while looking down at the floor.

"Do you guys want us here?" Riley asked while I got up

and stood beside her.

"I think we'll be fine," Mason answered. We said bye and left, heading for our room. We got in the elevator and as soon as its doors closed, we leaned against the wall and sighed simultaneously.

"Fucking hell," Riley sighed while running her hand through her hair.

"They'll figure it out," I said reassuringly while putting my arm around her shoulder and pulling her into me, kissing the side of her head. We stood in silence as the elevator moved up.

"I'm tired of being a referee," she groaned while hugging me as the elevator opened. I picked her up and carried her to the room. She was very sleepy and tired.

"You smell like me," I chuckled while setting her down, letting her open the door.

"I'm wearing *your* jacket," she laughed in response.

"Tired?" I asked and she nodded in response. "Sleepy?" I questioned.

"A little bit," she admitted.

"Just a little? You sure?" I asked as we knocked our shoes off and got into bed.

"Yeah, just a little," she replied while grabbing my hand and playing with my fingers. She put her hand up against mine, looking at how much smaller hers was than mine. She laced our fingers together and just stayed quiet. Her head rested on my chest as we lied in a comfortable silence.

She took a few deep breaths before calling my name. "Asher?" I hummed in response as she looked up at me. "Do you think we can ever be more than just- complicated?" she questioned, her voice soft.

"I don't know, but I hope we can," I confessed. I realized I was falling for her a while ago I just couldn't tell her.

"Good," she answered shortly.

That's all I get?

"Why?" I questioned.

She cleared her throat before looking back up at me.

"Because I think I'm falling for you," she whispered hesitantly while her eyes shifted from my eyes to my lips then back up to my eyes.

"Are you really?" I whispered in shock.

I never imagined that she'd feel the same way, let alone be the first to say it.

She nodded, "Pretty fast and pretty hard," she chuckled.

"Can I kiss you right now?" I blurted out.

She smiled, laughing slightly.

"Do you really have to ask?" she replied before grabbing my face and pulling me in for a kiss.

I'm going to be so in love with this girl.

She grabbed my collar and pulled me over to her side, not breaking the kiss while I propped up my elbows while she flicked the lamp off, dimming the room into darkness. She smiled into the kiss before pulling away.

"Night," she whispered against my lips. She gave me a small kiss before we very shamelessly cuddled and then dozed off.

I woke up to hear Ry groaning from the bathroom. I was about to get up and knock to check on her but she came out, pouting.

"What happened? Everything okay?" I asked while sitting up.

"Ali's calling me." She rubbed her hands over her eyes.

"Right now? At two am?" I asked, my voice hoarse.

"She's freaking out."

My brows furrowed, "Why?"

She drank some water before lying back down.

"They kissed." I rolled my eyes and turned my back to her, trying to go back to sleep. She called Ali and began talking on the phone. "Allison Jones, congratulations, you two have officially made up, now spare me the details. Talk tomorrow? I'm sleepy!" she whined into the phone while wrapping her arms around me.

"Allison! Please?" Riles pleaded while I ignored her and tried to get back to sleep. "I do not have a problem with him but please let me sleep," she huffed. "Yes, I swear, goodnight!" She finally hung up.

"Hey!" She tugged at my arm but I pretended to be asleep. "Bitch, I know you're awake." She tugged at me again. I bit back a smile and continued pretending. "Asher, I swear to god!" She pulled me with full force, having me face her.

"You're such an asshole," she laughed while I flipped over to lie on my back. "No!" she whined while climbing on top of me. She lied on top of me and put her arms around my neck.

I stayed frozen just to see what she does and she grabbed my arms and placed them around her before resting her head on my chest. I laughed before kissing her head and we dozed back off.

I woke up to Riley nowhere to be found. I groaned and sat up in bed when I heard the door open, creaking ever so slightly. Riley walked in, balancing two plates on her hands, with the keycard in her mouth.

She rushed over to the little table we have and set it down. "Good morning!" She said cheerfully.

Her hair was thrown up in a bun, she was wearing her pajamas, thankfully with my jacket thrown on top.

"I brought breakfast!" She grabbed the plates and got onto the bed, using her knees to crawl forward. I quickly grabbed my plate and made it easier for her while setting it on my nightstand.

"You brought me breakfast?" I asked, still not fully awake. Mentally at least.

"Yeah, of course," she said nonchalantly while sticking a piece of bacon in her mouth. "Go brush your teeth!" she spoke through a mouthful while nudging my leg with hers. I chuckled before going into the bathroom and brushing my teeth and splashing my face with some water and then heading back outside as it is.

In sweatpants and shirtless.

I got back onto the bed, lying on my stomach as I set my plate in front of me. "What do you wanna do today?" she asked while sipping on water.

"Well, I would like to start with a good morning kiss, maybe?" I asked.

"Get your breakfast in, it's the most important meal of the day after all," she smirked while finishing her food and putting the plate aside. She stood up and grabbed her clothes and went into the bathroom.

"Swimming?" I called out while eating.

"Walking around the city?" she called back.

She came outside with her hair in a high ponytail, denim shorts on with a black lace bralette.

"You're not going out like that, babe." I checked her out.

"Babe?" she chuckled while grabbing her grey cardigan. "Is that fine, babe?" she smirked.

"I fucking knew you had it," I laughed while finishing up breakfast before grabbing my clothes.

"Give me five minutes," I gave her a quick kiss before going into the bathroom to change.

CHAPTER FORTY

RILEY

"Look at that! That's such a pretty charm!" I exclaimed as I held the little Eiffel tower bracelet charm in my hand and looked at it closely before putting it back. We looked around the small shop for a little bit. It was a souvenir shop and we were just checking it out before heading back to get ready for the dinner that was being held.

Asher's hand left mine as he wandered out of the shop while I did too. I turned to find him when I heard him talking to the cashier. "Merci." He smiled while handing some money to the cashier before heading over to me.

"What did you buy?" I asked while we left and began heading to the hotel.

"This," he dangled the charm in my face. I gaped at him before a smile crept onto my face. "Give me your wrist." I held my arm up as he attached the charm onto my bracelet. My dad got me the Pandora bracelet a long time ago and I keep it on except for when I'm showering.

I like to add charms when I find them but I tend to get one

from each country I go to. The bracelet isn't an empty canvas but it's not weighed down by charms either. I have a decent amount.

This one wasn't a Pandora charm but it was just as pretty as one would be.

"Now I know it's not *Pandora* but..." he trailed off while shrugging. "You liked it, so I bought it."

I looked at it on my wrist before kissing him. I pulled away with a smile and we began walking back to our hotel. We got to the hotel to see Mr. Brown and Walker standing at the desk, talking to the receptionist.

"Merci!" Mr. Walker laughed before turning around and heading towards the elevator. We were walking right behind them and unfortunately had to go through an awkward elevator ride. "Where are you two coming from?" Mr. Walker asked suspiciously.

"We went to the souvenir shop and just the stores we have nearby," Asher informed them.

"And what did you buy?" he questioned further.

What does he think we were doing?

I held my wrist up, "A charm."

He then turned to Asher. "Mr. West?" he questioned.

He grabbed my wrist and held it up.

"A charm." He smiled at them. "Excuse us." Asher grabbed my wrist and pulled us away. I laughed while opening the door as we stumbled in.

"They will seriously kick one of us out of this room. They already know." I laughed while flopping on the bed.

"Open up!" Banging on the door was followed by Allison's impatient voice. I groaned and got off the bed, letting her in.

"How can I help?" I asked while flopping on the bed, putting my head on Asher's chest while hugging him.

"Get a room," Ali groaned before grabbing my ankles and pulling me to the edge of the bed.

"Hey!" Asher whined.

"Get up, loverboy. I need this room and my best friend so we can get ready."

Already? We have like three hours left!

"Oh! So I'm her loverboy now? You were calling me a dick yesterday," Asher rolled his eyes while getting up.

Ali's eyes widened while she stared at the ground.

"You heard that?" she asked in confusion.

He chuckled before kissing my cheek,

"See you later." He grabbed his clothes for tonight and left.

"So, which dress is the chosen one?" Ali raised her eyebrows at me.

"The black one. I'm gonna go take a quick shower, okay?" I said before quickly going into the bathroom and taking a shower. I washed my hair and put it two braids for the time being before stepping back out.

"Makeup?" I asked her while tightening the robe I had on.

"Can you do mine first?" she questioned.

"Sure, give me your makeup bag." She gave it to me and I sat her down on the couch. "What are we going for?" I asked.

"Well, it's a purple dress," she shrugged.

"Purple cut crease with glitter?" I asked and she nodded. I did her eyeshadow first, taking my time to make it look good then smoothly doing her face makeup.

"You can get started on your hair," I finished putting her lipstick on and then got started on my makeup. I did everything light and natural. I just put on some winged eyeliner and some lipgloss and I was done. I let the braids down and twirled two pieces from the front, tying them at the back.

Shit. I don't have any shoes to wear with this.

"I got you," Ali elbowed me while handing me a pair of heels. I looked at her wide-eyed.

"You brought heels on this school trip?" I asked in confusion.

She scoffed, "Bitch, as if! You're not the only one who went shopping with your boy today." She looked at me with amused eyes.

"At least I didn't drag him shopping for heels. We actually had fun and looked at things for both of us." I smiled sarcastically.

"Where do you think he got his clothes for tonight from?" she asked as we threw our heels on.

I laughed, "Oh shit! You picked it?" I asked in surprise. We stood up while I grabbed my phone and keys.

"Of course! How else do you think he'd look hot tonight?" she asked.

I rolled my eyes and sprayed perfume all over myself as the bell rang. I looked at the time and saw that it was seven-fifty-eight.

Two minutes till the dinner.

I went and answered the door to see the boys. "Gentle-men," I held the door open while letting them in. Mason walked in first, followed by Asher who apparently wasn't going to walk in. He leaned on the doorframe and just stared at me.

"Are you going to come inside?" I asked while fidgeting with my earring. Nervous habit. He didn't say anything just stared and I started feeling deja vu of the night we kissed. Just like that night, he kissed me again.

I quickly pulled away before swiping my thumb over his lips. "Lip gloss." I smiled as Ali and Mason walked over.

"Ready?" she asked.

Asher's arm linked with mine as we got the elevator, making our way inside. We clicked the button to the rooftop and talked on our way up there. We got up there to see the rooftop decorated beautifully. It had fairy lights strung around and the tables had one candle each.

It looked stunning.

But that's not what caught my eye. The view from up here did. I gasped while taking in the view.

"It's pretty isn't it?" I whispered to Asher beside me.

"It's beautiful." I felt him looking at me and I smiled. He began chuckling at nothing which made me turn to him in confusion.

"What?" I questioned.

"I'm gonna be able to say that to you as my girlfriend one day," he sighed, "And I can't wait for that day," he smiled down at me. "I really like you, Riles."

I'm falling in love with him.

"I really like you too," I whispered.

"Do you want to get a table?" he asked while locking his hand with mine.

"Sure." We took a table for two and saw that Ali and Mason were sitting at a table near ours and were having a great time laughing their asses off. I smiled to myself, happy that the two dumbasses found happiness with each other and were finally at peace.

"Do you want anything to drink?" Asher asked while standing up.

"I'll just take a coke, thank you." He smiled at me before heading inside. There was a bar counter set up on the inside for drinks. I pulled out my phone and took a picture or two of the view before going onto social media.

It had been about fifteen minutes and Asher was still

nowhere to be found. At first, I thought it was because there was a queue at the bar but then I saw pretty much everyone from our class up here.

"Hey, where'd Asher go?" Ali asked while sitting at my table.

"To get drinks," I said while resting my chin in the palm of my hand.

"And how long ago was that?" she asked while sipping on her coke.

"Fifteen minutes," I groaned. "Where's Mason?" I asked in confusion.

"He left his phone in the room so he went to go grab it," she replied.

Okay, that's it. I'm done waiting.

"Do you wanna come and help find Asher?" I asked while standing up.

"Sure," she shrugged while grabbing her drink and walking inside with me. As expected, he wasn't at the bar and wasn't outside either so where did he go?

"Do you want to check your room? Maybe he went to go grab something?" she asked.

"Maybe," I mumbled while walking towards the elevator with her. We turned the corner and my heart dropped. I couldn't breathe and my vision began blurring from the tears that were pooling in my eyes.

"Riles," Ali whispered hesitantly while resting her hand on my shoulder.

"I need to go," I whispered breathlessly while pushing through the few people that were coming upstairs and heading downstairs. I got into the elevators and pressed the button to the sixth floor immediately.

Ali wasn't able to make it through the crowd and just as the doors were about to close, someone's hand came in between, getting crushed between the doors, making them wince.

I quickly pressed the button and opened the elevator while wiping my tears. "I am so sorry!" I looked up to meet Kian's eyes.

"Hey," he smiled. His smile faded once he scanned my face.

"Riley!" I heard Asher scream but I was swift to pull Kian inside and close the elevator doors.

"What happened?" Kian asked.

"I saw him kissing Ashley."

Just as I began falling in love with him, he broke my heart.

CHAPTER FORTY ONE

RILEY

I just stood in silence as the elevator moved up. "Riley-" Kian began but I cut him off.

"Please don't." My heart was still racing and my breathing was ragged and at an uneven but quick pace.

"I'm gonna drop you to your room, okay?" he asked softly. I just nodded absentmindedly. The elevator dinged and opened and we stepped out swiftly. I picked up my pace and got to the room. I opened it and I already felt tears slipping out again. I blinked the rest of the tears away and grabbed my suitcase, throwing it up on the bed.

"Thank you for dropping me, you can go now." I sniffed while grabbing whatever was outside my suitcase and began throwing it inside, full of agitation and anger.

"Riley, Riley, Riley." He rushed over to me and grabbed my hands, pulling the stuff out and set it down, turning me to face him.

"What did I do wrong?" As soon as the words slipped my mouth, I broke down into sobs. I pretty much literally fell to the floor but Kian managed to catch me and sat me down on the edge of the bed.

"Riley, you didn't do anything wrong. Riley," he sighed and pulled me into a hug. I tried to get myself together when I thought about how Asher could walk in any second and I wanted to be out before that happened.

"I need to pack, I need to get out of here." I pushed him away and stood back up.

"Riley, where are you going to go? All the rooms are full." He informed me and I groaned into my hands.

"Do you know someone who doesn't have a roommate?" I asked while grabbing my pajamas. I went into the bathroom before he could answer and washed my face. I took all the makeup off and changed, leaving my hair as it is. "Do you?" I asked again once I stepped out.

He cleared his throat and cracked his knuckles. "Um- me," he stated.

"What?" I asked while folding the dress and throwing it in. I tossed the heels inside too, deciding to hand them to Ali later.

"Well, I picked Veronica's name and she hasn't been coming into the room. She didn't even come the first night. She grabbed her stuff and went with Ashley."

Say that again.

"They go out every night," he added.

"So, you don't have a roommate?" I asked while throwing my flip flops on.

334

"Nope," he shook his head.

"Well, now you do." I pulled the suitcase off the bed and grabbed my phone, throwing it in my pocket.

"What?" he asked in shock. "Riley, Asher wouldn't like that." His name was already making me tear up.

Riley, grow a fucking pair, get over it.

"Please don't cry," he sighed while standing up.

"I'm sorry. I shouldn't just decide I'm your roommate," I huffed.

"Kian, I really don't give a fuck what-" I choked up at his name. "What Asher thinks. Please?" I begged. "At least just for tonight. I'll try getting a new room tomorrow. Please?" I pleaded as knocks flooded the room.

"You're not getting a new room," he stated while standing up. "You can room with me." I let out a sigh of relief before giving him a small smile.

"Riley, open up!" Asher's voice boomed through the door.

"Room number?" I asked as we walked up to the door.

"Three-forty," he answered.

"I'll meet you there. Get away as soon as I open the door." I demanded before opening the door quickly. Asher looked at both of us in shock and Kian took that time to slip away.

"Did you two?" he asked.

I scoffed coldly, "No, Asher. I'm not gonna do what you did." I turned back inside to pack up my phone charger, laptop, it's charger, and all the toiletries I brought.

"You don't know what happened!" he argued while walking in. I shoved my toiletries into my bag.

"All I know is that you were kissing someone else. You were kissing Ashley after saying how we're going to stay loyal to each other! You didn't stay loyal to me!" I yelled while turning to him. "You left me," I stated.

"I'm right here! I did not leave you! I'm with you!" he argued.

"You left me the minute you kissed her," I said calmly. "Asher, I've seen you at your worst, okay? Your worst. And I never even fucking thought about leaving you. If you were going to leave me then why go this far? You took me for a date to the fucking Eiffel tower, you bought me the charm I wanted, you kissed me so many times, you made me feel special, you hugged me when I needed it and even when I didn't, you made me feel safe, Asher. You spent so much time with me and I loved it, every second. I loved you," I blurted out before I could stop it.

It's true.

What can I do now?

"And it sucks that I had to lose you to realize that, but it is what it is, right?" I gave him a sarcastic smile before zipping everything up in the bag.

"You don't think I love you?" he asked while stepping closer. "Please just give me one chance to explain what happened."

I sighed and folded my arms across my chest, "Five minutes is what you've got." I sat down on the edge while he kneeled in front of me.

"I went inside to get us drinks, I saw Ashley there and then I turned around to leave but before I could, Ashley called out my name. I thought I could get away and act like I didn't hear her but she grabbed my arm before I could step back onto the rooftop. I didn't have a choice, so I turned to her and she started talking to me. That went on for ten minutes.

Then she brought up the fact that she likes me and she tried asking me on a date for tomorrow. I told her that I wasn't interested in going anywhere with her. She asked me if I had a girlfriend, and I said no because we decided on no titles, then she asked if I was talking to anyone and I said yeah, I'm talking to you but it's kind of complicated. Once I told her again that I wasn't interested in going anywhere or doing anything with her, I was going to leave but she didn't let me.

She just grabbed me and kissed me. At first, I didn't realize what was really going on and at that time, you showed up and you ran into the elevator and I pushed her off and saw you. I tried to get to you but you closed the doors. I tried coming down here then and there but the other elevator was at the lobby and Mr. Walker saw me and began talking to me and I just couldn't get out of there. Allison distracted Mr. Walker and I came here as soon as I could, Riley, I swear I didn't mean to kiss her!" he spoke in a hurry, eager to get the truth out.

I looked down at him while his hands held mine in my lap. I swallowed the lump in my throat before answering.

"I call bullshit." I smiled before throwing his hands off of mine and standing up, eager to leave.

"Riley, please don't walk out that door." He grabbed my wrist and pulled me flush against his chest.

"Give me one good reason," I ordered.

"I love you," he whispered.

It breaks my heart that this is the moment and this is the situation we're in as he says those words to me.

"That's not good enough," I lied.

It was more than good enough and I would stay here in a heartbeat if I could. But I can't. I respect myself more than that.

"You love me," he said.

"I do. But I respect myself more." I grabbed my bag and began walking to the door.

"Riley, please don't leave me. Please!" he pleaded while standing in front of the door, blocking my way out. I looked up at him to see his eyes tearing up. "You said you'd always be here," he mumbled.

I cupped his face and ran by thumb over the one tear that fell from his eye. "Did you lie to me?" he whispered.

"I could never lie to you about something like that. Ever. I loved every minute that I spent with you, and every kiss that I shared with you." I wrapped my arms around his neck for one last hug and his grip on my waist was daunting.

It was scary that he wanted me to stay so badly and I meant so much to him in such little time. I loved him with every piece of my heart and I'm breaking those pieces down to millions right now, but I don't deserve this.

No one does. And this time, I have to put myself first.

"I love you, Asher," I whispered in his ear, "But it's over." I began to pull away but he wasn't letting me go.

"No," he shook his head, "I'm not letting you go." He picked me up and walked us straight back to the bed.

He sat me down before getting a death grip on my hand.

"I know it's not what you want," I whispered, "I don't want it either. But I have to do this, Asher. I have to do it for me." I hugged him again, tighter because I understood it could be our last and the seriousness of the situation dawned on me.

"It's not what you want, but you're going to be fine," I whispered before pulling away while he protested.

I grabbed my bags, and I was out.

CHAPTER FORTY TWO

ASHER

"She has the keys, bro. What do you want me to do?" I asked. It was the middle of the night. After she walked out, I dragged myself out of bed to change into something I could sleep in since that was my plan.

But i couldn't sleep and I really needed to go see her and fix things, but I didn't know where she went and before I made assumptions and went to Kian, I wanted to check Ali's room. So I walked out and went there to see if she was there and she wasn't, then I went to ask Ali where she was. Ali didn't know.

Shocker.

After that, Mason offered to walk me to my room because he wanted to have a word with me.

"Well, before we go down to get you another key card, I want you to tell me what the fuck happened?" he asked, shoving me into the wall and leaning on the other wall.

"I don't want to talk about it, okay. I need to go find her," I began to leave but he blocked my way.

"You can't! Not only do you not know where she is, but you also don't know what's going through her head right now. What if you go there and it just makes everything worse?" he questioned.

I scoffed at him, "Makes everything worse? How can things get possibly worse?" I chuckled dryly.

"Sometimes people just need space, Asher. Just to process things. Maybe she said something she didn't mean, in the moment and she needs time to realize that. She'll come around." He patted my shoulder.

"She's not going to fucking come around, Mase. I fucked up from what she knows! Bad! I know her like no one else does and she's not coming back unless I go and get her myself." I ran my hand through my hair in frustration while groaning when my phone dinged in my pocket. I took it out to see a text from Kian.

'She's in my room if you want to come and talk to her.' The party was still going on but Riles, Mase, Ali and I came back after the whole chaos that Riles and I went through. *'Room number three-forty.'* I put my phone in my pocket and sighed.

"I'm going to see her, I have to," I huffed before beginning to walk to the elevators.

"Are you sure? I'm not going to make you stay here, if you want to go see her then go. Just make sure you bring her back," he sighed and walked with me to the elevators. Both of us got into the elevator and went where we needed to. I got out and headed in the direction of Kian's room.

I met him in the middle of the hallway. "Dude, what the hell happened? She's been crying hysterically. You better fix it, Asher. The only reason I never tried to be with her is because I knew you wanted it a lot more than I did. If you hurt her this time, you're gonna lose her. I'm not threatening you or any other bullshit, I'm trying to help you because I see how deeply you're in love with her. You're fucking lucky to have her, I wish I did something earlier. Don't let her go."

He patted my shoulder and continued walking away. He liked her and I've always known that, but I've always respected the fact that he didn't try anything with her. He knows the difference between right and wrong and he's a genuine guy unlike almost everyone else I know.

He deserves someone a lot better than Kennedy and I hope he finds that. Just not with Riley. I can't lose her.

Not to him or anyone else.

I heard shuffling after I rang the bell. The door opened and she was wearing sweatpants with a rather large shirt. My shirt.

When did she take that?

"Did you forget something?" she sniffed before finally looking up at meeting my eyes.

She tried to slam the door shut but I put my foot in between. She groaned and finally opened the door. "What are you doing here? What do you want?" she sighed in defeat.

I didn't answer and I just kept staring at her.

"Is that my shirt?" I asked.

Dumbass.

"Do you want it back?" she asked while using my sleeves that were too big to wipe her tears away.

"No," I shook my head.

"Then what do you want?" she asked, sounding tired, exhausted and drained.

"You."

It's true.

She licked her lips, "Well, I'm sorry but that's not an option," her lips pulled into a thin line.

"It could be," I said.

"It couldn't." She shook her head while her voice trembled, breaking my heart.

"I love you, Riley," I sighed.

"I don't," she lied. "I can't." She shrugged slightly.

"Yes, you can. Have I ever lied to you? Why would I do it now? Now, when things are perfect between us," I stated.

"Were. Things were perfect between us," she corrected me. "You have lied to me, Asher. And the last time that you did, we lost each other for almost a year." My eyebrows furrowed in confusion and she took that as a chance to explain her words.

"You told me I was important to you, a long, long time ago. Then you went and told Jordan I meant nothing to you and I was a nobody. Then you went to Ashley and you left me. Not that we were ever together then, but I was there when you needed me, and then you left me when I needed you. You lied to me."

What the hell is she talking about?

What did I tell Jordan?

"Jordan? Like the Jordan that took my car back from the airport before we came here?" I voiced my confusion.

"What other fucking Jordan do you know?" she hissed.

Something is not right.

I *did* tell her she was important to me, I never told Jordan any of that and I never left her for Ashley. She's either misreading what happened before we stopped talking, or someone lied to her.

"Who told you this?" I asked.

"Told me what?" Her brows knitted.

"Who told you that I told Jordan that you meant nothing to me? Who told you that I went and dated Ashley? Who told you any of this bullshit that we lost each other over?" I asked while taking steps forward, making her take steps back into the room. I shut the door, still facing her.

"No one had to tell me! I heard your voice in the back of the fucking video!" she exclaimed before her eyes widened.

What video?

"Who told you, Riley?" I questioned.

"Nobody."

Lie.

"Who showed you the video?"

No answer.

"Who showed it to you?" I pinned her against the wall.

"J-Jordan," she stammered.

"He showed you a video?" I asked and she nodded. "Did you see me in it?" She shook her head. "But you heard me?" She nodded again.

She hesitated.

"Why did you hesitate?" I narrowed my eyes at her.

"I didn't." She doesn't have to admit it, but I saw that.

"Did *you* hear me, or did he tell you that it was me in the back?" I inched closer. She refused to answer and tightly sealed her eyes shut. "Tell me, Riley," I whispered in her ear. Her eyes snapped open and met mine.

"He said it was you."

I see.

"And who told you I was dating Ashley?" I interrogated. She shook her head. "You have to tell me," I whispered. "Who told you?" I asked again.

"Ashley," she sighed in defeat.

I closed my eyes and bit my lip, grunting in aggravation.

"And you believed her?" I questioned.

"Why wouldn't I? As far as I knew, I meant nothing to you and I don't now either." She tried sliding away but I grabbed her wrist in one hand and put my other arm around her waist.

"Riley, you know you mean the fucking world to me. You were and you are important to me. You pulled me out of dark times but you didn't let me in when you were there because you didn't trust me anymore. And I was fucking stupid for not coming up to you earlier. But I love you, Riley. You have to believe me, please?" I pleaded.

I noticed how her eyes teared up but she blinked it back. "Please come back to the room." I lifted her chin so her eyes met mine.

"Did you just come here to get me so I'm not sharing a room with another guy?" she whispered.

"Of course not," I shook my head. "I came here to get you because I love you and I don't want to lose you. I took you to the Eiffel tower, kissed you, bought you that charm, and spent all that time with you for a reason. Please come back."

She fell into thought.

Please say yes, please say yes, please say yes, I kept chanting in my head.

She sighed and pushed me gently. "Fine, I'll move back into the room, but we're not back together. I can't give it to you that easy," she stared down at the ground.

"Can I get a kiss?" I whispered.

She gave me a pointed look.

"One until you make it up to me, okay?" She raised her brows at me.

I smiled at her, "Promise."

She chuckled and shook her head before pulling me in for a long, hard, last kiss.

Until I make up to her.

CHAPTER FORTY THREE

RILEY

Asher carried my bags for me as we walked back to the room.

I'm still upset. I am still shattered from what I saw.

I trust that he told me the truth because like he said, when did he lie to me? And he doesn't have any reason to unless he wants to hurt me, which I hope not and so I doubt, but just seeing that- I don't know, it just shakes you up a little and it makes you fall into a downward spiral, trying to figure out if you did something wrong.

It made me wonder if I did something to drive him away.

I mean, she's Ashley and everyone knows she has a habit of throwing herself at guys but I didn't think she'd do something like that. I didn't think she'd stoop that low.

I hate her. With every bone in my body but I'm not mad at her. I'm a little disappointed in humanity but it's already done.

It only leaves me feeling... insecure.

Should I be trying harder? To impress him? Attract him? Or should I let it be?

I played hard to get for a little bit but he got me anyway. I do need to distance myself and as much as I don't want to, I have to. For me. We walked into the room and he set my bags down where they were before turning to me. He grasped my hands in his but I pulled them away.

"I can't. I need to put my guard back up, Asher. I let it down and you got your kiss, not like I didn't want it. But I need a little space."

He sighed and nodded before taking a step back.

"Okay, okay. I understand that," he said softly.

I bit my tongue and began tearing up again.

What is wrong with me?

He pouted slightly while looking at me. "Can I give you a hug?" he asked in a whisper. I bit my lip before blinking tears back.

This is going to be a lot harder than I thought.

"Okay, can you give me a hug?" he asked when I didn't respond. I sighed before wrapping my arms around his neck tightly. He wrapped his arms around my waist, clutching me close to him. "We'll be okay, Ry Ry." I smiled at the nickname. I missed it. I inhaled his scent and placed a small kiss on his neck before pulling away. I watched as he swallowed, his Adam's apple bobbing.

I let out a chuckle before grabbing a water bottle and drinking a large amount thanks to my dry throat from the crying. After that, we got in bed and just did our own thing on our phones. My phone dinged as I got a banner notification.

'I love you.' It was from Asher. I turned to him and gave him a pointed look. I texted back saying, 'I love you too,' before plugging my phone on charge and turning the lights off.

We slept facing each other but no talking and no touching, just distance.

I sighed as my eyes fluttered open. I opened my eyes slowly to see Asher already lying awake beside me, staring at me. I chuckled and hid under the covers. "How long have you just been staring at me like a creep?" I asked.

"About ten minutes," he laughed.

"What time is it?" I asked while peering my head over the covers.

"Almost nine," he smiled at me. "Arc de Triomphe awaits," he adjusted his position on his pillow.

"Do you want to shower first?" I asked while reaching out and grabbing my water bottle.

"Sure." With that, he stood up and went into the bathroom. I scrolled through my social media in the meantime. *Are you okay?* I read the text that Ali sent. *I'm okay. We're going to be okay.* I texted back.

I sat up in bed and threw my hair up in a bun since I wasn't washing it today and let out a yawn. I just finished grabbing my clothes when Asher walked out in a towel. I resisted the urge to roll my eyes, knowing that he walked out half-naked on purpose. "Really?" I deadpanned.

He just smirked. I grabbed my clothes and took them in the bathroom, taking a quick shower before stepping out and getting dressed. I threw on a little concealer since my eyes were puffy from all the crying I did last night and some mascara before applying lip balm and stepping out of the bathroom.

I grabbed a pair of socks and threw on my converse. I wore a pair of skinny jeans with a basic white off-shoulder top.

"Are you going to put anything on top of that?" Asher asked from his spot on the bed. I looked at my shirt.

What am I even showing?

"Um- no?" I phrased it like a question.

"The guys are going to look," he gave me a pointed look.

"At what? My sexy shoulders? Yeah right," I scoffed while grabbing my phone and slipping it in my back pocket. I turned to see him eyeing me. "Asher, come on," I whined.

He put his hands up in surrender.

"Okay, I just- I don't want people staring at what's mine."

I resisted a smile and just shook my head.

"Should we leave?" I asked while quickly pulling my hair in a side braid.

"Yeah, let's go." He stood up and put his phone in his pocket.

I grabbed the keys, and we headed out. We got breakfast per usual and got in the car.

"I'm sitting with her." Ali linked her arm with mine and sat us down before Asher could protest. The guys sat behind us while we began talking. "Did he explain?" she asked, keeping her voice low. I simply nodded. "Do you think he's telling the truth?" she questioned.

"I don't think he has a reason to lie, do you?" I asked. She took a moment to think before answering.

"How far have you two gone?" she asked bluntly. I looked at her in extreme confusion. "Because I have a feeling you're past the talking/complicated stage."

I sighed, "Well, we're past it but the situation now isn't any less complicated. I told him I loved him," I shrugged.

"You what?!" she shrieked.

"I said it too!" Asher popped up, standing in his seat behind mine.

"Asher, go away!" Ali clicked her tongue in frustration.

"But I want to sit with her!" he whined while resting his chin on my seat.

"Can't I get one ride with her?" Ali groaned.

"Fine," he huffed before sitting in his seat.

"Is he always so childish?" she asked me.

"Depends," I shrugged.

"Did she kiss him?" she asked.

"Yeah," I replied.

"Did he kiss her back?" she questioned.

How do I answer that? "I mean, not exactly but yeah, I guess?" I answered with confusion. She hummed in response before turning around, facing Asher.

"Did you kiss Ashley back?" she asked him bluntly.

"Oh my god," I mumbled, facepalming.

"Not really," he answered.

"It's a yes or no question!" Ali snapped.

"No, it's not! Our lips touched and she kissed me but I took a minute to comprehend! You tell me, is that a kiss or not?" he groaned at her.

"Guys, keep your voices down!" Mason hissed. I checked my pockets to see that I left my airpods.

Great.

"Did you make it up to her?"

I love being spoken about as if I weren't here.

"I'm trying, Allison!" Asher snapped.

"Okay listen up, if you guys want to argue and interrogate each other then please sit with each other, but please stop talking about me like I'm not sitting right here!" I turned to face Asher, sitting on my knees.

The bus jerked forward in an emergency break and before I could fall backward, Asher grabbed my wrists, making sure

I didn't go anywhere. He let go once the bus began moving smoothly again and a tense silence dawned upon his.

Asher broke it when he said, "Mason, go sit with her. I need to talk to Allison." I sat in my seat again while Ali huffed but switched seats with Mason nonetheless.

"You alright?" he asked me.

I sighed and said, "I'm fine."

Lie.

"So, you guys said the l-word." He tried starting a conversation.

"It's not a curse word, Mason." I chuckled.

"You know, he was planning on asking you to be his girl-friend, then Ashley ruined it." My head snapped in his direction.

"He was going to what?" I asked in shock.

"I wasn't supposed to tell you that," he mumbled, "Just know that he's deeply in love with you and- he genuinely hates himself for hurting you, Riley. I know he hurt you but he hurt himself a lot too. He's in love with you." Mason shrugged slightly.

"It's not good how we keep hurting each other," I sighed while leaning my head against the window.

"You two aren't *toxic*, don't even think about it. When did you hurt him?" Mase asked.

"A long time ago," I mumbled.

"They lied to you, I knew they did."

I asked, "You didn't tell Asher that it happened?"

"He was crushed over you leaving and saying you want him to stay away from you. I couldn't."

CHAPTER FORTY FOUR

RILEY

I sighed and grabbed my water bottle which I grabbed on the way out of the hotel and followed everyone off the bus. "I need to talk to you," Kian said while walking behind me.

"Okay," I nodded, slightly confused. We followed the class as the teachers led the way.

"Can you come here for a second?" He grabbed my hand and tugged at it.

What is going on?

I walked to the back of the line with him, a little secluded from everyone else. "Before I say anything, are you okay?" he asked me with concern.

"Yeah, I'm fine," I answered hesitantly. He gave me a pointed look before sighing.

"Okay," he nodded, "So, I'm guessing you understood that I told Asher where you were last night?" I nodded in response. "And you know that he loves you," he started.

"Did Asher put you up to this?" I interrupted.

"No!" Kian shook his head.

"So you called me here to talk about Asher?" I voiced my thoughts.

"I called you here to answer a question that you asked me earlier but truthfully this time," he sighed.

Oh no.

"You asked me if I liked you," he stated.

"And you said you didn't," I pointed out.

"Well um- I might have lied," he spoke hesitantly, "I'm not trying to get in between you and Asher but I just wanted to get it off my chest. I need to know that at least I told you," he shrugged slightly.

"Why did you lie earlier then?" I asked as we slowly trailed behind our class.

"It's kind of hard to tell the girl that you like, that you like her while she's wearing her boyfriend's jacket and her boyfriend glares at you, watching your every move. Plus, you seemed really happy with him."

He's not my boyfriend.

He wasn't then earlier.

"So, you like me?" I asked, raising my eyebrows.

"I do, I like you," he admitted.

I sighed, "You don't even really know me though."

He shrugged, "I don't really know you, but I want to."

How do I respond to that? "But I know I can't," he sighed. My brows furrowed and he began explaining.

"I'll never be able to match Asher. I'll never be able to love you like he can, like he does. You two are perfect for each other and you make each other happy and I see it even though you two don't see it. You especially. Just don't let someone like Ashley Simpson come in between."

I don't want to break his heart.

"And don't worry, you're not hurting me. I mean, we have time right? In the possible future, could I get a chance? Even though I doubt there will be an opportunity for me because he's not letting you go."

I feel so bad for him. He is such a nice guy and he deserves someone so amazing and great and loyal.

"Of course, you have a chance. Kian, you deserve someone that is willing to cross limits for you. Everyone deserves someone like that and I can't do that for you right now, and you know that. If you ever need me, I'll be here. You were there for me, especially last night. I hope you find the right person and stay happy with them," I gave him a small smile.

"I hope you stay happy with him." He looked at Asher while smiling at me.

I chuckled, "I asked for space," I looked down at the ground.

"Do you regret it yet?" he asked while chuckling.

"Very much, I miss him," I admitted.

"So go," he shrugged. I looked at him in confusion. "Go

walk with him, talk to him. Go." Kian is the nicest person I have ever met. He's not harmed anyone or wished anything bad upon anyone and I do hope he finds someone who loves him with all their heart and soul. It's just not me. "Go, Riley," he laughed.

I hugged him before listening and going up to Asher. "Hi," I said softly as we walked side by side.

"Am I losing you to someone else, Riles?" he asked me bluntly. I kept staring ahead as we walked, not looking at him.

"Who do you think you're losing me to?" I questioned.

"Kian," he sighed while looking at the ground.

"Nope. I already told you, I'm not going anywhere," I answered casually before taking a picture of the arc on my phone and continuing. "I'm just making you work for it," I said while shrugging.

"So you still need space?" he questioned.

No.

"Yeah," I lied, "It's better for us," I explained shortly.

"In what way? We hate this. We miss each other, Riley. Isn't it killing you?" he asked while pulling my arm and making me turn to face him.

"More than you know," I confessed, "But it killed me more to see you with her." I pulled away and continued walking by myself.

"You're not gonna be able to last as long as you think, you know," he said, making me stop walking and turn back to him.

"Why are you testing me?" I huffed.

"Because you're ignoring your feelings and in case you didn't know, it is awfully hard to stay away from you."

Don't fucking swoon.

"From anyone that you love, and you just happen to be that person for me."

Don't do it.

"And you don't know how awfully hard it is to see the person you love with someone else," I countered.

I'm allowed to be bitter.

He sighed, "I didn't kiss her back."

I rolled my eyes, "*Not really*, you said." I used his words. "You just took so long to comprehend that she got what she wanted." I arched an eyebrow at him.

"How long do you really think you can stay away from me?" he challenged.

I scoffed and folded my arms across my chest.

"Oh my god, you just can't help but get cocky, can you? I can't stay away from you, and I know that! But I'm going to make myself do it! Now you can either just be mature and at least talk to me normally, which I'm hoping you'll do, or you can just be a dick like you are now." I shrugged.

"I wanna kiss you so fucking bad right now," he spoke lowly.

I rolled my eyes, "Do you just like genuinely enjoying pissing me off? Is that what it is?" I arched an eyebrow at him.

"You have no idea," he smirked while stepping closer.

"Why? What is so entertaining about it?" I questioned.

"You don't know how attractive you are when you're mad at me."

What logic is that?

"Don't flirt with me." I deadpanned. He bit his lip while looking at me. "Don't stare at me!" I threw my arms up in frustration.

"When I'm away from you, you have a problem. When I get close, flirt or stare, then you have a problem. When I kiss someone else, then you have a problem. When I kiss you, then you have a problem. What do you not have a problem with?"

He is testing my patience.

"I don't have a problem with telling you to go fuck yourself," I sassed.

"Please marry me?" he smiled while walking right up to me.

"Please listen to what I'm telling you. At least sometimes." I turned around and walked away.

"Okay, okay, I'll stop!" he laughed while catching up to me. I sighed while rolling my eyes, biting back a smile. "Walk with me?" he asked.

I huffed, "Lead the way," I smiled sarcastically. We walked in silence when I felt him hold my hand. I jerked it away and elbowed him.

"Come on," he chuckled while throwing his arm around my shoulder, pulling me into his side. I clicked my tongue in frustration and glared at him while pushing him off. "Come here." I but did't listen. "Come here," he reached his hand out when I stepped away from him.

I gave in and walked over, letting him hold me close while wrapping my arm around his waist. We walked like that and spent the rest of the day as friends, maybe still a little touchy like we had been before Ashley happened but you can't let go of habit even though it's just happened over a short timespan.

It was early in the evening and we spent the day exploring the area near the arc and were now getting back onto the bus.

"So many kisses, such little time," Asher whispered in my ear as he sat down beside me.

"We already got that," I sighed while leaning my head on the headrest and closing my eyes. He linked his arm with mine and rested his shoulder on my head. I opened my eyes and glanced at him before Kian got on the bus and locked eyes with me.

I smiled at him before mouthing, 'Thank you'. He shook his head at me with a smile and took his seat towards the front.

He really just pulled Asher and me back to each other. I owe that to him.

Asher lifted his head and tucked a loose strand of hair behind my ear before kissing my cheek. I looked out of the window, blushing.

"Are you blushing?" he teased.

"Fuck you," I laughed.

— CHAPTER FORTY FIVE —

ASHER

This is so bad. Let me catch you guys up. Tomorrow is once again a free day. We're supposed to go to the water park but the other group from the other hotel is going first since it's going to be crowded and Mr. Walker doesn't want to take the entire grade when it's so crowded.

As expected, Tyler threw *another* party. And currently, Riley is drunk off her ass. Like, cannot properly function drunk. Like, cannot even get her ass up from the couch drunk. We had fewer people around this time and a lot more drinking this time. I took a beer which I don't know where Tyler got from or any of the other alcohol he has, but he does and instead of like last time when Riles took vodka and coke, she took shots.

She had six shots.

"You have pretty eyes," she giggled while poking my cheek.

"They're just brown," I groaned while standing up and trying to pull her up so we could get back to the room. It's currently two-forty-five am.

"They're hazel," she argued while whining and sinking in her seat.

"Riley, we need to get back to the room, please stand up." I tugged at her arm.

She groaned and stood up, only to fall back in her seat. "I'm tired," she groaned.

"You're drunk," I stated.

"No, I'm not. See, I'm perfectly- whoa!" she stood up too fast before falling back in her seat.

"Will you please listen to me?" I asked her patiently, talking slower as if she were a child so she would understand. She nodded eagerly. "Please *slowly* stand up. *Slowly*." She sighed and pushed herself off the couch slowly. "Okay, do you have your phone in your pocket?" I asked her.

"Yup," she said, popping the 'p.'

"Alright," I sighed before picking her up like a child. Her legs went around my waist while our chests were pressed together. She laughed before wrapping her arms around my neck and resting her chin on my shoulder.

I placed my hands on her thighs, pulling her up higher before walking to the door and out. She held onto me tighter, hugging me as I walked into the elevator. "You're gonna go to sleep as soon as we get to the room, okay?" I asked. She pulled her away and looked at me.

"I have to change," she mumbled.

"After you change, of course." I tucked a loose strand of

hair behind her ear as the elevator stopped and some people stepped in. It was a middle-aged couple. They looked at us and I instantly felt awkward. How do I explain why I'm carrying her like a child if they ask?

"Is she alright?" the woman asked me, looking at her with concern. Riley snuggled into me as the elevator continued going down.

"Yeah, she's fine." I nodded with a small smile.

"Are you her boyfriend?" The lady smiled at me. I heard Riley snicker.

"Yup, that's me," I answered awkwardly. The elevator dinged and they stepped out. It went one floor down and we were on our floor.

"Why'd you lie to them? You're not my boyfriend," she mumbled.

I sighed, "What was I supposed to say? I'm just a stranger that's carrying you in my arms?" I asked sarcastically. "Can you get the door?" I questioned.

"The keys are in my pocket, take it." I clicked my tongue before slipping my hand in her back pocket and grabbing the keys. I unlocked the door and walked over to the bed after getting the lights, and swiftly set her down on the bed. I kneeled beside her suitcase and grabbed her pajamas.

Black sweatpants with a grey cami. I handed it to her and she took the sweatpants but shoved the shirt away. "I don't want that one!" she pouted.

"Which one do you want?" I asked while looking at her open suitcase.

"That one!" she pointed at my open suitcase that lay beside hers.

"You want mine?" I asked in confusion. She nodded. "The black one?" I questioned. She hummed in response. I grabbed it and handed it to her. Once I handed it to her, without warning, she threw her shirt off. "Oh my god," I mumbled before turning around. I stayed like that until she told me to turn back around.

"You can look now, dummy." I heard her stand up before going into the bathroom. I folded her clothes and placed them with the rest of the clothes she's already worn on this trip. She came back out with her face washed and tired eyes.

She flopped onto the bed and snuggled into her pillow. I turned the lamp off after grabbing my clothes and going into the bathroom to change and brush my teeth. I came back into the room to see her twisting and turning.

"Are you okay?" I asked while getting in bed beside her.

"My stomach hurts," she whined.

"Are you feeling nauseous? Do you want medicine?" I asked with concern.

"No, I'm not nauseous," she groaned into her pillow.

"Are you on your period?" I wondered.

"No, Asher, I'm not on my period!" she hissed.

"I just thought you might have cramps," I mumbled.

"Oh my fucking god, fuck me." She let out a deep breath and ran her hands over her face. I still think she's having cramps.

Maybe I should try what I did while we still talked.

While we were friends before everything.

While we were friends, we were really close, obviously, and there have been times in the past where she'd have horrible cramps and sometimes I would stay the night and we would cuddle, which I know a lot of 'friends' don't do, but we did. It would help with her cramps and I liked her so I didn't bother stopping.

Her parents, however, didn't like it.

I wasn't allowed to see her for a while after her parents found me all snuggled up with her from the night before, but I got the chance to explain to her dad that I liked her, confused about it, but liked her nonetheless and he understood and let me see her again.

Her back faced me and I wrapped my arms around her waist. "Asher, I swear to god, if you're going to take advantage of my pain right now and-" I shut her up.

"Riley, shut up. If it doesn't help your cramps, which I know they are cramps, then I'll let go. Just try to sleep," I hissed. She huffed but stopped moping and closed her eyes. After a while of my hands around her waist and on her stomach, her breathing got steady and she fell asleep.

Soon after that, I did too.

I woke up to Riley getting back in bed.

Where did she go?

"What happened?" I questioned, my voice hoarse and low. She just stared at me blankly. "I was right, wasn't I?" I chuckled.

She smacked my shoulder. "Shut up," she hissed while getting under the covers.

"You *did* start your period, didn't you?" I asked, pulling the covers off of her.

"Asher, I am seriously going to kick you off this bed right the fuck now," she threatened.

"Awe, really?" I taunted even more. She glared at me and jabbed her elbow into my side. "Ow!" I winced as she pouted and turned her back towards me. "Awe no, no, come here!" I chuckled while wrapping my arms around her and pulling her back into my chest.

"Asher, let me go," she huffed.

"I'm sorry, I'm sorry. Come on, the cuddling did help with your cramps, come here." I laughed slightly while slipping my hand under her shirt and rested it on her stomach.

"Your hands are always warm," she mumbled while snuggling into her pillow.

"And yours are always cold," I mumbled sleepily. She looked at me over her shoulder with a glare. I laughed and wrapped my arms tighter. "Night," I whispered.

"Night," she replied.

I woke up the next morning to see Riley still fast asleep

beside me. She was clutching onto my hand while the other rested around her waist, on her stomach.

I slowly pulled myself away and got myself in the bathroom silently where I brushed my teeth and washed my face. I stepped out to see her slowly opening her eyes and waking up.

"Morning, sunshine." I smiled while stretching.

"How do I always wake up to you half-naked?" she asked in confusion. I laughed before walking over to her and lying down on top of her, my arms around her and my head in the crook of her neck. She threw her arms around my neck and took in a deep breath.

"Does your stomach still hurt?" I mumbled against her skin.

She nodded slightly. I hugged her tighter.

She huffed and pushed me off of her. "Space," she smiled before pushing me off.

I whined and groaned into a pillow while she went into the bathroom.

"Kill me!" she whined in pain.

I am so glad I'm a guy.

CHAPTER FORTY SIX

RILEY

I planned to stay in bed the entire day and nobody is going to change or challenge that.

"Get up." Ali walked in.

"Why?" I asked blankly.

"Because I'm bored and I want to hang out, get up."

I groaned, "Where's Mason?" I still refused to move.

"Where's Asher?" she arched an eyebrow at me.

The boys went to take a dip in the pool. I didn't go because mother nature paid a visit and Ali didn't go because she said she didn't want to hang out with the guys by herself because she'd get bored.

"It's not my fault they're not here, you should've gone with them." I clutched the pillow tighter to myself.

"And hear them talk about what exactly?" She gave me a pointed look.

I sighed, "There are other girls at the pool you know," I gave her a pointed look in return.

"Yeah, girls who say 'oh my god, did you see what he said to her?' and 'I don't blame him, she's such a whore!' um- no thanks," she scoffed in a high pitched voice.

"Please spare me?" I put my hands together pleadingly.

"Riley, I swear to god I-" she was interrupted by the door swinging open. Asher walked in with Mason behind him.

His hair was wet with his towel draped around his neck, looking as hot as ever and I didn't pay attention to Mason. Sorry. Not really.

"Hello," Asher smiled before lying on top of me and hugging me. Mason and Ali rolled their eyes and showed themselves out.

"You're making me wet!" I screamed even though I was hugging him.

He pulled away and looked at me with a smirk.

"Am I?" he teased.

I rolled my eyes, "Go and take a fucking cold shower, go!" I waved him off before snuggling deeper into my pillow as he went to shower. I was lying there with my eyes closed when I felt the bed dip beside me followed by a kiss on my cheek.

I shuffled before sighing and opening my eyes. "Do you want anything to eat?" he asked while resting his head on my shoulder. I simply shook my head.

"You didn't even have breakfast today," he stated. I just

looked at him. "Please eat something? I'll order it in for you," he sat up and grabbed the phone from his nightstand.

"I don't want anything," I whined.

I am pretty much the devil's cry baby when I am on my period, get used to it.

After the first two days, I'm usually fine. "Not even a chocolate muffin?" he glanced at me and my mouth zipped up.

"One," I held a finger up for emphasis.

"Okay," he chuckled before asking for one to be brought up to the room.

Get yourself a man that orders you chocolate muffins on your period, ladies.

The bell rang shortly after and he opened it. He got the small plate for me and lied on his stomach beside me. "Why are you staring at me like that?" I chuckled while taking a bite.

"Because I love you."

I sighed and shook my head before continuing to eat. I finished eating my muffin and sipped some water before deciding to get my ass up and shower.

"I'll be back," I mumbled before grabbing my stuff and going into the bathroom. I took a fresh set of pajamas.

Gorgeous outfit, I know right?

I took a swift shower, washing my hair thoroughly before heading back out to see Asher almost asleep. I tried to be as quiet as possible so I wouldn't disturb him but he shuffled and then he slowly opened his eyes and saw me.

"Hey," he smiled at me while waving me over.

"Hello," I sighed while climbing back into bed beside him. "Tired?" I asked while resting my head on his chest.

"Little bit," he replied.

"Take a nap?" I suggested.

He ran his hand through my hair.

"What are you going to do?" he questioned.

"I don't know," I shrugged slightly, "I'll read or watch something," I answered.

"I'll watch something with you, I'll probably fall asleep though," he chuckled lightly.

"Sure, feel free to fall asleep whenever," I chuckled while grabbing my laptop and opening up my Netflix.

"Oh, let's watch that one!" he pointed at my screen.

"You want to watch 'Breakfast at Tiffany's'?" I voiced in confusion.

"Yeah, I've never seen it and you really like Audrey Hepburn so, why not?" he shrugged.

"Alrighty," I sighed before clicking play and lying back down.

If you haven't seen that movie, I highly recommend it. It's a really cute, romantic, passionate and love-dovey movie. That might partly be my obsession with Audrey Hepburn talking. She was so beautiful and such an icon too. We began watching the movie, well, I did but he just drew patterns on my hand and my arm. After a while his breathing became steady and his arm fell limp beside mine and I knew he was asleep.

I continued watching the movie and once it was over the bell rang. I jumped at the loud noise and shot out of bed, not wanting the noise to wake Asher up. I tiptoed to the door and opened it to Allison, of course.

"What are you two-" she began asking loudly until I shushed her.

"Shh!" I put my finger to my lips. She raised her eyebrows at me while putting her hands up in surrender. "He's sleeping," I informed her.

"Girls day out?" she grinned at me. "Mason's sleeping too."

I sighed before contemplating it.

"Not out of the hotel. If you want to go to the rooftop or the pool deck then that's fine." I shrugged.

"Let's go to the pool deck, the sun's about to set so we'll watch it," she shrugged too.

"Wait a sec," I went back in and threw my flip flops on and came back out.

"Let's go," I sighed as we began walking to the elevator. We walked out to the deck and hung out there till the sun completely set and darkness took over to sky. We talked about a lot of things.

Mainly her and Mason and Asher and I. A little bit about changes once we get back to school and if there would be any and then we decided to head back a little before dinner time. We walked in and absentmindedly got into the elevator that was going down instead of going up.

The elevator opened at the reception and I heard a lot of shouting and arguing from the desk.

"Wanna check it out?" Ali asked me. I shrugged and we stepped out.

"How many times do I have to tell you that I don't know where she is?! I fell asleep and I woke up to her gone! I tried texting and calling but her phone is in the room!"

"Sir, have you checked the premises of the hotel?" the receptionist questioned.

"That is not my job! I'm here to ask for help in looking for her!"

Ali sighed beside me, "Oh boy. You better go."

I huffed and jogged up to the desk where I saw a panicking Asher who was turning pale and looked scared and terrified.

"What is going on?" I asked. He did a double take before sighing in relief and pulling me in for a hug. He pulled away after a short moment and looked into my eyes frantically. "Ash, are you-" he cut me off when he grabbed either side of my face and pulled my lips to his.

I froze and comprehended before kissing back slightly and then pulling away quickly. "You're okay!" he breathed.

"Of course I'm okay, what did you think happened?" I asked before looking at the receptionist apologetically before pulling Asher away with me. I noticed that Ali left and I was left with Asher.

"I don't know," he ran his hands over his face, "You weren't feeling well and I thought something happened to you and I didn't know where you went and your phone wasn't with you. I couldn't reach you and I just-" he took a minute to compose himself. "I thought something happened to you," he sighed while hugging me again.

I hugged him back tightly before clearing my throat and talking hesitantly. "You kissed me," I stated. He looked away and looked at me nervously.

I'm melting.

"Sorry," he pulled away, scratching the back of his neck awkwardly. I bit my lip in thought before asking him a question I had.

"Can I let my guard down for a moment?" my voice barely came out.

He nodded.

I took a few breaths before slamming the stop button on the elevator and grabbing his collar, smashing my lips onto his.

I allowed myself to take a minute to soak in the heated moment before pushing him away rashly and pressing the button again, having the elevator move upward again.

We both were panting while I leaned against the wall.

"Guard back up?" he asked as the elevator dinged and opened.

"Yup. Back up." I breathed before we stepped out and walked awkwardly.

CHAPTER FORTY SEVEN

RILEY

We got to the room, still in silence. We have roughly thirty minutes until dinner and we have to stay in the same room until then, so how are we going to deal with the awkward silence?

"I really want to kiss you," he mumbled under his breath. I began stammering. Our eyes met and I guess he got the message because he picked me up and placed me on the desk before standing between my legs as we fell into a heated makeout session.

That went on for a *while*.

We both broke away, panting and breathing very heavily. "Are we good?" I asked hesitantly, not even knowing what that question really meant.

"We're good," he breathed. He stepped away, allowing me to step down. "We should get to dinner," he panted.

Why so early? We still have- oh my god.

I glanced at the clock to see we only have fifteen minutes

until dinner. I took a deep breath or two before grabbing the key card and my phone before heading out with him, *low and behold*, again in awkward silence. We got to the dining area and we split up. I went to get food with Ali while he went with Mase.

"Why is there suddenly so much sexual tension between the two of you?" Ali asked bluntly.

"There is?"

Who the fuck am I playing dumb for?

"You know there is, come on." She gave me a pointed look.

"I don't know. Things are just rough," I shrugged slightly.

"Like intimately?" she questioned. I looked at her with wide eyes.

"Ali!" I exclaimed.

"What?" she shrugged. "It's no secret you both miss each other but your ego is too high," she scoffed.

"*My* ego?! He's the one who kissed someone else, am I just supposed to let it go?" I asked rhetorically.

"Obviously not, but don't stay away if you don't want to if you physically can't!" she emphasized.

"If I couldn't then I wouldn't even be trying to stay away," I argued.

She rolled her eyes, "You definitely just made out with him before coming down here," she gave me another pointed look.

How in hell?

"No, I did not!" I lied. "We are not on terms that allow us to do that!"

She sees right through me right now, that's for sure.

"You are not on terms that allow you to control yourselves. You're mad at him and that's making you more attracted to him. Admit it." She arched an eyebrow at me. "And, you're playing hard to get and he's getting more attracted to you," she shrugged. "It's like hooking up with feelings."

No, it's no- maybe a little.

"Maybe a little, am I right?" she smirked.

"I did not think that out loud." I glared.

"You didn't but I know you, honey." She knows me a little too well. "How many times so far?" she raised her brows.

I shuffled uneasily before answering, "Thrice." I resisted a groan.

She hummed in response,

"Hmm, I thought it would have been more." She handed me a plate.

"Bitch," I smacked her shoulder. "I have more self-respect than that."

She glanced at me, "I know you have self-respect but is it more than your love for him?" she asked.

"It should be," I answered.

"It should. But is it?" she questioned. "You can work on it

over time. I'm sure he'll help you with it, he's mature enough to do that."

I hope he is.

"It's killing you, please kiss and make up. Well, you've already kissed so, please just make up." She said as we grabbed our food and sat at the table. I sat with Ali and Asher sat opposite to me.

"Why is there so much sexual tension between you two?" Mason asked.

Here we go again.

I ducked my head down with my hand over my eyes. "Because we're attracted to each other but aren't talking," Asher answered bluntly and I looked up at him in shock.

"So you're hooking up with feelings?" he questioned further. I didn't even have time to answer.

"Yeah," Asher shrugged. His eyes met mine and slowly widened. He smacked his hand over his mouth and sank in his seat. "I didn't mean to say that out loud," he mumbled.

"But you did, huh? That's very interesting," I spoke sarcastically.

"Riley," he sighed.

I rolled my eyes and quickly finished up the little bit of dinner that I put on my plate and excused myself.

"Night, guys." I stood up, ready to leave.

"Wait!" Asher quickly stood up and began following me

while I began picking up my pace. I looked at him as we stood in front of the elevator, waiting for it to arrive. "Are you mad?" he asked softly.

I smiled to myself. "I'm amused," I replied honestly.

"You are?" he asked in surprise as we entered the elevator.

"I said the same thing to Ali. Well, she forced it out of me but still," I shrugged as the doors closed and the elevator began moving up.

"So that's what we do now? Hook up with feelings?" he arched an eyebrow at me.

"I guess that's what we do now," I shrugged as the elevator stopped in between and the same old couple from that one time stepped in.

"Oh, hello again!" the man laughed.

"Hi," I chuckled while Asher just smiled at them.

"I *still* feel like we're interrupting something," the lady said quietly.

"You're not, trust me." I laughed.

"Young love," she sighed and shook her head.

What is that supposed to mean?

I shrugged it off and we stepped out on our floor, wishing them goodnight. "Something is wrong with that lady, I swear to god. How the hell does it look like anything is going on between us?" I didn't mean it, I just knew it was going to rile him up and that is amusing.

His actions are.

"I mean like seriously? What goes through their head when they think that-" he interrupted me by pinning me to the wall and kissed me.

That wasn't amusing but that was something.

I kissed him back, obviously, and then I smiled because I'm winning in my head. Not that it's a stupid challenge, but it feels good to know that I'm wanted. It's good to know he loves me as much as I love him, even though I don't show it as much.

I opened the door that I was leaning against and walked backward with him taking steps, following me in.

I chuckled to myself while setting my phone down. He was leaning against the door which he closed and was just watching me. I threw my hair up in a high ponytail and began walking into the bathroom.

He kept staring until I shut the door to brush my teeth and wash my face. I opened the door and came out to see him still standing there. I turned the lights of the bathroom off and shut the door but before I could walk to the bed, he stuck his fingers into my waistband and pulled me closer, pressing his lips to mine again.

He kept taking steps forward while I took them back until my back hit the wall. I placed my hands on his chest to push him off but he grabbed my wrists and pinned them against the wall. I began taking steps forward, backing him up into the bathroom before pushing him in and closing the door.

I heard him sigh which made me chuckle before I got into bed. He came out, in sweatpants and nothing else. I checked him out which made him smirk. I grabbed my shirt and tugged its edge, watching as his face dropped.

I smiled before letting it go and getting under the covers, turning the lamp off. "You wanted more," he whispered into my ear.

I turned to face him. "You wanted more and so you wish I wanted more, but no. You wanted more," I whispered back. His finger traced my shoulder, down to my arm before he sighed and retreated his arm.

I didn't like that he pulled it back but he did and so I'm gonna let him think I don't care. And then he turned me to face him. He hovered over me while trailing kisses from my jaw down to my neck until I pushed him off and pretended to be asleep for a while until I genuinely dozed off into a deep slumber.

I woke up before him and felt like being a little more wifey than usual so I got him breakfast in bed. I got him french toast with chocolate milk.

Better be grateful, bitch.

He woke up with messy hair, as usual, and a very hot morning voice, also as usual.

"Someone's being wifey," he chuckled while snuggling into a pillow.

"Wake up, honey," I said sarcastically before he sat up and took the plate from my hands. He looked at me for a long time with a smirk.

"What?" I asked in confusion. He looked at my neck and pointed to his neck with his finger.

My eyes widened in realization.

I went downstairs like that, in front of everybody.

CHAPTER FORTY EIGHT

ASHER

"Just stay back?" Mason suggested.

"She's going to have to be the only one staying, they're not going to let someone stay with her," Ali said, "Someone with a valid excuse," she sighed, "You could just come with and not swim? Do you want to come?" she asked Riley. We were currently up early and talking about the water park that we're heading to today.

Riley was kind of hesitant about coming because she is on her period but if she stays back, she'll be by herself the whole day since no one has an excuse to stay back and keep her company. We came over to Ali and Mase's room because we both had nothing to do. We're leaving later than usual because we won't be there for that long so there's no point in going early only for a few hours and then have nothing to do for the rest of the day.

"I don't know, it's a crowded and chaotic place," Riley sighed.

"Are your cramps okay? You can hang out with me by the pool over there?"

I don't want to go without her.

"Yeah, I guess I can do that," she shrugged.

"It's settled then, we'll hang around here until we have to leave and then we'll be gone for about two to three hours, what about after we come back?" Mason asked.

"Well, we'll freshen up and then we can go to a cafe or something," I shrugged. We settled on that before Riley and I headed back to our room. She sighed as we got into the elevator and leaned against the wall.

Something wasn't right.

"Are you okay?" I asked in concern.

"Yeah, I- I'm fine," she was taking quick short breaths, panting almost.

"Riles, are you sure? Do you need water?" I asked, taking steps closer to her, grabbing onto her arms to keep her steady.

"No, I'm fine." That is not convincing. Especially with her turning pale.

"Riley!" I grabbed onto her as she began falling to the floor. I have no clue what is going on with her. The elevator opened on the fifth floor.

Who's room is the closest?

Mr. Brown. I swiftly picked her up and went to his room. Five-fifteen. I rang the doorbell way too many times with my elbow. He opened the door with an irritated look in his eyes until he saw me and his eyes widened.

"What happened?" he opened the door and let me in.

"I-I-I don't know. I don't know. She was fine a little while ago but in the elevator, she began turning pale and uh- I think she just suddenly passed out, I don't know what's wrong with her," I explained.

"I'm going to ask for a doctor and call Mr. Walker, please take her up to your room. We'll be there shortly." I nodded in understanding and picked her up, quickly taking her up to our room.

Should I give her water? Is that bad? Is it safe to give her water?

The phone in the room rang and I answered it quickly. "Sir, we've spoken to the doctor and we're going to need you to lay her flat and give her a little bit of water, not too much," someone from the desk called. "A doctor will be there shortly." I hung up and lifted her head slightly, giving her some water. A little bit.

A few minutes after that, a doctor walked in with Mr. Brown and Walker behind him. "Step aside please." I heard him addressing me but I couldn't move. "Excuse me, please step aside," he said more sternly. Mr. Brown grabbed my shoulder and pulled me back.

The doctor sat beside where she lay and checked her heartbeat first. Then her eyes and her breathing pattern. "Can I get a bottle of water?" Mr. Walker handed him one. He lifted her head like I did and gave her water. He pulled away and glanced at his watch. About a minute later he did the same thing.

And then again after another minute. This went on until one-fourth of the bottle was done. Her eyes fluttered and she shuffled before slowly gaining consciousness. She took a few slow, deep breaths before beginning to slowly sit up.

"Slowly," the doctor helped her up. He sighed and placed the bottle on the table beside her.

"Have you eaten anything today?" he asked her. She slowly shook her head. "And how many fluids have you had today?" he questioned.

"I'm not too sure," she answered very drowsily and softly.

"Well," he began, "From the looks of it, you've had none." I watched her carefully. She knew she didn't have anything. Why would she do that?

"She passed out due to dehydration. She doesn't have enough fluids in her body and because of that she lacked energy and something as simple and walking around for a little bit caused her to lose consciousness," he addressed us. "She needs to rest and have a lot of fluids. Juices, water, anything you like," he turned to her.

"Get some food in your system and take some rest. If this happens again, here is some medication to give to her if she's dehydrated. I recommend you stay with her and keep an eye on her," he looked at me.

I nodded while blinking slowly.

"Thank you so much," I sighed.

"Thank you," the teachers spoke from behind me.

"No problem," he smiled before getting his stuff and being walked out by Mr. Walker and Brown. We stayed in our spots in pin-drop silence. I had my arms folded across my chest while I chewed on the inside of my cheek and she looked down at her hands which rested in her lap. I inhaled before pouring her a glass of water and handing it to her. She slowly drank consistently.

I sat on the edge of the bed with my elbow propped up on my knee, and my chin resting in the palm of my hand. I closed my eyes and took a deep breath. I knew that a tear slipped down my cheek.

"What the hell is wrong with you?" I wiped it away quickly and turned to face her.

"I didn't do it intentionally," she still wasn't looking me in the eyes.

"You've been up since eight and you haven't had any food or water. It's been eight hours, Riley," I sighed. "You're already physically tired and in pain for the last three days and you haven't been eating much anyway, so I don't understand why you're not even drinking water."

I was more than angry with her. I was relieved but beyond angry.

"How was I supposed to know that my body is too weak to handle no water for eight-" she looked up and her eyes met mine and she processed that I was crying. "I'm sorry," she whispered.

"Don't say sorry to me. You're the one passing out, I don't care," I lied while standing up.

"Asher-" she quickly said and began standing up but she couldn't even bring herself to move. I huffed before going back to where I was sitting. "Why are you crying?" she asked softly while leaning her head against the headboard.

"When I couldn't find you that day, I was a fucking mess because I thought something happened to you. Today, something actually did. Riley, when you mean so much to someone, you have to take care of yourself, if not for yourself then for that person. How would you react if I passed out like that?" I asked her.

I'm still tearing up.

She stayed quiet. "Please be fucking careful." My voice cracked.

"Sit here," she patted the spot beside her in bed. I huffed before going and sitting there. She took a deep breath before pushing herself up and sitting on my lap, straddling me. She wiped my tears before hugging me tightly.

"I'm so sorry," she whispered. I sat still, not hugging her back. I am so upset with her right now. She pulled away and grabbed my arms, placing them around her waist.

"Don't be a dick. I said I'm sorry," she spoke slowly, hugging me again.

"I hate you," I mumbled while hugging her back.

She pulled away and looked at me.

"Do you really?" she asked, worried.

"No," I sighed while pulling her back into the hug. "Riley, I love you. Just please don't do that again," I ran my hand through her hair.

"I'm so sorry," she mumbled.

"It's okay, just get some rest. I'm staying in with you." I stated. I lied her down beside me.

"I'm sleepy," she snuggled into the covers.

"Take a nap, I'll be right here," I kept running my hands through her until she fell asleep. I lied down beside her and draped my arm around her waist. That was one of the scariest moments of my life.

I felt like I was about to lose her right then and there. This isn't the first time she's passed out due to dehydration.

I remember when it happened while we were friends, it was just as scary then.

And I hated it just as much then as I do now.

— CHAPTER FORTY NINE —

RILEY

I woke up from my nap to Asher sleeping beside me. I don't understand how I passed out. Yeah, I hadn't eaten or had any water but that shouldn't have made me pass out. It's happened once before when I was already sick but I'm not sick now. I shrugged it off and grabbed my phone. I was about to open social media when he grabbed my phone and placed it out of my reach.

"You're supposed to rest, not use social media," he mumbled sleepily.

I huffed before turning to him,

"If I'm just going to be in bed, I need something to entertain me," I explained.

He sighed and turned to me. He was lying on his stomach, arms tucked under the pillow on his right cheek, now looking at me.

"You just passed out a few hours ago and you want to be entertained?" he asked in disbelief.

"I'm fine now," I reasoned.

He rolled his eyes, "Have some water," he said before sticking his face into the pillow. I sighed but had some water nonetheless. "If you want to be entertained then you can talk to me," he rested his head in my lap.

"Hmm, about what?" I asked while scratching his back.

"About anything," he mumbled. I was about to say something but he spoke up again. "I think you should eat something now, order something," he got off of me. I knew that he wasn't going to rest until I ate so I sighed in defeat.

"Order me whatever, I'll be right back." I began getting out of bed.

"Where are you going?" he asked in a rush.

"To the bathroom," I chuckled. I went to the bathroom, did my business and came out to see him hanging up.

"I ordered you a club sandwich with fries and iced tea," he grinned at me. I smiled before getting back into bed. My phone rang and I picked up.

"Hello?" I asked.

"Honey, are you alright?" my dad's panicked voice spoke through the phone. It's around nine-thirty there.

"Yeah dad, I'm fine why?" I decided not to tell him.

"What do you mean why? You passed out!" he exclaimed.

"Who told?" I sighed.

"Asher did! What happened? How did you faint?" he questioned. I glared at Asher.

"I was just dehydrated," I played it cool.

"*Just* dehydrated? Honey, please take care of yourself. Just because Asher's taking care of you doesn't mean that you don't have to."

Okay, since when?

"Please be careful," he sighed.

"Yes, dad," I said softly.

"I've got to run, bye honey," he said quickly.

"Bye," I hung up. "Did you have to tell him?" I turned to Ash.

"He's your dad, Riles. He has to know."

I hate that he's right.

"Do you want to call the doctor to check up on you?" he asked with concern.

"I'm okay, Asher. I'm fine now." I watched as his face eased a little at my words before he ran his hand over his face. The bell rang and we both got a little startled. He sighed and answered, bringing in the tray.

He set it down in front of me before taking a fry and grabbing a shirt, putting it on. "Eat up," he spoke.

"All of it?!" I asked in disbelief.

"Two sandwiches," he picked up one of the four. Two for him, two for me. I sighed before beginning to eat.

We ate while talking about random things. Once we were done, he placed the tray outside and came back in. He sat against the headboard while grabbing his laptop.

"What do you wanna watch?" he asked.

"Shrek," I snickered sarcastically. He actually clicked it. I laughed before wrapping my arm around him and resting my head on his chest. We watched the whole thing, laughing at nothing at times and everything from the movie and then it was over.

Our bell rang as the movie ended and Asher went and got it. Ali rushed in with Mason. "Are you okay? I heard what happened," she sat beside me.

"I'm fine," I sighed for the billionth time.

"Have you eaten?" she asked.

"Have you met him? Did you think he would let me go without eating after that," I spoke while looking at Asher who was leaning against the wall and talking to Mason.

"You're seriously crazy," she looked at me.

I clicked my tongue, "I didn't know. I wasn't hungry or thirsty and it just happened, Ali," I huffed.

"Okay," she put her hands up in surrender. "She just be careful in the future," she said while standing up. "Take care," she smiled at me before leaving with Mason. Asher sighed and crawled into bed beside me.

"Why is everyone so mad at me even though I'm the one that passed out? I didn't get this mad at myself," I mumbled under my breath.

"Because people care about you, maybe a little more than

you care about yourself which probably isn't the best thing but..." he trailed off.

"Maybe people shouldn't care about me as much then," I groaned before sipping on some water. He clicked his tongue before resting his head on my shoulder and holding my hand in his.

"I don't care what you think, people will keep caring about you. Especially me." He kissed the back of my hand.

"Dinner is in a bit, you should probably go down with Mason," I suggested quietly.

"Will you come?" he asked.

I shook my head in response,

"I'll just order a little bit in."

He lied down beside where I sat.

"Then I'm not going either. I'm not leaving you here by yourself," he drew circles on the back of my hand.

"I'll be fine, Asher. You should hang out with Mase, you haven't in a while," I explained.

"*I will hang out* with him tomorrow. You're a little more important right now after what happened," he gave me a pointed look.

"That's not fair," I pouted.

"Life's not fair," he shrugged. "Order in dinner," he demanded. I huffed and grabbed the phone. I ordered a fruit salad for myself with a mini bowl of spaghetti and Asher just asked for some pasta. The food came in and so did Mase and Ali with their dinner plates.

"You guys didn't show up so we did," Mase shrugged while they sat on the edges of the bed.

"Sorry for being a little harsh earlier but you really scared me," Ali addressed me.

"Oh, you have no idea, he lost it," I jabbed my thumb in Asher's direction. He looked at me in disbelief.

"What did he do? Cry?" Mason asked sarcastically. I turned to Asher. I didn't wanna blurt out yes and then have him get mad at me.

"Yeah actually, I did," he admitted.

"Are you serious?" Mason asked.

"One-hundred percent. I thought something happened to her, it scared the hell out of me," he sighed.

"And that, ladies and gentlemen, is what they call love," Ali sighed before eating a spoonful. "Would you cry if I passed out?" she asked Mase through a mouthful.

"Why would you pass out?" he asked in confusion.

"True," she shrugged nonchalantly. Asher and I gave each other a look before I shook my head to myself.

They are such idiots.

We were all done with dinner and were just chilling around and talking. "Do you think she'd like it?" Mason asked me. He was telling me about how he planned on taking Ali to a shopping street near our hotel.

"I think she'll love it. Just make sure to bring her back before you go bankrupt," I joked. We laughed it off before Ali came and sat with me.

"So, what were you two talking about?" she questioned not-so-subtly.

"You'll find out soon enough, patience my dear," I teased.

"Should I be preparing myself for something?" she arched an eyebrow at me.

"I don't know," I shrugged.

"Riles," she spoke warningly.

"I don't know, Ali. He was just telling me how much he likes you, I don't know about anything else. I would tell you," I lied. I would tell her if I was concerned but I'm not. I trust him with her and I think she does too.

"Guys, I think we should head back. It's getting pretty late," Mason stood up to leave.

"Are we going anywhere tomorrow?" Asher asked while walking them out.

"No, it's just a chill hotel day. Students are free to go wherever they like," he replied.

"Night guys!" I called out.

"Night!" they answered in sync. I heard the door close while I stood up to go brush my teeth. I did that and then Asher went in to do the same before snuggling beside me in bed.

He looped his arm through mine while I plugged my phone on charge. "What are you doing?" I laughed before turning the lamp off.

"I wanna cuddle," he pouted.

"What do you wanna do? Be the little spoon?" I asked.

He shrugged before turning his back to me.

I laughed but wrapped my arms around him nonetheless.

— CHAPTER FIFTY —

RILEY

I woke up sometime in the middle of the night, to Asher gone from beside me, the bathroom door shut with the light creeping out from the bottom while hearing him faintly mumbling to himself.

What the hell is going on?

I decided to give him a moment and stayed in my spot, trying to go back to sleep, but now I wanted to know what was going on. Which is exactly why I threw the covers off of me and walked over to the bathroom. I was about to knock on the door when he swung it open, taking a few steps back after seeing me.

"Are you okay?" I asked.

He nodded frantically, "Y-yeah. Do you need to go to the bathroom?" he asked while holding the door for me.

"Um- no? Asher, are you sure you're okay?" I asked while holding his hand but he pulled it away.

"I'm fine," he answered shortly.

"Is there something you want to talk about?" I pressed further.

"I probably shouldn't do this in the middle of the night," he whispered under his breath.

"Do what?" I asked, getting more and more nervous by the clock.

"There's something I need to talk to you about," he began. My head automatically went to the worst thought possible.

Is he ending things?

"Okay," I said slowly, "Do you wanna sit down?" I asked while taking steps towards the bed. He followed and sat beside me on the edge of the bed.

"I didn't want to do this here," he groaned while running his hands over his face.

That's not helping my thoughts.

At all.

I stayed quiet because maybe he just needed a minute to compose himself and then it'll all be over in a minute. I'm preparing myself here. "Okay," he grabbed my hands and held them in his lap.

"You know that I like you a lot. I've fallen way too deep. And I've been thinking about this for a while but I just- I don't know how to do it." He paused.

He is definitely ending things.

"Riley," he looked into my eyes.

"Hmm?" I mumbled.

"I know it hasn't been long. At all. But I just- I have this thought looming over me that we're going to- we're going to get back to town and our normal lives and everything that's happened between us will all be over."

No, it won't.

"And I don't want that to happen," he continued. So he's ending things now to get things over with?

Did this have to be done the day I passed out? Because I might just pass out again.

"So I thought I should ask you something that could help sort of, I don't know, figure out how serious we truly are." I am so confused. I guess he saw that on my face because he spat it out. "Before I ask,"

Seriously?

"I need to know, are you still mad at me?" I shook my head in response. "Okay good," he sighed. "Riley, will you be my girlfriend?"

Hold on, what?!

"I'm sorry, *what?*" I asked in pure shock.

"I know, I know, this is not how I wanted to do it, I wanted to wait till we got to see the Eiffel tower again and I could take you back there but I just couldn't wait until then because the anticipation of what your answer would be was eating me alive, it was killing me and I-" I cut him off.

"Breathe!" I exclaimed.

He took a deep breath. "I just wanted to say, whatever your answer is, I'll understand. It might be too soon."

No, you dumbass, it's not.

For me at least.

"What do you think my answer is?" I wanted to hear his thoughts.

"Well, I'm hoping for a yes but there could be a difference in what I hope and what you will say so..." he trailed off nervously.

Am I the only one who finds his nervousness adorable?

"You think I'm gonna say yes?" I questioned.

He hesitated, "Yes?" it came out like a question.

"You're right," I nodded.

"Okay," he said, sounding disappointed while looking down at our held hands in his lap before his eyes snapped back up to mine. "Whoa, wait what?" he asked in surprise.

"You just asked me to be your girlfriend and I said yes," I stated.

He shook his head, "No, I know that but..." he trailed off with a smile slowly forming on his lips. "Can I kiss you?" he asked.

"I'm a little sick so you probably shouldn't-" I began answering but he cut me off when he kissed me.

Okay then.

I allowed myself to savor the moment before gently pushing him away. "Back to bed," I bit my lip to hold back a smile and got back under the covers, blushing like crazy. He just sat in his spot and sighed while smiling to himself like an idiot. I shook my head and closed my eyes as I felt him lay down beside me.

I dozed off, not before feeling his arm wrap around my waist.

I woke up to feel fingers running through my hair and obviously, I knew what was happening. I shuffled and turned to face him with a smile spreading on my lips. I opened my eyes, squinting slightly at the sun that was seeping through the windows before throwing my arm around his waist with a sigh, closing my eyes again and leaning my head on his chest.

He chuckled before grabbing my arm. "We have to wake up." He drew circles on my arm.

"Mm-mm." I lightly shook my head.

"Mm-hmm," he began pushing me off of him.

"No!" I whined, my voice more hoarse than usual since it's the morning.

"Riley, we have to go." He kissed the top of my head after chuckling.

"Where are we going today?" I sighed in defeat before sitting up and drinking some water. Don't want a repeat of yesterday now, do we?

"We are going to Champs-élysées," he sighed.

"So I should be taking quite a bit of money, got it," I nodded while getting out of bed. I stretched before tying my hair up in a bun and walking over to my suitcase while Asher went into the bathroom to shower.

I picked my outfit and lounged around until he came out. Once he did, I grabbed my clothes and walked past him, into the bathroom. As I slipped past him, his hand latched onto my arm when he pulled me in for a kiss. It was a quick kiss and so I swiftly pulled away before going into the bathroom, locking it and beginning to shower and get ready.

I came out with damp hair and my skinny jeans with a tank top on. I let out a sigh before throwing socks on with my pair of Adidas superstars and running my hand through my waist-length hair.

What do I do with all that hair today? I decided on leaving it down to air dry a little more and maybe later I could throw it up in a high ponytail or something. "Ready?" he asked, not looking up from his phone which rested in his hand.

"Yup," I inhaled while taking the key, my phone and putting them both in my back pocket. Before I forget, I took the money that I was taking for the day and grabbed my wallet, slipping it into my other back pocket. He stood up with a sigh before looking at me and checking me out.

"Well don't you look charming?" he smiled while walking up to me.

"Well, this charming lady is hungry, let's go," I dragged out my words while pulling him out of the room. We walked to the elevators hand in hand. We got to them to see Ashley standing there, waiting for it as well.

Keep your fucking composure, Riles.

I clenched my jaw while grinding my teeth, deciding to ignore her since that is probably the most mature and logical thing to do. "Hi," she said in her annoying-ass, bitch-ass voice. Neither of us replied so she cleared her throat and said it louder this time.

I closed my eyes tightly and let out a sigh, "Hi," I said bitterly.

Why am I still pressed over what happened?

"I wasn't talking to you," she glared at me.

"Nobody here wanted to talk to you so please do us a favor and shut the fuck up," I said being unpredictably straightforward. I did not know that was coming out of my mouth, I swear. The elevator opened in front of us and we quickly slipped in while she simply stood there in shock.

"Bye," I said in a sickly sweet voice while waving as Asher closed the elevator doors. I let out an agitated huff while he chuckled while kissing the side of my head. "Shut up," I pushed him away.

"What did I do?" he asked as we walked to the dining area. I just took a deep breath and resisted a groan. "Oh come on," he laughed while locking my hand in his. I shook my head and chuckled.

We walked in before Ali and Mase today so we got our food and took our seats. As soon as we began eating, an overly-excited Ali came into view.

"I'm stealing her for the day. We're shopping today honey," she shimmied.

Oh boy.

Here's the thing, I like shopping, I do, but let me tell you with Allison Jones, it is a completely different experience.

CHAPTER FIFTY ONE

ASHER

"I'm stealing her for the day. We're shopping today honey," Ali shimmied.

I narrowed my eyes at her slightly.

"Um- no you're not," I countered.

"We're not shopping?" Riley asked in confusion.

"You're shopping but she is not stealing you for the day," I explained.

Ali huffed while Mason brought both their plates.

"This isn't a couple's trip you know, I'm allowed to hang with her," Ali rolled her eyes while sitting down.

"Why can't we all just hang out and shop together? We'll split up occasionally when we're buying specific things?" Mason suggested.

"Exactly," Riley agreed. I shrugged before turning to Ali with a raised eyebrow.

"No," she shook her head. "I want a girls day out. We need

to catch up," she explained. I sighed while resisting an eye roll.

"Mason, do you have a coin?" Riley asked out of nowhere. He looked at her in confusion before pulling one out nonetheless and handing it to her. "I'll flip a coin, the person who wins gets the first half of the day with me. Fair enough?" she raised her eyebrows and looked between both of us. We both nodded hesitantly. "Who wants to pick?" she asked while placing the coin on her finger with her thumb tucked underneath.

"I'll pick!" Ali said quickly. I simply shrugged. Riley tossed it and Allison picked. "Tails." Riley caught the coin smoothly.

"Tails it is," she sighed.

She turned to me and said, "Sorry," she shrugged slightly while smiling. Ali smirked before getting back to her food. We ate while talking until it was announced that we have to leave. We got up and headed to the bus.

We walked into the bus and Riley got into the window seat but before I could sit beside her, Ali squeezed past me and quickly sat down. She looked up at me with a wicked smile.

"Not even on the bus?" I asked. Is she being serious?

"You always get to be with her in the bus, it's my day," she arched an eyebrow. I huffed before sitting with Mason in the seats behind theirs.

"She is one annoying-" Mason cut me off.

"Watch your tongue," he warned.

"One annoying best friend of my girlfriend," I mumbled.

"Girlfriend?" he asked in shock.

"Who's girlfriend?" Ali's face popped up as she knelt on the seat facing us.

"What girlfriend?" Riley's head popped up in front of me.

"My girlfriend," I smirked at Ali.

"His girlfriend?" she demanded Riley.

"His girlfriend," Riley nodded.

"My girlfriend," I smiled.

"His girlfriend," Mason nodded.

"Your boyfriend?" Ali asked Riley.

"My boyfriend," she nodded.

"Her boyfriend," I nodded.

"Her boyfriend?" Ali asked in shock.

"Her boyfriend," Mason concluded.

"Each other's girlfriend and boyfriend?" Ali asked.

"Each other's girlfriend and boyfriend," we said and nodded in sync. This is so confusing yet somehow so clear.

"Why was that so confusing?" Riley thought out loud.

"I have no idea," I chuckled.

"Spill," Ali demanded while grabbing Riley's arm and pulling her back in their seats, not allowing her to face me.

"How'd you do it?" Mason asked while fidgeting with his fingers.

"Randomly in the middle of the night, completely opposite to how I planned, like a fucking nervous wreck," I concluded, stating the facts.

"Did she like it?" he asked.

"Are you okay?" I asked in confusion.

"I don't fucking know how to ask her," he sighed in frustration.

"I see how it is," I huffed. "Just do it. Next time you have her alone and you guys are having a moment, just do it." I explained.

"What do you mean a moment?" he asked in confusion.

"You'll feel it. A special moment. Just do it the first chance you get because it's now or never, brother," I patted his shoulder. About ten minutes after that, we reached our destination. We all got off the bus in a single file before sighing and stretching while looking around.

"Students are to meet back here in one and a half hours. You're all now free to go." Mr. Brown announced. I kissed the side of Riley's head while she threw her arms around my waist.

"I'll see you in thirty?" I asked since that's the halfway point.

"No, you won't. We said half of the day. Not the time spent here," Ali smirked while dragging her away. I sighed while rolling my eyes this time. Riley looked at me with her lower lip sticking out, pouting with puppy eyes.

"I love you," she reached her hand out to me while Ali pulled her inside.

"I love you," I walked up to her and kissed her quickly, making her smile before they walked in and I lost sight of them.

"Doesn't she get too clingy?" Mason asked as we strolled in. I nudged him with my elbow.

"Watch your tongue. That's my girlfriend," I warned.

"It's just a question," he mumbled.

"She's attached" shrugged slightly while my hands rested in my pocket. "So am I."

He chuckled,

"She's a cry baby from what I see." That's offensive.

"So am I when I'm with her. Watch what you say, Mase." I said a little gruffly while we continued to walk.

"I didn't mean to be offensive, it's a good thing you two are like that. It's adorable," he shrugged.

"It feels really good to know that someone cares about you so much and is so in love with you. Just wait till you and Ali get like that," I scoffed.

"Do you think she's the one for you?" he asked me.

"I do," I admitted. "You will too, for Ali," I nudged his shoulder teasingly.

"I don't know man," he began. "I like her a lot, I really do. I just- I don't know if we'll last," he mumbled.

"What do you mean?" I asked in confusion.

"We're so different. We argue a lot whether they're serious or not and sometimes I don't know how to handle her. She's too much for me," he sighed with stress.

"If she's too much for you then why are you asking her to be your girlfriend?" I questioned. He didn't answer. "Please don't tell me you think becoming official will help fix things," I sighed in disappointment.

"Will it not?" he asked hesitantly.

"If it's not working now, putting a title to it won't help it. It'll just add more social pressure," I stated.

"So then what do I do?" he questioned.

"You tell her how you feel and both of you try to make it work. If it still doesn't work then it's not meant to be." We continued walking.

"That means we break up if it doesn't work, right?" he asked.

"Do you really *want* it to work?" I asked since I had a feeling he doesn't.

"Mason, if you don't then don't drag it along. Don't make her hurt more than she needs to." He nodded in understanding before we walked around in comfortable silence. This is going to be a long motherfucking day.

"Have you ever thought just maybe-ee-ee, you belong with me-ee-ee, you belong with me." Ali and Riley came into sight with linked arms, looking drunk while stumbling and singing.

We were back at the bus waiting for a few people to come back. Riley almost fell and I got to her in time to grab her and hold her up. "Are you drunk?" I asked her softly.

"A little bit," she whispered.

"What did you have?" I asked while taking her into the bus, Mason following with Ali behind me.

"Tequila," she giggled.

"Where?" I asked in disbelief.

"Tyler brought some," she shrugged. Of course, he fucking did. "You're on the phone with your girl-" she began yelling but I smacked my hand over her mouth.

"Shh!" I hissed. She looked at me with wide eyes before biting my hand. "Ow!" I winced before pulling it away.

"Don't shush me!" she whisper yelled.

"Riley Rose Blakely. We are on a school trip. You're not allowed to have alcohol. Do you hear me?" She nodded. "So now, until we get back to the hotel, you will keep quiet and sit with me. No more yelling." She nodded slowly.

She was seated in the seats at the very back while I was kneeling in front of her. "I love you," she said quickly as if it were her first time saying it.

I chuckled while looking down at the floor. She grabbed my face and pulled my lips to meet hers. We kissed for a while until people walked into the bus.

"Come on," I pulled away before taking her hand and pulling her up, taking her to sit with me.

She sat in the window seat and rested her head on my shoulder, hugging my arm. I kissed the top of her head before resting my head on top of hers.

"I love you," I whispered.

She took in a deep breath, sighing out loud.

"And I love you, Asher West," she said. She giggled, "Even now when I'm drunk."

This amazing girl is all mine.

CHAPTER FIFTY TWO

RILEY

I woke up to my head pounding while I lay in bed in my pajamas.

What the-

"You're awake! Here you go," Asher handed me an Advil. I swallowed it down with water before running my hand through my hair and letting out a sigh.

"Where's Ali?" I asked, falling back onto my pillow.

"I think she's still sleeping," he informed me while crawling into bed beside me.

"What the hell happened?" I asked in confusion.

"You and Ali got drunk. By the time we came back here you and her fell asleep so we carried you guys in." That makes sense. My eyes shot open when I processed things.

"Who changed my clothes?" I questioned.

"What?" he asked in confusion.

"Who changed my clothes? I left in something completely different, I remember that." I looked at him accusingly.

"I did, of course. Don't worry, my eyes were closed as far as I remember," he smirked. I pushed him off the bed. "Ouch!" He got back into bed.

"What time is it?" I rubbed my eyes.

"It's almost seven," he stated. "You knocked out at about two since we got there at twelve."

"I was asleep for that long?" I asked in shock.

"Yup," he nodded. "You took a little bit of the time I was supposed to get with you today," he pouted while resting his head on my stomach.

"We have all night," I laughed while running my fingers through his hair.

"Question is, what are we going to do?" he asked with a sigh.

"I don't know, we'll figure it out." I shrugged. "We should have a self pamper spa day, don't you think?" I asked while scratching his back.

He laughed, "What?" he asked.

"Yeah! That's what we should do tonight. Once we're back from dinner," I laughed while grabbing my phone.

"Dinner, which is in thirty minutes?" he asked.

"Mm-hmm." I nodded. "What about until then?" I asked while sitting up and throwing my hair up in a bun.

"We could just make out?" he suggested. "Not that we should but we could," he shrugged slightly.

"Oh, you're being serious?" I asked in surprise when he didn't finish with a witty remark or a sarcastic comment.

He shrugged, "You can think whatever you like," he smirked before getting off the bed.

"What is that supposed to mean?" I asked in confusion.

"You can think whatever you like," he shrugged. "Do you wanna watch something?" he asked while pulling out his laptop.

"Sure," I shrugged as he lay beside me and opened up Youtube. We watched some videos until it was time for dinner. I got up with Asher and placed my phone and keycard in his pocket since the sweatpants I was currently wearing had no pockets.

"Can I ask you something?" I asked as we got into the elevator.

"Sure," he agreed.

This might be personal.

"You don't have to answer it. Why do you smoke?" I questioned, my voice soft and quiet. I felt him stiffen beside me and turned to see his eyes slightly wide.

"I used to smoke as an escape," he sighed. My eyes widened at his words.

"*Used* to?" I asked in confusion.

"I haven't touched a cigarette since that day with you in

the printing room," he said quietly. Neither of us said one word or made one move, we just stood there in an eerie silence.

"Why?" I whispered.

"Because I liked you and I didn't want to do something that you despised. I didn't want you to despise me."

I inhaled deeply before turning to him and kissing him.

I pulled away when the doors opened and a ding echoed through the elevator. I felt his hand hold mine before he smiled and we walked out and to the dining room. We got our food together and sat down to see Mason and Ali already seated together. Ali looked nervous for some reason and so did Mason.

What is going on?

We all ate while making conversation and once we were done, Ali pulled me aside. "I'm about to end things with him. I'm breaking up with him," she said frantically.

"Wait what? Why?" I asked in confusion.

"Things aren't working Riles," she sighed. "I like someone else," she admitted. I raised my eyebrows at her, waiting for her to tell me who she's talking about.

"Is it Kian?" I guessed.

"What? No! He likes you!" she said with disgust at the thought of liking him. Okay if it's not him then this can't be good. He's the only good guy here.

"It's Tyler," she sighed.

"What?" I yelled. Many people turned and looked at us weirdly.

"Are you fucking serious? Tyler? The Tyler who flirts and checks out every fucking girl he sees?!" I hissed at her, keeping my voice down.

"I know! I know!" She threw her arms up in frustration.

I sighed, "Have you thought about where you're going to sleep after you break up with him?" I asked her.

"Well- Tyler's been rooming with Kennedy," she replied.

"What does that have to do with this?" I asked in confusion.

"And um- I asked her to switch."

Are you fucking kidding me?

"Wow Ali, I am so glad you told me first," I said sarcastically while rolling my eyes. "Well, you seem like you've got everything under control. But just asking, don't you think it's a little hypocritical for you to fight with him earlier when we thought he slept with Kennedy and now you're sending her to room with him?" I questioned.

"Yes, it is very hypocritical but I can't help who I like!" she exclaimed.

"Okay, okay," I put my hands up in surrender. "You do you," I sighed, covering my disappointment in her taste in guys.

I am never taking her advice on who's cute or not, ever again.

She likes Tyler! Gross and disgusting Tyer!

"Can we head back now?" I asked with a sigh. She nodded

and we got back to see Mason and Asher talking about something very serious.

"We need to talk," Ali and Mase said to each other at the same time.

"We're gonna head out," Asher sneaked out of his seat and pulled me to the elevators, leaving them to it. "Who does she like?" he asked me.

"Tyler," I sighed.

"That is fucking disgusting, that guy is a walking STD" his nose scrunched up.

"What about him?" I asked.

"It's not any better. Kennedy," he answered.

"Oh great!" I threw my arms up. "There might be a time where we have to hang out with those two if we love our friends," I groaned into my hands.

"I love him but not enough to tolerate her," he sighed.

"I am not sticking around Tyler," I said, completely grossed out.

"Maybe it'll blow over?" he tried to be optimistic as the elevator opened.

"Let's hope it does," I sighed as we walked to our room. I flopped straight onto the bed, letting out an exhausted sigh.

"Now what?" he asked while flopping down beside me. We turned to look at each other before I stood up and went into the bathroom. I wrapped my hands around the edge of the counter and looked at myself in the mirror before sighing.

I bit the inside of my cheek before looking around all the shampoo, body wash and that stuff that the hotel itself gives you. "Face mask, face mask, face mask," I mumbled under my breath while my eyes scanned the shelves. I know hotels don't usually give face masks but some occasionally do so I'm hoping this one does. "Got it!" I exclaimed before grabbing the two packets I found and taking them to the room.

"Okay," he chuckled while I handed him the packets and grabbed a headband to push his hair back. "Do I really need to put that on?" he asked while looking at the headband in my hands.

"Yes, you do," I replied while slipping it on his head. I used my fingers and applied the face mask on him while he just sat there staring at me. "What are you looking at?" I asked without looking into his eyes and focusing on applying that face mask.

"You," he answered.

"Really? I had no idea," I replied sarcastically.

"Riley," he began while I hummed in response. "I wanna take you to the Eiffel tower one more time at night before the end of the trip," he sighed.

"Okay," I said slowly, slightly confused. "We have a lot of time till the end of the trip though," I pointed out in confusion.

"I don't." I stopped moving for a second and looked at him with confusion.

"What do you mean?" I asked.

"I had Mr. Walker book an early return for me. I can't stay here for so long, I have to get back to work."

What?

"What work?" I asked in confusion.

"At Garage Town."

It's a mechanic repair shop in town.

"Since when do you-" he cut me off and explained.

"I took a job there before we got here. I need to get back."

Why didn't he tell me earlier?

"When?" I sighed.

"Three days from now."

— CHAPTER FIFTY THREE —

RILEY

"That doesn't leave us with much time," I said while focusing on the face mask and avoiding eye contact.

"I'll be there at the airport to pick you up," he replied optimistically.

"Yeah," I finished applying the face mask on him and stepped back, looking in his eyes. "But you won't be *here*," I answered a little bitterly before going into the bathroom to apply the face mask on myself. I leaned against the sink and looked down sighing. I heard him sigh before he walked into the bathroom. He walked up to me and held my face in his hands.

"What am I going to do here?" I sighed.

"You're going to have fun," he smiled slightly.

"I wanted to have fun on this trip *with you*. Not alone," I mumbled while looking away, pushing his hands off.

"You're not going to be alone, you'll have Ali, Mase, Kian, everyone will still be here," he chuckled slightly.

"Everyone except you." I looked at him.

"Facetime, we can facetime?" he suggested.

"Can I kiss you over Facetime?" He didn't answer. "That's what I thought," I turned to the mirror and applied the face mask on myself. He sat on the counter, watching me.

"Why do you have to go?" I asked once I finished while sighing and turning to him.

"Frankly, to make money," he scoffed.

"So let me come with you?" I asked.

He immediately shook his head, "You're here to have fun, with or without me."

No.

"No, I'm here to have fun *with* you," I countered.

"You didn't come here as my girlfriend," he stated.

"I came here and became your girlfriend so why would I let you leave?" I questioned.

"Because I have to go," he chuckled while hopping off the counter and picking me up, seating me on it instead.

"And I don't want you to go. That doesn't mean I don't want you to make money, but if you're going just let me come with you," I pleaded.

"You've been dying to see this place since you were a kid, Riles. I can't take that chance away from you," he looked down at the floor.

"I've seen enough of it. I don't want to see the rest without you here with me," I replied.

"We can talk about this later," he huffed.

"We don't have time," I stated.

"It's only for a little while," he sighed.

"I can assure you, it won't feel like a *little* while," I scoffed.

"What are you going to do at home? We don't have school or any work to do, you're just going to sit at home?" he questioned.

"I am going to come to work with you. We are going to get ice cream after or go on little dates. We're going to spend the nights at each other's watching movies and talking all night even though you'll probably doze off midway. We're going to be together and hang out," I replied.

"I'm still working at the diner, Riles. When are we going to have time?" he sighed.

"We're going to *make* time," I huffed, "I'm coming with you."

"No, you're not."

"Yes, I am."

"No, you're not."

"If you don't let me come with you, I'm not letting you take me to the tower." I set an ultimatum.

"That's not fair," he gave me a pointed look.

"Yes it is, you want to take me somewhere and I'm not letting you just how I wanna go somewhere and you're not letting me," I pointed out.

"You're not letting me take you to the Eiffel freaking tower. I'm not letting you go home," he stated.

"I've seen the tower so obviously that's not why you want to take me. If you're going to be at home then I'd rather be there with you than be here alone," I explained.

"I want to take you because I want the last thing I do here to be with you and to be special," he sighed.

"It can be the last thing we do here," I stated. "Asher, I swear if you don't take me with you I will fly back the next freaking day," I huffed.

"No, you won't."

He rolled his eyes.

"Try me." I challenged.

"It's too late to book your ticket," he clicked his tongue.

"Don't look for excuses!" I spoke through gritted teeth before pinching his arm.

"Ow!" he winced.

"I am coming with you," I said slowly.

"Okay," he sighed in defeat. "I'll have Mr. Walker book your ticket," he said, making me smile. "Happy?" he asked.

I nodded while grinning ear to ear. He smiled to himself. "Can you take this off now?" he asked while pointing to his face.

I nodded again, taking a cloth and running it under warm water. Once I took his off, I took mine off too before washing my face and brushing my teeth which he had already done.

I got to the bed to see him scrolling through his phone. I crawled into bed and he put his phone down, giving me his undivided attention. I wrapped my arms around him, resting my head on his chest.

He grabbed my wrist and tugged at it and I climbed on top of him, my chin resting on his chest.

"Why is your hair so fluffy today?" I laughed while ruffling his hair.

"It's not," he laughed.

"Yes it is, what did you do?" I laughed while squeezing his face together.

He pushed my hand off and laughed, "Nothing."

Liar.

"Did you use my shampoo?" I asked while looking at him suspiciously.

"No, I've been using the hotel's, Riley," he laughed.

"Look at me."

And he did.

"Did you accidentally or on purpose, use my shampoo?" I interrogated while biting back a laugh.

"Maybe," he smiled while trying to turn away and hide his face.

"Awww," I pinched his cheek while cooing teasingly. I lifted myself higher and planted a kiss on his cheek.

He flipped us over so he was hovering over me before holding my wrists in one hand and using the other to tickle me.

"No!" I screamed through laughter while kicking all over and laughing. "Please, please, please!" I exclaimed when he gave me a break. I was still smiling and laughing when he kissed me.

He pulled away after a while and said, "You are really stupid to leave Paris to come back home with *me*," he chuckled before lying beside me.

"You are very stupid to think for a second that I would choose to stay in Paris over coming home with you," I spoke mockingly.

"Just think about it, Riles. One last time. Are you sure?" he asked again.

"Yes," I sighed, "I am sure." I nodded while playing with his fingers.

"Okay," he sighed before kissing the back of my hand. We sat in silence until I started laughing.

"What?" he chuckled.

"You used my shampoo," I laughed again. "You could have just asked, I would have said yes," I chuckled while flipping over and lying on my stomach.

"Really? Are you sure about that?" He gave me a pointed look.

"Yeah. I mean, it's just shampoo," I shrugged. "At least

your hair smells nice now," I twiddled my thumbs.

"Should I be offended?" he chuckled.

"No, it just smells better now," I shrugged cockily.

"It smells like vanilla," he pointed out.

"Which is better than whatever the hotel gave," I stated. We were lounging around when our doorbell rang.

I went to answer it and saw Mr. Walker. I froze in my spot and ran to the bed. "Mr. Walker is here."

He rang the bell two more times. "You have to get it, the room is on your name," I whispered. The bell rang again.

"I'll be right there!" Asher responded before jogging over to the door, answering it hastily while I hid in the bathroom.

"Mr. Walker, hi. How can I help?" he asked, playing it cool.

"We're doing a check on the rooms. I believe you all are rooming with opposite genders, so just checking." I gulped while getting into the shower and pulling the curtain.

"Where's Mason?" I heard Mr. Walker question.

"He's um- he's in the bathroom," Asher lied. I unlocked my phone which I managed to grab and called Mason.

"Hello?" he asked while I heard shuffling.

"Mr. Walker is doing room checks, you might have to act like you're in the bathroom," I whispered.

"Fine," he huffed before I heard two knocks on the bathroom door.

"Mr. Sparks are you in there?" he called out. I put the phone to the door and on the speaker.

"Yes sir, I'm here!" Mase spoke through the phone.

"Alright," Mr. Walker sighed. I ended the call and sighed in relief, leaning against the wall. "I would like to see your suitcases."

Are you fucking kidding me?

What is with this guy?

"Sure," Asher agreed.

Okay, what the hell is he thinking?

Last I checked Mason did not wear dresses.

"What about his suitcase?" Mr. Walker asked.

"He has it locked," Asher lied.

When did he lock it?

"Privacy reasons?" Asher guessed.

"Hmm," Mr. Walker hummed in suspicion.

God help us.

CHAPTER FIFTY FOUR

ASHER

"What the hell was that?" Her head peeked out of the bathroom with relief written all over her face.

"Someone definitely hinted him, there's no way he could have known," I sighed while leaning against the wall.

"Um- are you sure about that? People made it pretty obvious that they had a certain person they were sticking with. We, for one, definitely did." She walked out and flopped onto the bed.

"Oh shit," I shot out of the door, chasing Mr. Walker down the hall. "Mr. Walker!" I called after him.

"Yes?" He turned to me with confusion.

"I would like to talk to you about something," I began. "I was wondering if I could get another ticket back to town for someone," I said awkwardly.

"For who?" he questioned.

"Um- Riley," I answered.

"Elaborate," he demanded.

"She wants to come back with me. I understand that this is a school trip and she is required to be here, but she can't be held here against her will and if she doesn't want to stay then she needs to be sent back." I shrugged a little.

"She is required to be here unless her reason for wanting to go back is valid, which as far as I know, not wanting to be here anymore, is not."

Since when did Mr. Walker become such an asshole?

"And why exactly is my reason valid?" I questioned.

"Would you like your ticket to be canceled?" he arched an eyebrow at me.

"Mr. Walker, my ticket can be canceled or hers can be booked, but as you know, we're not kids. If needed, we can book our own tickets and get ourselves back home. Can't we?" I smirked.

"I need her reasoning, either way, Mr. West." He gave me a pointed look.

"She *wants* to go back. It's as simple as that. I'm hoping you understand," I raised my eyebrows, waiting for him to answer.

"I'll have her ticket booked by tomorrow morning." He rolled his eyes before storming off.

Someone woke up on the wrong side of the bed.

I sighed and walked back into our room, closing the door and leaning against it with a sigh. "Where did you run off to? You scared me," she walked over to me while letting her hair down.

"I went to ask him to book your ticket," I sighed while pushing myself off the door.

"And?" She asked with hope seeping through her voice.

"He was stubborn, I don't know what's up with him today, but he said yes nonetheless," I shrugged nonchalantly.

She squealed before kissing my cheek and hugging me tightly. "Jesus," I mumbled as she wrapped her legs around my waist and jumped into my arms. "Okay babe," I chuckled while carrying her to the bed.

She didn't let go of me still and so we tumbled onto the bed because no shit, what else would happen?

"Oh my god, what are you doing?" I laughed while flipping us over so she was on top. She lied on top of me, humming in satisfaction when she got comfortable. "I never thought you'd be this excited to leave Paris and come back home," I mumbled while drawing circles on her lower back, under her shirt.

"I'm excited to go back home and be with *youuu*," she stretched out her words.

"Even though the majority of the time, I'll be fixing cars and taking orders?" I chuckled.

"Yup, even then," she nodded before kissing my cheek again.

I cannot stress enough how lucky I feel. It feels amazing to have someone so head over heels in love with you, to know that someone would be willing to do anything for you and you would do the same.

It's a blessing to find a girl who loves you and who you fall in love with. I fell in love with her and she loves me. I am so in love with her.

"You're getting a stubble, shave tomorrow," she mumbled sleepily before dozing off.

I smiled before letting my eyes droop closed.

I woke up to her gone from beside me while the shower water ran. The bathroom door opened and she strolled out. "Catch!" she tossed my can of shaving cream at me. I managed to catch it before it hit my face.

"Right now?" I groaned.

"Come on, we have today to ourselves so I want my clean-faced boyfriend with me, get up!" she threw a pillow at me before going back into the bathroom. I walked in there while she was drying her hair with a towel.

I brushed my teeth as she began applying moisturizer and sunblock. I finished brushing my teeth as she finished braiding her hair. I applied shaving cream on my face and she immediately began laughing at me. I poked her side, making her squeal and then shut up.

"Wanna do it for me?" I handed her the razor.

"No thanks, that's uh- too risky," she chuckled nervously.

"Why?" I laughed.

"Because if I cut you then I will have a panic attack so yeah," she said nervously, trying to play it off.

"You're not gonna cut me, here." I placed the razor in her hand.

"Oh, no no no, Asher. I seriously shouldn't-"

"Riley, you will not cut me. Here you go." I chuckled before grabbing her waist and placing her on the counter, standing between her legs. She took a deep breath. I chuckled before grabbing her resting hand and holding it.

"Come on," I laughed.

"It's not funny," she laughed at herself. "Okay," she sighed before I tilted my chin up and began shaving. "Turn the tap on," she turned to the tap after a few shaves to clean the razor.

"Yes ma'am," I laughed. She began talking to me while focusing and by the time we were done, I had a clean face and not one cut.

"You did it!"

"I did it!" we screamed at the same time.

I washed my face before turning to her for a kiss. "Now what are we doing today?" I asked while helping her to her feet and following her to the room.

"Absolutely nothing," she smiled while flopping onto the bed.

"You got me up and shaved for nothing?" I asked in disbelief before groaning into my pillow.

"I want to walk through the city with you again." She held her chin in the palm of her hand while lying on her stomach, propped up on her elbow, rocking her legs back and forth.

"Then let's go," I smiled while getting up.

"Put some clothes on," she narrowed her eyes at me. I laughed before throwing a shirt on and heading out with her. Since it was just going to be us two, we both dressed casually and took some money with the key and our phones of course. We left the hotel, decided to get our brunch outside in a cafe and just aimlessly walked around until we had a certain location in mind.

Which was never.

As we were exploring, if you say, we stumbled across the same souvenir shop as earlier, the one where I bought her the charm. "Wanna go back in there?" I asked as we peeked in through the glass windows.

"Sure," she shrugged. We walked in, looked around together for a while before splitting up. I was looking at some bracelets, handmade by a thread before I found one I liked. It was a simple black braided bracelet and I liked it but I left it there and continued walking around.

"Find anything?" she asked once we met in the middle after ten minutes or so.

"Nothing," I shook my head.

"Okay, let's head out?" I nodded and we left. We were

walking in comfortable silence and about five minutes later she said,

"You lied to me."

Confusion graced my face.

"About what?" I asked. She opened up her wallet and took out the bracelet.

"I saw you looking at it. Why didn't you just buy it?" she asked while grabbing my wrist and tying the bracelet around it.

"I don't need to have it, I just thought it was cool," I chuckled.

"If you find something that you think is cool in Paris, you buy it. You never know if you'll come back," she shrugged before locking her hand with mine as we continued walking. I glanced at her with a smile tugging at my lips as we strolled into a cafe.

"Can I just get water please?" she asked while pulling money out.

"Make that two." I paid for us both before she could. I felt her eyes on me while I refused to look at her because I knew this was going to be about letting her pay.

We walked out and she immediately asked, "Why didn't you let me pay?" she huffed.

"Because we are out on a date and while I know you can

pay, I like to be a gentleman and pay, do you have a problem with that?" I turned to her while huffing.

She looked at me with a smile. "No, I have no problem at all," she shook her head slightly.

"Shall we?" I held her hand, leading the way.

── CHAPTER FIFTY FIVE ──

RILEY

Time jump- Their last day in Paris.

I woke up to Asher still sleeping beside me. I checked the time on my phone and when I saw the date, reality struck and I realized that it was our last day here and at six tomorrow morning, we're flying back.

Now you see, my initial thought was to let him get rest because last night we had a movie marathon but I want to make the most out of today.

"Hello, good morning!" I ruffled his hair. He groaned and shuffled but did not wake up.

"It's our last day here, come on," I shook him up a little.

"Asher West, wakie, wakie," I chuckled.

"Okay, get up." I deadpanned.

"Maybe he doesn't want that morning kiss then," I whispered to myself, loud enough for him to hear before beginning to get out of bed but he grabbed my wrist and pulled me back, into a kiss.

"Good morning, did you sleep well?" I asked sarcastically.

"After you kept me up watching Mean Girls, definitely. I slept like a baby," he smiled before kissing my forehead.

"Now listen here, today is our last day. Everyone is getting the day off but I want to do something so that I know I did everything I wanted to on my last day in Paris." I explained.

"And I wanna take you to the tower tonight," he replied.

"So during the day, we are going to go to the closest mall we have, we're going to walk around and eat our meals and then tonight-" he cut me off.

"Tonight, I'm taking you on another date."

I nodded with a smile, "Sounds like a plan." I grinned.

"Now let's get up and start by swimming?" he asked.

"Sure," I laughed while getting out of bed and grabbing my swimsuit. I got ready first and once we were dressed in swimwear and had applied sunblock, we got to the pool where we met pretty much everyone.

"Where are- oh my god!" I screamed when my eyes landed on Mason and Kennedy snogging.

"Ew!" he groaned beside me.

When I looked where he was, which I shouldn't have, I saw Ali and Tyler doing the same.

"What is wrong with the world?" I groaned in disgust before taking his hand and getting into the pool.

"We have got to do something before we have to leave.

Otherwise, all we're going to see when we get back at school is well- that," Asher sighed.

"Um- okay. Confession," I laughed awkwardly. "Ali and Mase are um- how do I say this? They're cheating on Tyler and Kennedy. If it can be called cheating," I mumbled.

"What? With who?" he questioned.

"With each other," I answered, clearing my throat.

"How do you know this?" he asked.

"Allison told me," I said quietly.

"If they're seeing each other again then why did they break up?" he pressed further.

"Well you see, that's a funny story," I chuckled. "They couldn't let each other go." I laughed it off.

"So why not get back together?" he asked in confusion.

Has Mason told him nothing?

"Tyler is sort of, kinda, in love with Ali and uh- Kennedy is in love with Mason," I blurted out. "Hasn't he told you? Why am I the one giving this information out?" I whined.

"No, he hasn't told me! So do Mase and Ali like *each other* again?" his eyebrows furrowed.

"Not exactly," I breathed. He just looked at me, waiting for me to elaborate. "You seriously need to question your best friend," I mumbled. "They're sort of um- *this should not be coming from me*- they're sort of friends with benefits, oh my god kill me." I hid my face in my hands.

"Hasn't it only been like five days?!" he exclaimed.

"I don't know! I just- I- I highly recommend that we find a new set of friends," I huffed.

"They're going to try this friends with benefits thing and they're going to fall in love. Again." He rolled his eyes.

"What makes you say that?" I questioned.

"They are super alike. They're meant for each other."

True.

"Do you think we could last if we were friends with benefits?" I thought out loud.

Probably shouldn't have asked that.

"What?!" he asked in shock.

"I'm- I am not suggesting that we do it! I'm just wondering."

Kill me.

Please.

Just do it now.

Now would be nice.

"We haven't had-" I cut him off.

"I know! I know! Just uh- forget I asked," I waved my hand dismissively.

"Do you want to?" he smirked at me.

"What?!" Believe me when I say my eyes widened quite a bit. "Could you repeat yourself?"

Why am I so nervous?

"Do you want to?" he repeated. "Do you think you're ready?" he asked.

This is incredibly nerve-wracking.

"A- are you?" I asked back.

"I'm ready when you are, which is why I am asking," he replied.

"D-do you- do you want to?"

I am stuttering like the fucking fool I am.

"It doesn't matter if I want to. It matters if you think we're ready for it."

Why is he so good with words?

"I think we should just leave it up to the moment," I blurted out quickly.

"Okay," he chuckled. "You don't have to be so awkward," he wrapped his arms around my waist and pulled me closer.

"It's nerve-wracking," I mumbled.

"I know," he replied. "Wanna head back out?" he asked.

"Yeah." He got out of the pool and helped me out before we got to the elevator. Then we pretty much went on about our day, like that conversation never happened. We both showered, got dressed before heading out for the day. We took an Uber to the nearest mall to us where we shopped.

Well, I sure as hell did.

He bought some clothes here and there, a hoodie which I demanded he buy so I could steal later, of course. And we were currently having lunch.

"About that conversation," he began.

"Do you have to bring it up? I don't know what I was thinking I-" I began blabbering but he interrupted.

"You don't have to freak out, Riles. We're not little kids. Just uh- out of curiosity. Would you ever consider..." he trailed off questioningly.

Ha, my turn to poke and tease.

"Do you want me to say yes?" I asked in a taunting tone.

"Am I supposed to want you to say no? You're my girl-friend," he countered.

Fair enough.

"I mean, would you want it to be me?" he asked hesitantly.

"Yeah," I nodded.

"Really?" he asked, slightly surprised.

"Am I supposed to say no? You're my boyfriend," I smiled. "Wanna change the subject?" I asked after a moment of awkward silence.

"Yeah, he laughed.

~~~

"Thank you!" We called after the uber. We had just gotten back to the hotel so we could get ready for our little date and then pack and get as much sleep as we could till six. We got up to the room, making conversation that always flows between us and once in the room, we began getting ready.

I took all my stuff in the bathroom and he just got ready in the room itself until we switched at the end when I needed to put on shoes and he needed to do his hair. "Ready?" I called out just as he appeared.

"Ready," he smiled. I stood up, grabbed my purse, phone, wallet and we headed out.

"Starting with dinner?" I asked as he held the door open for me while I slipped into the uber.

"You bet," he smiled, climbing in through the other side. We got to the restaurant, had a great meal and stayed there for a long time. Then came the tower. It glimmered. Boy did it glimmer.

"I love you. I am so glad this trip happened even if it was *extremely* last minute an- and I am so glad I picked your name and you agreed to stay and yeah we had that rough patch but I really wanted to thank you for giving me that second chance. If it wasn't for that, we probably wouldn't be here. I love you, Riley."

He squeezed my hand thrice.

"If you didn't pick my name that night, I would never have gotten the chance to really understand and find out what it's like to be with you. You make me feel loved in a way no one else has and I just- I want to thank you for showing me what love is."

I squeezed his hand back thrice while keeping my gaze on the glittering tower.

"You know, I used to think I can't be loved because no one ever stayed," he chuckled coldly. "But you did. And I love you for it." He turned me to face him before pulling me in for a soft kiss. "Remind me to punch Jordan when we get back," he said after we broke away.

I laughed as the tower glimmered for the last time for now.

Here I am in Paris, standing in front of the Eiffel tower, with the boy I loved, then hated, now I love again.

I guess that's what happens when you get stuck in Paris.

The city of love.

And lights, of course.

Printed in Great Britain
by Amazon

61804792R00261